SUDDENLY
A SUCCUBUS

THE AURELIUS ARCHIVES: BOOK ONE

NYX NYGHTINGALE

Suddenly A Succubus

Content Warning: This book contains explicit sex.

Copyright © 2025 by Nyx Nyghtingale

For permissions, contact: *NyxNyghtingale@gmail.com*

Cover Art by Linda Bulickova | Noeran

Cover Lettering/Design by Nyx Nyghtingale

Scene Break Image by Freepik

ISBN 979-8-9923715-0-5 (Print Edition)

ISBN 979-8-9923715-1-2 (eBook)

www.nyxnyghtingale.com

CONTENTS

I

THE MORNING AFTER

Amara paced back and forth in her room, repeatedly clenching her hands as she tried to steady her breathing. Thoughts raced through her head, each one trying to find meaning before another pushed it away. Her long brown hair, so perfectly curled the night before, was now a tangled mess. It bounced around with each frantic turn before she finally crashed back to her bed.

"Amara, you idiot!"

Her voice echoed through her room, her eyes absent-mindedly tracing cracks in the ceiling. Grabbing a nearby pillow, she used it to muffle a scream, then an angry sigh. A few minutes later, she reluctantly pulled it off her face and tossed it to the floor. She sat up to look around, her cluttered room suddenly feeling wrong.

Standing up, she moved to the window to let in the morning sun. Wincing slightly as the light hit her face, she opened her laundry basket and started picking through the piles on the floor.

Her pajamas could stay on; it was Sunday. She grabbed loose clothes from Friday's classes, throwing them into the hamper, and kept moving. Various shoes went back in the closet, as did a few outfits that had been put together but ultimately rejected. Her backpack was slumped in a corner, papers haphazardly pushed in.

Amara rolled her eyes before dumping the backpack's contents on her bed. There was no doubt one of her friends had 'borrowed' some of the answers for the week's assignments while everyone else had been doing their makeup.

She spread the papers out on her bed, then sat in the middle of them and pieced together which assignment went in which folder. It was nice to have mindless labor, paying just enough attention to her tasks to avoid thinking about more pressing issues. Her breathing had calmed, and by the time she'd zipped her back-pack closed she already felt much better about the state of her room. She went to place the backpack on the chair in the corner.

And that's when she saw it: the dress from last night.

Last night.

Memories rushed into her head, replaying the start of her evening. After more than a year of classes, the stress of college had finally gotten to Amara. Her friends had convinced her to go to a party—her first ever. They picked out outfits, pointed out which guys were single, and helped her do something special with her makeup.

My makeup! Fuck!

Amara checked her pillow, finding it smeared with foundation. She groaned again, then headed for the bathroom. She put her hair up, hip checking the bathroom door open before starting the sink. She paused, then turned the shower on too; as much as she loved her apartment, it took forever for the hot water to kick in. Makeup wipes in hand, she pulled together the courage to look in the mirror.

Golden-brown eyes stared back at her, almost unrecognizable through the heavy eyeliner. They seemed exceptionally vibrant today, as if they were glowing. She loved their color, how they perfectly matched her darker complexion. She quickly took off her eyeliner, then the rest of her makeup.

Her eyes trailed down and lingered on her lips; traces of lipstick still clung there, though some had worn off. She wondered if the rest of it was still on his—

Stop. Stay focused, Amara.

She pulled her gaze away from the stranger in the mirror, then washed her face with unusual vigor. Her own face gradually returned, and looking in the mirror felt easier. Her eyes still seemed unusually bright, but that hardly seemed to matter. By now the shower was ready, and she quickly stripped down before stepping in.

Hot water poured over her, and she felt a sense of calm returning. She nudged the faucet warmer, then started her routine. There was barely room in the shower for all her products, but thankfully she had no roommates to battle for space. The steam surrounded her, fragrances mixing together to help her relax.

Start at the beginning, Amara. The party was a good idea! I should have let Tessa talk me into it earlier. No doubt she'll be rubbing that in my face for weeks. Assuming she remembers last night at all.

Amara laughed, now remembering she'd lost count of how many drinks her friends had finished. She had been tempted to join them, but decided to play it safe, a decision Nick had supported.

Nick. Is he just as stressed as I am? Will we still be friends after this?

After meeting in Junior High, Nick and Amara had become fast friends. They'd initially bonded over a love of outdoor exploration, but quickly learned that they also shared interests in movies, shows, and everything else that teenagers define their lives with. They'd supported each other through awkward crushes, poorly timed acne, bad breakups, and dozens of other minor catastrophes. Their friends often joked they were secretly in love, but there had never been any truth to those rumors. In fact, Nick and Amara had talked about dating several times, but it never felt right. They worked best as friends, and they were happy to keep it that way.

So how did last night happen?

More memories surfaced, replaying the night once she arrived at the party. Dancing with friends in the basement, guy after guy, and the occasional girl, trying to make a move. None succeeded, as usual, but the attention had certainly excited her. Surrounded by hormones, she might as well have been drunk; an itch had appeared, one normally satiated by toys and vibrators. Before she could question herself, she had dragged Nick upstairs, locking them both in one of the Jade Palace's empty bedrooms.

Don't re-open that door, Amara. Just...not now. Think about something else; anything else. Is your homework done?

Her thoughts drifted back to her classes, thinking about the assignments she'd packed away earlier, mostly finished but still needing some final touches. As eager as she'd been to step away from the world of studying last night, there was no denying she loved school. Her classes kept her excited and engaged, and she'd never once regretted her choices.

Amara had fallen in love with photography at an early age. Her mother had thrown her a birthday party, and despite the many presents Amara had received, her attention had been held captive by the disposable camera her mother had used to document the party. A few weeks later, after burning through multiple such cameras, her mother had finally caved and bought her the real thing.

Through photography, Amara had grown fascinated with presentation, with the different masks people wore to express themselves. Sometimes these masks were defense mechanisms, sometimes they simply made it easier to fit in at school. Amara's goal as a photographer had always been to strip away those masks and discover the person underneath. Over the years, she'd grown incredibly skilled at doing this, and the process had also given her plenty of graphic design skills.

This fascination had led her to declare a major in Marketing, with a focus in social media. The internet was positively saturated with people wearing masks, and Amara felt that her background in photography, along with her myriad graphic design skills, would pair nicely with a major that encouraged grabbing people's attention.

Steam filled her senses, pulling her thoughts back to her immediate surroundings. Grabbing another bottle, she continued her routine. Rich lavender helped ground her thoughts, and she focused on her body, on how good it felt to pamper herself. As she massaged her legs with fragrant body scrub, she became acutely aware of how sensitive her skin felt.

Is this because of last night?

Every part of her felt alive in a way she'd never experienced before. The connection between her mind and her body was stronger than ever, and she wanted to explore that connection. She gripped her thighs, massaging them before moving higher. Her fingers teased her waist, her chest, and finally lingered on her neck. The itch was returning, stronger than ever.

Feeling brave, Amara dared to remember what happened last night.

She had locked herself in the room with Nick, his puzzled look turning to excitement as he realized what was happening. After pushing him to the bed, she pulled her dress off and tossed it aside, eager to feel another person against her skin.

She pushed her shower hotter still, losing herself in the sensation. Water ran down her back, her chest, retracing where Nick's hands had been just hours earlier. She let her own hands wander, finding that same path. She pushed her breasts together, teased her nipples the way he had, then continued down. A gasp escaped her lips as she ran her fingers over her sex, teasing her clit with small circles.

The next few minutes were electric; the way her body responded to her hands felt incredible. She continued teasing herself, water cascading down her body as her soft moans echoed through the shower.

Amara had been a virgin before last night, but was intimately familiar with how to get herself off. Her body trembled as she moved closer to her entrance, fantasizing about how good it felt to have someone else inside her. Slipping a finger in, her toes curled as she felt the first hints of an orgasm start to build.

And then it vanished.

There was still pleasure, but it seemed further away the more she tried to reach for it. She gave herself another minute of soft exploration, hoping it would re-appear just as suddenly, but it never happened.

That's what your toys are for, Amara.

She groaned in frustration, upset she couldn't get herself off. Summoning the strength to hold her libido at bay, she resolved to finish her shower as quickly as she could. The water felt lukewarm again, but she was surprised to see it couldn't get any hotter.

Making a note to check up on this later, Amara dried herself off and eagerly left the shower. She returned to her bedroom, pulling out a shoebox from under her bed, filled with exactly what she needed. Vibrators, dildos, a few butt plugs she hadn't yet worked up the courage to play with—everything to make a woman sing. She pulled out her favorite, a relatively small vibrating dildo that hit all the right places.

Sinking back into bed, she resumed the exploration she had started in the shower, remembering what it was like to have someone touch her, kiss her, pleasure her. She bit her lip as she moved her toy between her legs, teasing her clit once more, but taking it slow. The vibrations surged through her body, and she closed her eyes, willing herself to surrender to the release she so desperately needed. Spreading her legs, she pushed the toy inside. She moaned loudly, savoring every inch as it drove deeper. An orgasm couldn't be far off now. Her hips started meeting the thrusts of her hand, the toy moving in and out while the vibrations continued to build. She pushed the toy harder, increasing its power as she brought herself closer...

Until she lost it again.

Exactly like in the shower, all the pleasure that had built up dispersed without warning. She could still feel everything—the toy, its powerful vibrations, her sensitive clit—yet somehow everything was out of sync. It was as if her body was rejecting its normal forms of pleasure, searching for something else that wasn't there.

Or...someone else?

Amara shook her head, shocked she was even thinking about it. Nick was her best friend. Last night had clearly been a mistake, but she couldn't get it out of her head.

Maybe that's the problem? We need to talk, to reset everything to normal!

It was the best guess she had, and there wasn't much else to do today. With another groan of frustration, she tossed her toy aside and pulled her pajamas back on. Grabbing her phone, she pulled up Nick's contact info and froze. Their messages from last night stared back at her.

Nick: 8 PM right? Your place?

Amara: Yup! You gotta see what the girls did with me, I barely even recognize myself!

Nick: Wellll you're also willingly going to a college party, so I already don't know who you are XD

Amara: Oh shut up and text me when you're here idiot

Nick: Here!

It all seemed so innocent now. Could things go back to the way they were? Did she want them to? There was definitely a lot to talk about, but it had to start somewhere. She iterated a few times before deciding to keep it short and simple.

Amara: Hey, I'd like to talk about last night. Come over?

Heart pounding in her chest, she had no idea what to expect. Would he be angry? He had seemed into it but what if she just caught him by surprise?

Stop overthinking this, Amara. He's Nick! He's the most understanding guy you know, he'll get it.

Taking a deep breath, she exhaled slowly just as his response came in.

Nick: I think that's a good idea. Gimme ten.

Amara was thankful Nick was true to his word, but that didn't stop the ten minutes from dragging. By the time he texted again, she'd rearranged the throw pillows on her couch dozens of times. When she opened the door, she was pleased to discover she didn't have to force a smile, and his grin seemed equally genuine.

They stared at each other awkwardly for a few seconds before Amara finally moved in for a hug. It still felt right, and Amara was relieved as she pulled him into the room.

"You're looking well," she chimed, closing the door. "Glad you made it home safe!"

"Thanks! And, uh, you too, obviously." He laughed nervously, but the words seemed to come easily enough.

Amara vaulted the couch and curled into her favorite spot, patting the cushion next to her. Nick opted for the long way around which, given his size, was probably for the best.

"So. I don't want to tiptoe around this. We're adults, right?" Amara paused, waiting for a nod before continuing. "We...we had sex." Saying it aloud felt odd, but strangely comforting at the same time.

Nick took a breath, likely mulling over his words before speaking. "We...did, yes. I want to say that I'm sorry if things got out of hand. I wasn't thinking straight; I think I had a bit too much to drink. If you want to just forget it ever happened, I'm happy to do the same."

Amara chuckled as he stumbled through the words; no doubt he'd been practicing them all morning. "Hey, I didn't say I wanted to forget about it. People have sex all the time! Is it a little odd that my first time was with you? Sure, but at least it was with someone I trust, right?"

He laughed too, the stress in his shoulders relaxing somewhat. Amara noticed that she felt drawn to him, as if it were wrong for them to be this far apart.

"I suppose you're right. Do we want to change anything? In the past we've agreed we weren't interested in dating. Is that still true?" Nick asked.

Amara bit her lip as her eyes lingered on him; something was different now; she just couldn't define it. "I think my opinion hasn't changed. You're a great guy, Nick, but we both know it wouldn't work. No matter which way I look at it, I don't have those kinds of feelings for you."

He relaxed further, sinking into the couch as relief took hold. "I'm glad we agree! I've been worried about losing you; losing your friendship." He looked at her again, the tension gone, only this time Amara noticed something else—the itch was back.

Amara started recalling memories from last night, and she found it more difficult to focus on what her best friend was saying. He seemed to be on another nervous rant, maybe about something else that happened at the party? Her eyes had broken with his and were tracing down his body, wondering what kind of underwear he had on.

"—and she seemed really nice but obviously the evening took a bit of a turn, so...Amara? You alright? You're zoning out on me." Nick leaned forward, content to stop his story there.

"Y-yeah, I'm...fine," she muttered unconvincingly, her legs twitching as she tried to pin them together.

"Look, I can tell when something is bugging you, and—hey!"

Amara cut him off, her needs bubbling to the surface. She pushed him back as she straddled him, grasping his shoulders as his breathing quickened. Her instincts taking over, she leaned in and kissed his neck, biting it gently as she started grinding into him.

"Amara, what's gotten into you? Are we...are we leaving this alone or not?" He spoke quietly, frozen with nervous energy as she kept exploring his body.

"Nick, I...I need this, I need you. I've been so pent up all morning; my toys did nothing," Amara pleaded with him, her eyes desperate as she played with the bottom of his shirt.

As they looked at each other, an understanding formed.

Nick had been holding his hands out, trying not to touch Amara, and he slowly moved them to her waist as he spoke. "S-so one more time, but nothing of it, right? We're just friends having fun?"

A devilish smirk grew on Amara's face. She didn't bother to justify Nick with an answer, instead pulling his shirt off and tossing it away. She rested her hands on his chest, and the two kissed once more. The taste of his lips excited her, but she couldn't stop herself from moving away to tease his neck. Each kiss felt new and exciting, and when she moved closer to his ear, she softly bit it, enjoying Nick's quiet gasp.

Finally, Amara pulled away from him, taking off her own shirt and throwing it next to his. She leaned forward, letting him explore her in return. His lips traced her neck, moving down to find her breasts, then her nipples.

She bit her lip, her breath quickening as she played with his hair, urging him to continue. As he softly bit her, she moaned, her legs squeezing him in excitement. Finally, she tapped his neck, silently asking him to stop before she pushed herself off. She slid down to the floor, taking a pillow with her and settling on top of it.

She leaned in, her breasts pushing against the bulge in his pants, and began kissing his chest. Each kiss took her further down, and soon her fingers had hooked into his pants and were pulling them down.

Amara licked her lips as Nick's cock came into view, and she knew this was what she needed. She kissed the tip before opening wide and sucking him in, both of them moaning in pleasure. Grabbing his legs, she steadied herself as she bobbed her head up and down, savoring every inch she could fit in her mouth.

His hands moved to cover hers, and he moaned loudly again as he threw his head back. His body was already twitching, and Amara briefly worried that she might push him over the edge. Strangely, her worry disappeared as quickly as it arrived. Reading his body language felt almost natural, and a little voice in her head whispered that she could continue like this and not risk ruining her own fun later.

"So...obviously I'm pretty new to this, and last night was a little rushed," she said, kissing the tip as her hand massaged his shaft. "What feels good?"

Nick looked down, their eyes meeting as she teased his cock. "I...like long strokes, a little slower, I guess?"

She nodded, adjusting her movements to match his desires.

"And I like hearing things."

"Hearing things? Like, dirty talk?" Amara tilted her head inquisitively.

"Definitely dirty talk, but also anything? I like hearing moans, gagging, things like that."

"You're so bad! You want to hear your best friend gagging on your cock?" Amara teased, letting her lips surround his tip a few more times.

"W-well I didn't mean...only if you want to!" He shifted uncomfortably as she teased him.

Amara thought about it for a second, then decided it was time to push herself in ways she hadn't last night. She took a deep breath, then pushed her head forward to take his cock deeper. She felt it brush against the entrance to her throat, and she gagged in surprise.

"Fuck, that's harder than it looks." Amara wiped her chin as she caught her breath. After a second, she tried again, only to meet with the same results.

"Hey, no need to push yourself." Nick looked down and smiled, a hand brushing her cheek in reassurance. She let her own hand rest on his, then smiled as an idea formed. She took his hand, moving it to the back of her head.

"I want to see what you like," Amara said, and moved her hands to his hips, preparing herself. "Make me pleasure you, Nick."

With a small nod, Nick grabbed some of her hair. He pushed her down, and she prepared to gag again, but he pulled back before reaching her throat. His tip now barely in her mouth, he began guiding her up and down his shaft. It was slower than she would have expected, each stroke long and sensual. After a minute, she squeezed his thigh, telling him she wanted more.

His grip tightened, and the next time he pushed her down, it was slightly deeper. Amara gagged, feeling him pull back instinctively. She squeezed again, telling him to continue, that she wanted this. Another push, another gag, and this time she heard a moan. His cock twitched in her mouth, and he started moving her slightly faster. Her head moved up and down, and each time he pushed her just far enough to make her gag, but never further. She realized she could easily let him push this far, and the gagging noise alone would excite him.

Amara began to vocalize how much she was enjoying herself, her moans joining his. Each time she gagged, she played it up to fuel his excitement.

This continued for another minute before Nick suddenly pulled her off, his breathing erratic. "Fuck, Amara, I need to stop. I don't want this to be over quite yet."

"I couldn't agree more," Amara replied, her breathing as heavy as his. "Maybe...you should return the favor?"

Nick nodded, obviously enthusiastic. He helped her up, watching intently as she pulled her pants off. Amara winked at him, playfully showing off her ass before collapsing onto the couch.

"So, do you have much experience with this?" Amara slowly spread her legs, exposing herself completely.

"You know I haven't dated many people," Nick moved to the floor, kneeling on the pillow, "but yeah, one of them really liked oral."

"Well, don't disappoint me!" She giggled as he drew closer.

She felt his lips on her thighs, her breath catching as he began exploring. Her legs grew more sensitive the higher he went, and each kiss caused her to shudder. When his tongue finally found her clit, she gasped loudly in pleasure.

She reached down, tracing her fingers through his hair as he teased her. Every inch his tongue explored felt divine, and her breathing quickly grew erratic in response. She pulled him closer, desperate to feel more, her hands holding his head tight.

"Nick, I...use your fingers," Amara gasped, shivering, as Nick's hands ran up her legs. He teased her thighs again, his nails drawing lines on her skin before they found her pussy.

He teased her entrance, his finger massaging the edges as he continued licking her clit. Her hips pushed against him, begging for more, but he continued holding back. Amara swore she could feel him smirking, and her body was growing more insistent by the moment. She was seconds away from grabbing his hand and taking what she wanted, but her thoughts were cut short when he finally pushed into her.

She bit her lip, moaning as he pushed deeper. He slowly moved in and out, matching his thrusts to the rhythm of his tongue. She whimpered whenever he threatened to leave her, and each time he would pause before pushing back inside. She knew her orgasm was close, and she began thrusting her hips to try to match his rhythm. In her excitement, she accidentally pulled away too fast, his finger slipping out and breaking the spell.

The moment lost, Amara looked down at Nick, and they locked eyes. "Fuck, sorry, I didn't mean to...I was so close!" She groaned in frustration as she fell back against the couch.

"Hey, nobody said sex had to be perfect." Nick leaned forward, grabbing her hands. "Besides, it's not like I'm going anywhere; I haven't cum either. Here, I've got an idea." He helped Amara up, the two now standing. They traded places, Nick now taking the spot on the couch as Amara stood over him.

"Oh, I see where this is going," Amara whispered, her excitement returning. "Want me back in control?"

"Honestly, I just think you should call the shots so we can get you to cum...but yes, I also want to watch you ride me," Nick laughed.

She moved closer, straddling him before falling onto her knees. She was able to reach underneath her and feel Nick's hard cock, still aching for more. Feeling it twitch, she lined it up with her pussy and slowly teased the tip. She sank down, gasping as his cock pushed into her, inch by inch.

The feelings from last night returned, the thrill of having someone else deep inside her. She tensed her legs, trying to find her balance as she started bouncing up and down on Nick. His hands moved to her waist to help steady her. She lifted up, savoring the feel of his cock moving inside of her, then pushed down. It took a few minutes to get used to the motion, but soon she was picking up speed. She moved faster, her clit throbbing with each hard thrust, and her breathing quickened in turn.

Amara grabbed his shoulders, using him as leverage as she fucked him harder. She could feel her orgasm approaching, and she had waited far too long for it.

Strangely, as she looked down on Nick, she began to sense that he was close to cumming too, maybe even closer than she was. His cock was pulsing, eager to unload in her, and she was desperate to feel it. She remembered his words from earlier, and she knew what would push him over the edge.

"Nick," she leaned in, whispering into his ear, "I want to feel you cum! I want you to fill my pussy!"

Her words clearly got to him, and he shuddered with excitement. Amara continued to fuck him, riding him hard as she kept whispering to him. Finally, it was too much for Nick, and he tensed.

"Fuck! Amara, I—" Nick couldn't finish his thought, his words stuck in his throat as his cock erupted.

The feeling of his cock pulsing, cum pushing into her, set her off too. Her moans filled the apartment, joining Nick's as they rode their orgasms together. Her body twitched, the pleasure overwhelming her senses, and it felt like every nerve in her body was firing. What she was feeling now put every orgasm from her past to shame; her toys seemed like shallow imitations of the real thing.

It took a while for her to finish cumming—another first—but eventually the pleasure started to fade from her body. Her chest was still pounding from the exertion, and she forced herself to take several large breaths.

After a few minutes, when their breathing had evened out, she relaxed her grip on his shoulders. She leaned back, sighing, as she realized her itch had completely vanished.

Amara stood up, a little unsteady, and stretched her arms high above her head.

"That was exactly what I needed!" When she looked back at Nick, he still seemed to be putting himself back together.

"I...that was certainly unexpected." He shifted on the couch as he spoke.

"Look, with how good this was, I don't know if I can give this up just yet!" Amara spun around in glee, letting herself imagine all the devious things she wanted to try.

"Amara, I think you—" He tried to start a thought, but she was too giddy to let him finish it.

"I mean, think about it, we're both single! What's wrong with friends blowing off steam, right?"

"Amara, I really think—"

"It's good exercise, and I imagine we can only get better with practice!" She turned toward Nick as he stood, wondering why he didn't seem as ecstatic as she did.

"Amara!" Nick stood and grabbed her shoulders, holding her still. "You need to look in the mirror, now!"

Caught off guard by his sudden shift in tone, his concern spread to her. She moved to her bedroom, and twitched slightly as something brushed against her ankle. Soon she was standing in front of her tall mirror, her freshly pleasured body on full display.

"Nick, I don't see anything. I guess my eyes are still weirdly bright?" She looked back at her friend, whose eyes were still frozen in concern. He held up a finger and spun it, wordlessly telling her to turn around. As she did, her expression changed to mirror his, the shock apparent.

On her lower back, roughly at the base of her spine, a long, red appendage had suddenly taken root. It was thick at the base, grew slightly thinner as it extended, and the end of it flared into a sharp point, almost like a spade. It rested near her ankles, and when she flinched in surprise, so too did this new part of her. With an errant thought, she envisioned it moving, then watched as it did exactly what she told it to.

"Nick," Amara turned to her best friend, her voice shaking, "Why do I have a tail?"

2

A DEMONIC DISCOVERY

A gentle breeze drifted across the quad, its presence scattering the early autumn leaves that had just started breaking free. The large field, directly in the middle of the Aurelius University campus, was home to dozens of large oak trees. Students regularly came here to study and relax with friends, though Amara was having difficulty staying focused. Every few minutes she found herself scanning the field, scared that she might find a student looking at her. Thankfully, nothing seemed out of the ordinary, but that could change at once if anyone saw her tail.

In the past, Amara had taken pride in looking her best every day, picking cute outfits that complimented her style. Her tail, however, prevented her from wearing almost everything in her closet. She'd ruined an old pair of leggings by cutting a hole for her tail, which sat quite low on her back, and an oversized sweater hopefully hid everything from view. If nothing else, she was thankful autumn was here, as the chill temperature gave her an excuse to bundle up.

She was holding the end of her tail tight inside the pouch of her sweater. Wrapping it repeatedly around her waist was the only way to keep it hidden, but it still felt incredibly bulky. Every so often she would give it a squeeze, hoping to discover it had disappeared, but it remained frustratingly present.

Her mind wandered back to yesterday, to the moment she had first learned about her body's new addition. At first she had been frozen in disbelief, but soon after had succumbed to a full-blown panic attack. Nick, used to keeping her grounded during these times, had done his best to keep her calm.

When the initial panic passed, they had run through some rudimentary tests. They confirmed her tail could register touch just like the rest of her, and she was able to move it at will. Moving it around felt awkward, as if trying to run on a leg that had recently fallen asleep, but she had a surprising amount of control over it.

In the end, she had fallen asleep early. The combination of physical exertion and emotional outburst had brought her to utter exhaustion.

Though she hadn't seen Nick since last night, they had been texting constantly. Their current plan was to meet at the library later this week, once Nick could find time in his schedule. Of the two, he was much more studious, and she hoped he could figure out what was going on.

Why is this happening? And why now?

A hand grabbed her arm and she jumped in surprise.

"Hey, Amara, you okay?"

Shaken back to reality, Amara looked up and forced a smile. "Sorry, I must have spaced for a second there." She was currently sitting on the grass, leaning against a tree. Across from her, sitting in the middle of a pile of books, was Vee.

The two girls met every Monday before their shared Chemistry class. The lab was scheduled in a late time slot, so they both had gaps in their schedules. Spending the time together meant they could enjoy each other's company, but also hold each other accountable for schoolwork.

Vee smiled, then pulled her hand back. "That's alright, I was just checking. It looked like you wanted to take some pictures, but you've just been staring into the distance for the last few minutes."

Amara looked down at the camera in her lap. She pulled her hand out of her sweater, resting it on the grip of the device. She needed a distraction, something to focus on besides her strange new limb. She looked up at Vee, whose attention had turned back to her homework, and decided to shift her focus to her photography.

She turned the camera on, raised it up, and started taking test shots. The digital camera automatically adjusted its own settings, but Amara always tweaked things slightly once it finished. As nice as the camera was, it didn't always capture scenes the way she saw them. The lighting in the first shot was flat, the focus in the second was centered on the wrong object, and after a few more shots, she'd adjusted to the current environment.

Looking through the viewfinder, she aimed the camera at Vee and took a picture. The warm autumn light perfectly highlighted Vee's brilliant blonde hair, which ended just above her shoulders. Her eyebrows were furrowed, her bright blue eyes focused on whatever problem she was solving at the moment.

Amara examined the test photo, decided that the camera settings were up to her standards, then deleted it. She shifted slightly, set up a better angle, then spoke up.

"Hey, Vee!"

Vee looked up from her homework, saw the camera, and laughed. Her response had been exactly what Amara was hoping for; a genuine reaction, something impossible to fake. Vee's smile was gorgeous, just like the rest of her, and her face was framed by light reflecting off a building on the other side of the quad.

"This for an assignment?" Vee asked. Before Amara responded, she raised the camera for another picture, and Vee happily obliged.

"Not this time." Amara continued her impromptu photoshoot, letting Vee decide on poses. She liked giving Vee the freedom to choose. It often made the pictures more dynamic, though the energy didn't quite compare to the spontaneous nature of that first shot.

The two of them, as well as their other close friends, Chloé and Tessa, met as freshmen last year. Aurelius University mandated that all new students take a specific elective designed to encourage community, and the class was focused on introducing people to each other. There had been dozens of group projects and eye-rolling icebreakers, but the class had ultimately worked as intended. The four of them had been inseparable since being grouped on day one.

Vee and Amara had gotten along especially well. They both attracted a fair number of suitors, and while this made perfect sense in Vee's case, Amara had never quite understood the attention directed at her. Still, whenever she spent time with Vee, she always felt good about herself. Vee was smart, kind, well-spoken, and effortlessly confident; the more time they spent together, the more that attitude rubbed off on Amara.

When they'd first met, Amara had been jealous of Vee. She was taller by a few inches, and seemed incredibly comfortable with her toned, athletic body. As their friendship grew, that feeling had eventually faded, with Amara deciding she preferred her own, curvier features, along with her more prominent bust. Now, as she continued taking Vee's picture, that feeling of jealousy returned, this time wishing she could have a normal, tailless body.

"If you get any good shots, can you send them to me? I'm always happy for decent pictures of myself." Vee struck a few more poses, each more ridiculous than the last, but the session was cut short when another breeze passed through the quad. It dislodged a leaf from a nearby tree, which immediately flew into Vee's face. Amara's quick reflexes scored her the perfect shot, but the laughter that followed prevented her from taking any more.

"Vee, check out your face! You look ridiculous!" Amara said, turning the camera's screen towards her friend. Vee began laughing as well, and it took several minutes for them to calm down.

"Alright, my turn," Vee said, reaching for the camera.

"Wait, what? That's not how this works, I'm the photographer."

"I don't care, turnabout is fair play. Now come on, hand it over."

Amara grumbled, but eventually relinquished her hold on the camera. She trusted Vee with it, but desperately didn't want her own picture taken. She knew better than to argue with Vee, however, and tried to strike an engaging pose.

"C'mon, Amara, just act natural," Vee said.

"How am I supposed to do that?" Amara asked. "No matter what I try, I can't force natural behavior, it'll always be staged to some extent."

"Okay, well, then you should learn how to pose." Vee set the camera down, then slid closer. She grabbed Amara's chin, moving her head side to side. "Which do you think looks better? Your left or your right?"

Amara blushed as Vee moved her around. "I dunno, right?"

"Amara, you're a photographer, how do you not know these things? Haven't you ever run tests by taking pictures of yourself?" Vee tilted Amara's head so that her right side was on display, then held up a hand to tell Amara to stay still.

"I, um... don't really like how I look in pictures," Amara muttered.

"Okay, straighten your back, head up, then angle your chin down slightly... perfect!" The camera clicked a few times, and every so often, Vee would shift to a new position. "Amara, no joke, you look fantastic. Here, come take a look."

Amara released her breath and her posture before she moved closer to Vee. They now sat side-by-side, but she made sure not to get too close; she still had a tail to hide. As Vee turned the camera around, and Amara saw the pictures, she reluctantly agreed with Vee. "Alright, you win this one. I don't look half bad."

"Not half bad? Amara, you're gorgeous!" Vee threw an arm around Amara's shoulder and pulled her close. "Okay, last photo is a selfie. Smile!"

Amara froze up, split between two trains of thought. Initially she was terrified that Vee had pulled her close, and did her best to wrap her tail even tighter. She then remembered that trying to take a selfie with a real camera was a terrible idea, and watched as Vee struggled with the grip. Amara was shocked the camera didn't fall, but the absurdity of the moment got the better of her. She relaxed against Vee, smiling and laughing as the shudder clicked.

"Alright, if you're done abusing your camera privileges, we have a chem lab to get to," Amara said, grabbing the camera back before slowly starting to pack it away.

"Abusing? Please, those pictures are amazing." Vee grabbed her things as well, neatly placing books and homework into her backpack. "I don't understand how you don't see it, Amara. Is that why you haven't dated anyone since college started?"

"I mean, maybe?" Amara zipped her camera bag closed. "I know people are interested in me, but it always feels insincere. Like they're flirting with the person they think I am or want me to be. Every time I try to picture myself with someone, it doesn't feel right."

"Personally, I was hoping you might meet someone at the party." Vee seemed ready to continue talking, but stopped abruptly. When Amara looked up, she caught Vee looking at another girl, one who was walking straight towards the two of them. This new girl was shorter, with medium-length brown hair, and she was being followed by three other students.

"Look girls, it's Vee," the brunette said, smirking to her friends. "I saw you at the Palace on Saturday, did you manage to find a guy more appropriate for you?"

Vee rolled her eyes, and Amara stepped back to avoid getting sucked into the confrontation. "For the record, Tania, I don't give a shit about Derek. Pretty much anyone on campus would be a step up compared to him."

Tania laughed. "Please, we all know what you're doing. Playing hard to get makes you look like a desperate high schooler. Just stay out of my way, alright?"

Before Vee could respond, Tania gestured to her friends that she wanted to leave. She quickly walked past Vee, conveniently bumping into her on the way past. The other students followed quickly, and once they'd left, Amara moved closer. She placed a hand on Vee's arm to comfort her, then asked, "What was that about?"

"Ugh, it's so stupid. Tania's trying to get with Derek, but since I'm his current fascination, she thinks I'm standing in her way."

Amara scowled as she thought about Derek. His family was notoriously wealthy, and his father was the most influential person on the school's board of directors. Derek took full advantage of his position, and had essentially turned the campus into his own personal playground. Students and faculty alike bent over backwards to keep him happy, while those who stood in his way frequently regretted it. Supposedly, the last teacher to give him a poor grade had lost tenure within a year.

A few weeks back, Vee had run into Derek at a party, and she'd become somewhat of an obsession for him. He desperately wanted to hook up with her, and he refused to accept that she wanted nothing to do with him.

"Seriously? Ugh, I can't believe people actually want to spend time with that asshole. There haven't been any incidents recently, have there?"

Vee shook her head. "Not really. I got pretty lucky, and he wasn't at the Palace when we were there. Look, I'd rather not talk about that, if it's alright. What about you? I mean, it was your first party ever, and you still haven't told me anything about it! It seemed like you were having fun dancing, but I lost track of you shortly after that.

Amara swallowed nervously. "Uh, yeah, it was neat. It took a lot out of me, though, and Nick ended up walking me home early."

"Hm, that explains why he went missing too. Shame; he and I were really hitting it off." Vee said with a smirk.

"Wait, that was you?" It was Amara's turn to lean in, eager to get more details and thankful for the distraction. The two continued gossiping, sharing details about the party, and Amara confirmed her suspicions that Vee was interested in Nick. She'd suspected something for a while, but it was impossible to convince Nick to make the first move.

Today's chemistry lab was nothing special. The impressively bland tone of the professor was tolerable only because of Vee's presence, but thankfully most of their activities were self-guided. Their conversation bounced between gossip and pH levels as they worked through the assignment, and eventually it was time to pack up.

Amara took over the cleaning, washing out all the beakers and tools while Vee finalized the notes and turned their papers in. When Vee returned, Amara had just finished washing her hands, and left the water running for her. Grabbing the soap, Vee moved her hands under the water, then immediately jumped back.

"Ah, fuck!" Vee yelped. "Amara, this water is scalding hot!"

Amara ran over, grasping the handles, but she paused briefly. Everyone nearby was looking at Vee, so Amara quickly ran her hand under the water. Surprisingly, it felt fine; she would have guessed it was slightly warmer than room temperature had it not just burned her friend.

"Here, this should be better, come run some cold water over it." Amara finished adjusting the water as she called Vee over. "It was fine when I was cleaning up; I think I just left it running too long."

"That feels nice, thanks. I don't think there's any real damage; it just caught me by surprise."

Vee finished washing her hands, hopefully none the wiser. Amara sighed in relief, happy her friend was okay, but made a mental note to tell Nick about this.

Once they cleaned up, they said their goodbyes, and Amara started the long trek home. The incident at the lab had her thinking about Vee, the concern for her friend outweighing the confusion over what had happened.

Spending time with Vee always cheered Amara up, and today was no exception, but the feeling faded fast once they parted ways. She wished she could have Vee's confidence, but compliments about her appearance only went so far when she also had a mysterious new limb twitching uncomfortably under her sweater.

With a heavy sigh, Amara pulled up some music on her phone, then strolled out into the brisk autumn air.

Well, I've officially survived my first day as a... whatever I am.

Before knocking on the door in front of her, Amara took one last look at her outfit. She still struggled to find clothes that fit comfortably around her tail, and she desperately wanted to avoid cutting up more leggings. Thankfully, she had no shortage of cute, oversized sweaters, and she had made it through today's classes without incident.

Is this really a good idea? I know I promised Tessa I'd hang out with her today, but it's not too late to back out. I could say I'm sick!

Amara sighed. She knew she wasn't going to bail. As scared as she was of being found out, she loved her friends and wanted to keep pretending she was normal. The more time she spent alone at home, the more she feared spiraling into another panic attack.

Plus, one of Tessa's partners was an amazing chef, and Amara would never dream of passing up a chance to eat her food. Her stomach was already grumbling thinking about it.

As she thought about her stomach, she inevitably returned to thinking about the tail wrapped around her midriff. It hadn't moved for most of the day and was starting to cramp up. With a quick look up and down the hallway, she nervously released her tail long enough to wrap it in the other direction. Although the process only took a few seconds, it felt like an eternity as she nervously looked at the myriad other doors in the hallway.

With her tail safely under wraps, Amara finally knocked on the front door. When it opened, she looked up to see not Tessa, but Raine.

Raine was, to the best of Amara's knowledge, the person that had been dating Tessa the longest. They had short dark hair, a prominent silver septum ring, and hints of a mustache on their upper lip. The two had met last year and, after several weeks of hooking up, decided to start dating. Eventually, they'd welcomed other people into the dynamic, and from what Amara could remember, their polycule currently had four people in it.

"Amara! How 'ya doing?" Raine asked, pulling Amara in for a hug.

After panicking briefly, Amara squeezed her tail as tight as she could while also hugging with just her upper body. "Hey, Raine! I'm good, as usual. What about yourself? The facial hair looks like it's really coming in!"

Raine pushed the door further open, gesturing for Amara to come inside. They ran a finger over their top lip before responding. "You think so? I feel like I haven't noticed a difference, but *someone* says I should wait to get my testosterone levels checked before upping my dosage again."

Now that Amara was inside, she smelled fresh onions and peppers frying in the kitchen. She also saw a small column of steam rising from a rice cooker, and Sydney was standing over the stove with a handful of spices. "Yeah, 'cuz you just upped your dosage, like, two months ago! You've got to wait longer than that! When I started hormones, I always waited a minimum of three months, sometimes longer," the chef said. Her long brown hair was tied up in a ponytail, and she was energetically bouncing back and forth to the music coming from a small Bluetooth speaker.

"Ugh, you're such a killjoy," Raine said sarcastically. They walked over to Sydney, playfully kissing her before moving to the couch in the living room.

From down the hallway, another voice shouted, "Is that Amara?!"

"Yes!" Raine called back. "Think you can spare the time to come say hi? Or would you rather spend another hour in the shower?"

Tessa walked into the living room holding a small towel, which she was using to dry her short, jet-black hair. It was completely shaved on one side, replaced with a small collection of intricate runic tattoos. Excessively detailed eyeliner decorated her face, which was also adorned with a small collection of piercings. Black sweatpants hung off her hips, likely a few sizes too large. They seemed on the verge of falling off, and the straps of her thong were visible above the waistband. She also wore a simple, purple tank top, though she hadn't bothered putting on a bra after her shower; Amara saw hints of her friend's nipples peeking through the fabric.

"Oh, shut up, Raine," Tessa said, throwing her towel at her partner. She then turned her attention to Amara, running in for a hug. "Amara! You have to tell me all about Saturday! You looked so fucking hot in that dress, I'm still having wet dreams about dancing with you."

For the second time since arriving, Amara found herself manipulating an incoming hug. She quickly pushed Tessa's arms up over her shoulders and broke off the hug as soon as she could, blushing heavily as she tried to ignore her friend's lewd comment. "I mean, I'll tell you everything, but don't get your hopes up. I didn't really do much."

Tessa turned around, grabbing Amara's hand and dragging her to the couch. As they walked, Amara's gaze wandered down to her friend's body. Tessa was the shorter of the two, and had less curvaceous features, but she was still incredibly attractive. What she lacked in physical presence she more than made up for with her attitude; she was the most sociable of Amara's friends, constantly going to parties, hooking up with new people, and trying to get others to join in the fun. Amara had always appreciated Tessa's energy, though she'd never quite gotten used to that energy being turned on her.

Ever since they'd met, Tessa had flirted with Amara nonstop. It was almost impossible to have a conversation without her sneaking in a sexual proposition. The attention never failed to fluster Amara, especially since she'd never thought about Tessa that way.

Until now, apparently.

Without even realizing it, Amara found her eyes tracing the curves of Tessa's body, following the straps of her thong as they disappeared into her pants. A familiar itch reappeared in Amara, tingling between her legs as she imagined what Tessa might look like without those pants.

What am I thinking? There's no way I can be this horny already, I had sex twice this weekend, and it's only been two days since then!

Shaking her head, Amara shifted her attention back to the apartment around her. She jumped on the couch opposite Tessa, who pulled her legs under her before leaning forward. "C'mon, gimme the deets! What happened? Did you meet anybody? Fuck anybody?"

"Tess, I already told you not to get your hopes up. Nothing happened!" Amara sighed, leaning back on the couch before continuing. "I hung out with you and the girls for a while, and dancing was a lot of fun. There were definitely a lot of people trying to hit on me, but I politely turned them all down, and eventually I just got a little overwhelmed. When I left you guys, I went and found Nick, then we walked home so I could go to sleep."

At least, I wish that's what happened. There's no way in Hell I'm telling Tessa that I slept with Nick.

"Bullshit! You can't be serious!" Tessa said.

Raine moved closer, sitting between Amara and Tessa before speaking up. "No need to harass the poor girl, Tess. Not everyone takes to parties as easily as you do."

"Okay, but giving up after a bit of dancing? Why even bother going out?"

"In case you've forgotten, Tessa," Amara started, "I barely even wanted to go to this party. If you, Vee, and Chloé hadn't ganged up on me, I never would have considered it. Besides, I did have fun dancing, and it was nice to get all dressed up!"

Tessa groaned loudly, dramatically throwing her head over the side of the couch while swinging her legs into Raine's lap. "Ugh, I can't believe we're friends."

Amara's eyes instinctually moved to the dramatic motion, but with Tessa hanging off the armrest, her gaze was drawn to her friend's small bust. Her nipples were still easily visible, and the soft curves of her breasts seemed eager to invite Amara's imagination.

Fuck, what is wrong with me? I've never needed to masturbate more than, like, once a week, and now I can't even stop myself from fantasizing about Tessa?

With a loud grunt, Tessa sat back up, and Amara quickly diverted her eyes. If Tessa caught her checking her out, she'd never hear the end of it. "Okay, well, if nothing else, you have to let me give you a tarot reading," Tessa said, pulling a box off the coffee table.

"It can't be a full one, Tess!" Sydney called out from the kitchen. "Dinner's almost ready!"

"Okay, I'll be quick! Just a single card, so we can check in on how you're feeling." Tessa opened the box, pulled out a deck of cards, and began expertly shuffling them. Amara watched as she tossed the cards back and forth, focusing on her dexterous hands. Would she be just as skilled using her fingers for something else?

Stop it, Amara!

When Tessa finally finished, she swapped places with Raine to sit next to Amara. "Alright, put your hand on the deck, and think about the party."

Amara did what she was told, casting her thoughts back to that fateful night. The dancing, the attention, the overwhelming itch. Slipping her friends to grab Nick, then pulling him into an abandoned bedroom in the Palace. Tessa had given her readings before, and she knew what to do next. She cut the deck, moving the top half to the bottom, then pulled the new top card and held it up for Tessa to see.

"Oooh, spooky," Tessa whispered.

"What? What'd I draw?"

"You pulled the thirteenth Arcana. Death." Tessa was smiling now, clearly excited about the draw. "Are you sure nothing weird happened at the party?"

"Positive!" Amara said, praying that Tessa didn't notice her blushing. "What does Death mean, again? I remember that it's not literal, but that's it."

"No, you're not about to die," Tessa said. "At its heart, Death often represents change or rebirth. You can't take steps into the future without leaving something behind. That person, the past version of you, dies to make way for something new."

Amara had never been particularly spiritual, and couldn't even remember if her mother had ever tried to bring her to church, but a chill ran down her spine as she turned the card around. A stylized grim reaper, its scythe held aloft, stared her down as she reflected on Tessa's words. She didn't quite know what to say, and certainly didn't want to risk her friends finding out what had really happened. "Why is thirteen considered unlucky, anyways?" Amara asked, trying to change the subject.

Raine spoke up first. "That's actually pretty hard to pin down, especially since it's more commonly a fear in western civilization. I often see people cite the Last

Supper, where the person who betrayed Jesus was the thirteenth person at the table."

"Nah," Tessa said, "it's because of the patriarchy."

"Tess, you say that about everything," Raine said.

"That's because it's always true! In ages past, the number thirteen was viewed positively as a symbol of femininity. Women, on average, tend to have about thirteen periods over the course of a year. It's also considered the number of the witch. Early practitioners of witchcraft tended to form groups, or covens, of thirteen people. When those early cultures got stamped out, the men in charge decided that thirteen was unlucky because of those associations. So yes, men ruin everything."

Before Amara could respond, Sydney spoke up again. "Bold words from someone who's openly bi."

"Okay, look, I can't control who I find attractive, alright?" Tessa protested. "Besides, I date women and enbies like, ninety percent of the time. Sometimes men are just more fun as casual hookups, you know? Besides, I think that fucking stalker has turned me off men for a while."

"Wait, you have a stalker?" Amara asked, surprised.

"Ugh, I hate talking about it, but yes. Some little twerp that's into goth chicks won't leave me alone. I think I've taken care of it for now, but he's a slippery little fuck, so who knows."

Tessa had always been flighty, but Amara was shocked that she'd never heard about this stalker before. Trying to get personal information out of Tessa was always a pain in the ass, but this seemed like the type of thing she would have been openly bitching about with her friends. Amara was about to ask another question when she was cut off by Sydney.

"Dinner's ready!"

Eager for dinner, and knowing that Tessa would probably refuse to elaborate anyways, Amara jumped up from the couch and grabbed a bowl. This was one of Amara's favorite dishes, it was a rice dish packed with veggies and chicken, though Sydney had a bad habit of adding too much spice for Amara's liking. She was intrigued, then, when she bit in and found the dish to be unexpectedly tame. It was every bit as delicious as she'd expected, but the heat she normally feared was nowhere to be found.

Tessa and Raine joined her seconds later, and soon everyone was eating. Interestingly, when Tessa took her first bite, her eyes immediately went wide in surprise. "Wow, that's got more kick than usual. Did you drop the whole spice jar in by accident?"

"Oh, shoot," Sydney said, staring into the distance as she scanned her memories. "I might have been distracted by Amara showing up when I was spicing it."

Wait, this is spicier than normal? Shit. First yesterday's incident with the hot water, and now this?

"It's not bad, just caught me off guard. Whew." Tessa grabbed a fresh drink from the fridge before returning to her meal. On her way back, she slapped Amara on the back and said, "You holding up alright? You've got the wimpiest tolerance of all of us!"

"Um, yeah it's pretty hot," Amara muttered. "I think I might be getting used to it, though, so no worries, Sydney."

Sydney quickly finished a bite before responding. "How is your spice tolerance so low, by the way? I always thought Hispanic cuisine was generally on the spicier side of things."

Amara cocked her head, then quickly remembered that Tessa's partners knew almost nothing about her family life. What little of it there was, at least. "Oh, I'm not entirely sure what I am. My mom always seemed to cook pretty typical American stuff."

"What about, like, holidays? Birthdays? Family gatherings?" Raine asked.

"I didn't really have anything like that," Amara said softly, "it was just me and my mom. I don't know anything about her family, I'm pretty sure she doesn't like them. My dad was never a part of the picture, so I didn't get any relatives from that side either. Though, even if my mom were Hispanic or something, we never celebrated any holidays outside of the popular American ones."

Sydney reached across the counter and grabbed Amara's hand. "I'm sorry, I didn't mean to pry. Hey, at least you've got us now! We can be your new family!"

Amara forced a smile as she squeezed Sydney's hand in return. Talking about her family, or her lack of one, was never her favorite topic. She'd always felt somewhat detached, like she didn't have anything she truly belonged to, though it was a feeling she'd gotten used to over the years. "Aww, well, I couldn't ask for better siblings!" Amara said, trying to lighten the mood.

Everyone at the counter laughed, though Tessa jokingly rolled her eyes as she did. Raine noticed this and playfully elbowed her. "C'mon, Tess, lighten up. If you can't handle a little found family dramatics, you're going to hate Sydney's movie choice tonight."

Tessa narrowed her eyes. "What are you planning?"

A devious smirk lit up Sydney's face, and she finished her food in a hurry before running to the bedroom. "You all get comfortable! I need a sec to set it up!"

"I didn't realize tonight was movie night, that's exciting!" Amara said. The thought of enjoying friendly company while being able to easily hide her tail in a heavy blanket sounded like a dream come true. She made her way to the couch, eager to steal the corner with the thickest blanket, then settled in. Raine and Tessa joined her moments later, and everyone watched as Sydney emerged from the bedroom with a large plastic box. Various cords dangled from it, and it took Amara a moment to recognize what she was looking at. "Is that a VCR?"

Sydney set everything down in front of the TV, then turned to the group on the couch. "Ladies and enbies, friends and partners, today you have the utmost privilege of watching a masterpiece from 1993, preserved in its original format: Homeward Bound!"

Tessa groaned. "Really? Silly animal movies?"

"Homeward Bound?" Amara asked. "I don't think I've heard of that one."

Sydney seemed to take this as a personal attack, and gave Amara a quick synopsis of the movie while she plugged in the ancient piece of hardware. After several minutes of troubleshooting, a grainy picture appeared on the TV, and the movie started. Sydney jumped on the couch, squeezed between Tessa and Raine, and turned up the volume.

It was an incredibly simple movie. Two dogs and a cat were trying to make their way home through the wilderness, facing down dangerous wildlife and various other hardships. It wasn't the type of movie that Amara typically found interesting, but as the story continued, she became completely enthralled. She forgot about her tail, and the apprehension from the last few days vanished as she grew more absorbed in the movie. She celebrated every tiny victory, gasped at every new challenge, and prayed desperately that everyone would make it home safe.

In the final stretch of the movie, the older dog fell into a muddy pit and was too weak to climb out. The other two animals were forced to continue without him, and Amara was furious at the movie. Would the filmmakers really be so cruel? The movie was almost over, and the pets were so close to their home!

When the first pet reunited with the family, Amara couldn't stop herself from laughing with joy. Then the second made it home, and everyone turned to look at the forest. The other dog was nowhere to be seen, and his owner started to give up hope. Just then, the music swelled, and the last pet limped over the hill. With the final reunion, Amara completely broke down. She was sobbing uncontrollably, soaking the blanket she had borrowed. The movie ended happily, with everyone safe and sound, and the credits rolled.

"See? Was that so bad?" Sydney said, teasing Tessa.

"I guess it was alright. Amara, what did you—holy shit, are you okay?" Tessa turned to Amara, surprise in her voice.

Amara, who was still in the middle of her unexpected breakdown, did her best to say something between sobs. "It was so cute! They just wanted to be home with their family!" Her entire body was shaking, and she had no idea why she'd been so affected by the movie.

Raine was sitting next to Amara, and they gently put their arm around her shoulder to give her somewhere to cry. Amara fell into their lap, the heavy blanket hiding her tail, and spent another five minutes trying and failing to stop her waterworks. By the end, she'd been crying so hard that she also started laughing, the absurdity of her reaction finally hitting her.

Eventually, she managed to pull herself together, though not before burning through half a box of tissues. She slowly sat up, pulling the blanket tight, and blew her nose one last time. "Um, I guess I liked the movie, Sydney," Amara said, forcing a smile.

"You doing alright Amara?" Tessa asked. "Like, seriously, what was that?"

"Fuck if I know. I'm just as shocked as you are." Amara rubbed her eyes, taking a deep breath before heavily sighing. Now somewhat lucid again, she checked the time on her phone. "Whew, is it already that late? I should probably get going."

"Awww, that's a shame," Sydney said. "I'm glad you enjoyed it though! I've never had a choice of movie affirmed quite this dramatically before!"

Amara happily said goodbye to everyone, making sure to keep their hands away from her stomach as they hugged. Once finished, she gathered up all her things and headed home. She spent the entire walk trying to figure out why that movie had hit her so hard, but every time she thought about the ending, she started tearing up again.

She finally decided to give up altogether, instead pulling out her phone to text Nick more updates. They'd finally found a gap in his schedule, and were planning to meet in the library tomorrow after classes.

Two days down, Amara. You can do this.

After wandering around the library for a while, Amara finally found Nick huddled in a secluded corner. He had stacks of books on the table, with a laptop open in the middle. His brows were furrowed in concentration.

His light brown hair was fairly curly, but he typically kept it short; he claimed it was too difficult to manage when it got long. The one time he tried, their junior year, Amara had thought the long hair flattered his sharp features nicely. His deep green eyes darted back and forth across the pages, and his arm propped up his face as he read. He was hunching slightly; no doubt the library chairs weren't the most comfortable for someone close to six feet tall.

Nick had wrestled in high school, and while he didn't play sports anymore, his body was still quite athletic. His muscular frame was sometimes hard to notice, due to his uninspired wardrobe, but today he was wearing a button-down flannel that was quite flattering.

Amara moved in, sitting down across from him and tossing her backpack to the floor.

"You know, normal people use the internet these days. Heard of it?" Amara grabbed the nearest book, pretending to read it upside down as she stared at Nick over the top of it.

"Very funny, Amara, but my roommate is hogging the room again. Plus, a lot of the books I need for my classes are locked behind paywalls." Nick put his book down and leaned back, stretching his arms behind him. "Not to mention all the books that haven't been properly digitized yet, especially on older campuses like ours."

"Whatever, *nerd*." Amara rolled her eyes. "What is all this anyways?" She gestured to the stacks cluttering the table.

"I've been here for a while, so it's a combination of most of my classes. Calc, History, all stuff you hate." Nick leaned in, his eyes more focused as he changed the topic. "And of course, some research about your... condition. How are you holding up? Anything new? Weird?"

Amara set her book down as she quieted her voice. "Other than, I don't know—my fucking tail?" She sighed, planting her head on the table before groaning. "I'm sorry, you don't deserve that. I've just been so stressed since Sunday. Every time I catch someone looking at me, I'm scared they'll see it."

Nick reached across the table, grabbing her wrist. "Hey, I get it. I'm confused and scared too, and this isn't even happening to me." He squeezed again before letting go. "So, nothing else? Just the tail?"

Amara switched to leaning on her elbows. "Ugh, I think I almost burned Vee during our lab. I was washing my hands, and left the water running for her, but she shrieked and said it was practically boiling." She pushed her head into her hands, sulking. "I'm starting to think my building doesn't actually have issues with its water heater."

Nick paused, thinking to himself. "So now, it's just the glowing eyes, the tail, and a tolerance to heat. That would make sense." He started rummaging through the books on the table, looking for one in particular.

"Make sense? Did you figure out what's happening?" Amara had to remember to keep her voice down.

"I've got a theory—the book is here somewhere." Nick moved a stack of books to the floor as he kept digging. "Have you looked into this at all?"

"I tried! I learned a lot about a group of fighter pilots in World War Two called the Red Tails; it was pretty inspirational."

Nick glared at her, likely not surprised she had gotten distracted.

"Hey, you *know* I'm terrible at research."

"Well, maybe if you actually focused on what's around you," he muttered, grabbing the book under her arms and turning it right side up, "You'd find something useful once in a while!"

Nick triumphantly held up the book, its tattered hardcover reading *A Complete History of Demons and Demonology.*

Amara stared at him in disbelief. "Nick. You *can't* be serious."

He leaned in again, matching her gaze. "Let me walk you through it, okay? Keep breathing, focus on my voice, I'm here with you." He guided her through a familiar routine, keeping her grounded as he opened the book.

"So, we don't have a lot to go on, but the tail is a pretty big clue. There are a lot of stories from mythology about creatures that are mostly human, except for the addition of a tail."

Amara kept breathing, in for two counts, out for four. A steady rhythm, one Nick had helped her piece together over years of friendship.

"Often, the tail is based on an animal. Satyrs have horse-like tails, kitsune have fox tails, things like that. There's very little overlap, which makes it helpful to figure out what you're dealing with."

She squeezed her tail through her hoodie, listening to Nick intently.

"Now, yours is pretty unique, and doesn't really match up with an animal. It does, however, match a lot of descriptions of various religious demons." He flipped through pages, showing off different depictions of hellish creatures. Many of the demons depicted had smooth, red tails, with flared spades at the end.

"Okay, I guess that makes sense. But this book is huge! How are we supposed to narrow it down?" Amara's eyes lingered on a picture of a snake offering a woman an apple.

"That stumped me for a bit too, but then I remembered another detail. When did this start happening?"

"It was right after the party. Right after I finally had sex!" Amara shifted in her seat, leaning closer to Nick.

"And with that in mind..." Nick flipped to a dog-eared page, "meet the succubus. A demon that gains power and energy from sex."

Amara picked up the book, properly this time, and spent the better part of the next hour reading everything she could. She wasn't the fastest reader, but with the scope of her research narrowed, she was able to be much more productive. She managed to find another few books Nick had missed, but also a few websites that proved helpful.

The amount of information she found was staggering. Myths about demons have existed for as long as humanity could tell stories, and every source seemed to have a different interpretation of the succubus. However, there seemed to be several commonalities amongst all the stories, and Amara did her best to track those ideas, hoping they might give her an idea of what was happening.

Most obviously, succubi were sexual creatures. They needed sex to survive and often relied on trickery to get it. Sometimes this involved shapeshifting, sometimes they invaded people's dreams to prey on their unconscious minds. Some stories claimed that succubi simply wanted to eat cum and tempt men into cheating, while others claimed that they consumed the souls of their victims. No matter the interpretation, every source agreed that sleeping with a succubus, even once, could have disastrous consequences.

Amara lingered on this thought, reading and rereading several lines of text describing the various ways people could die by sleeping with a succubus. "Hey, Nick. Have you felt any different since this weekend?"

Nick looked up from his book, then furrowed his brow as he cycled through his memories. "Not really?"

"Hm. Okay." Amara didn't bother elaborating, and returned to her research.

The next thing she learned was that succubi always seemed to be women, but some books referenced a male counterpart called an incubus. She didn't find any actual differences between the two, other than incubi being far less represented.

I'll bet the authors were just a bunch of pervs. Doubt there was a lot of opportunity for sexy demon porn way back in the day.

The first hour came and went, and she continued reading. Succubi always seemed to have tails, but they usually also came with horns and wings. They had power over dreams, and could usually summon and control fire. Mind control came up frequently as well, but seemed to be limited to victims the succubus had already slept with. On a similar note, supernatural charm seemed fairly common: the ability to magically coerce someone into feeling sexual attraction, regardless of personal taste.

Out of curiosity, she slightly lowered her book and peeked over the top at Nick. She'd been trying to wrestle her libido all week, and she tried to project those thoughts onto him to see what happened. After a few minutes of concentrating, nothing seemed to change, and she gave up.

Eventually, her stomach rumbling, she was forced to start packing up. Her mind was racing from all the new information, and she moved slowly as she cycled through it all.

"So, how are we feeling? Better or worse?" Nick asked, returning from dropping off his last pile of books.

Amara's eyes lost focus, staring into the distance as she pondered his question. "You know how monster movies always have that one scene? Where the heroine finds an old library and learns all about the thing trying to kill her? It's like I'm living that movie, but I'm the monster." There was a slight hitch in her voice, which she countered with another deep breath.

Without realizing it, she found herself stuck in Nick's arms as he pulled her in for a hug. "Hey, you are *not* a monster. So what if you're not quite human? You're a good person, full of love. Nothing can change that." He squeezed tight, letting a few moments pass as their breathing started to synchronize. "Let's move to the next thought. Push forward, leave the stress behind."

Amara exhaled, listening to his advice as he guided her through her scattered thoughts.

"I'm glad we've got a working theory. I feel like I've established some parameters, and this doesn't feel as scary." Amara took care to speak in a steady tone, giving voice to her feelings to keep them from overwhelming her. "But, Nick, there's *so* much conflicting information! Some cultures say succubi mostly operate in dreams, and others say they walk among us, changing shape as they please! One book says they just want to eat cum all day, and another says they actually feed on human souls. *Souls*!"

Nick sighed, pushing her away slightly before tilting her head toward his. "Well, a lot of these stories are hundreds of years old, and most people assume it's all made up anyways. Can't say I'm surprised." He handed Amara her backpack, slinging his own over his shoulder.

They started toward the main entrance, but Amara only took a few steps before pausing. An unforeseen side effect of all this research was that she'd been thinking about sex constantly, and her libido was particularly feisty. "Nick, wait up, I've got an idea!" She grabbed his hand and pulled him in a different direction.

Confused, Nick let Amara drag him through the library, dodging between shelves as they went. He took care to be quiet, unsure what the plan was.

"So, this library has a basement, mostly used to store older materials. Ancient newspapers, books too tattered to put out, stuff like that." Amara finally stopped when they reached a small door, which creaked ominously when she pushed it open.

"And you're hoping to find more information down there? I thought we were calling it so we could get dinner?"

"Oh, shush, let me finish. Anyways! When they remodeled, they added a second staircase downstairs. It's much easier to find, which means this one is basically never used anymore!"

As the door closed behind them, what she was saying became obvious. The lights weren't even on, which Amara addressed. A series of lights hummed to life, bathing the area in a dull orange hue. Many of the handrails were covered in dust, their paint chipping and falling to the floor.

"Amara, as much as I love a good architecture lesson, how do you know about this? I thought libraries were for *nerds.*" Nick pushed her in jest as he started down the stairs, his steps echoing off the yellowed tiles.

Amara started after him, pushing him back as she raced ahead. "I know some-one who used to work here! Heard a lot of fun gossip!" She paused at the landing between the staircases, turning to face Nick again.

He caught up to Amara, her body blocking the second set of stairs. "I'm still waiting for the point of all this, Amara." When he looked down at her, he noticed her eyes were glowing.

"The point, Nick—" she laid her hands on him, suddenly pushing him up against the wall, "—is that I want to say thanks!" She moved closer, wrapping her hands around his chest as she pulled him in for a kiss. Her hands wandered, first exploring underneath his shirt, then moving down as they started undoing his pants.

"I mean, what kind of succubus has never swallowed cum before?" She smirked deviously, kissing his neck before sliding down onto her heels. Her hands hooked into his pants, pulling them down just enough to free his cock.

"I-I mean...here? What if someone finds us?" Nick muttered, his cock growing harder by the second as she wrapped her hands around his shaft.

"I think it's kind of exciting!" She leaned in, licking him from base to tip before locking eyes again. "Now are you going to complain all day? Or let a beautiful girl suck you off?"

"F-fuck, Amara, you know that's not what I'm saying..." Nick shivered as her tongue explored him, precum forming on the head.

She kissed the tip, his precum decorating her lips as she pushed forward. His cock slid inside her mouth, and she moaned in pleasure as she felt how much he was enjoying this. She bobbed back and forth slowly, her tongue working the head every time she pulled back.

Amara could feel her own arousal building, but she was too focused on the task at hand to bother undressing. Shifting slightly, she moved to her knees instead of squatting, and found it much more comfortable; here, she could really savor this experience. Her hands moved back to his cock, grabbing the base and accentuating each pass her mouth made with a gentle squeeze.

She was enjoying taking her time, no longer in a rush to lose her virginity or scratch an impossible itch. The feel of her mouth wrapped around him was incredible, and she loved every small grunt he made as she pleasured him. Taking a deep breath, Amara pushed forward a little more, feeling his cock push against her throat. A soft gag escaped her, and she pulled back, grinning.

"It always looks so easy in porn," Amara whispered, slowly stroking his cock.

She licked it from base to tip again before opening wide, slapping him on her tongue. She smirked as she watched his face contort with pleasure, then took him back in her mouth again. She continued sucking, long strokes as far as she could comfortably go, each time gagging ever so slightly; she was determined to fit more of him in. The sounds of her gagging echoed through the staircase, accompanied by Nick's heavy breathing as she kept testing her limits. Nick's cock grew increasingly wet as she sucked, and she felt it was time to be bold.

With a deep breath, she pushed down hard. She relaxed her throat, willing it to open and let his cock inside. Another gag, much louder than the rest, reverberated around her as she felt the tip push deeper into her. She managed to hold herself down for a few seconds before finally pulling back, a look of satisfaction on her face.

"Fuck! I think I'm getting good at this!" She giggled as she went back to stroking his cock, precum dangling off her lips. She locked eyes with Nick as he glanced down.

"Amara, I don't know how much longer I can last!" His breathing was erratic, and he was attempting to steady himself on a nearby railing.

Eager to finally taste cum, Amara redoubled her efforts. She went back to sucking with long, slow strokes, building up a rhythm. She moved her hands to his hips, holding him tight as she let her mouth take full control of his cock.

Down, relax the throat.

Up, breathe.

Down, feel the entrance give.

Up, tongue his cockhead.

Down, a little deeper.

Up, feel his body quiver.

Amara moaned as she kept going, thrilled she was getting better at opening her throat for Nick's cock. Her hands slid behind him, working harder to pull him in as she sucked.

She wanted to feel more of him, and a devious thought crossed her mind. Without moving her hands, or stopping her mouth, she uncurled her tail from around her waist, letting it slide out of her sweater. As she freed it, Amara looked up and was surprised to see Nick looking down at her. The last two times they'd fucked he mostly kept his eyes closed, lost in the moment. Now, however, he watched keenly as Amara presented her tail, whipping it back and forth behind her. It moved closer to Nick, coming to rest near his ankle before starting to curl around it. The tail crept higher, covering more of his leg, until Amara ran out of length. She felt her eyes flare with passion, and suddenly she knew that Nick only had moments left.

She pulled back, taking one last deep breath, then pushed toward Nick. Her hands and tail held him perfectly still as she felt her throat open again, completely swallowing the rest of his cock.

"Fuck!" Nick yelled, one of his hands moving to Amara's head. His body tensed, quick waves of pleasure shooting through him as he finally orgasmed.

Amara moaned as she felt his cock pulse, and she pulled back so just the tip was in her mouth. Load after load pumped into her, filling her mouth with his cum. She was shocked at how delicious it was, and she eagerly swallowed every drop he gave her. Her whole body tingled, and she felt a wave of heat pulse out of her body. A strange flicker of light danced around her head, but she had trouble focusing on it, instead eagerly tonguing Nick's cock for the last few drops of his cum.

Surprisingly, despite having received no pleasure of her own, Amara's itch seemed to have faded somewhat.

Nick relaxed his grip on her head, and she realized just how tightly he had been holding her. She took his cue and pulled her hands off his hips, her mouth letting his cock free as she moved her head back. Her tail loosened its grip as well, though she gave it one last flex out of curiosity.

"Fuck, that was fun!" Amara took a deep breath, standing up and stretching her arms. She watched as Nick pulled his pants back up, slowly regaining his composure as he dressed himself. Moving in, she gave him a quick hug from the side and kissed his cheek. "Thanks for the snack. I hope you enjoyed it as much as I did!"

"Believe me, that was fantastic." Nick finally returned her hug now that he was fully dressed. "Now, do you want the good news or the bad news first?"

Amara pulled back, eyeing him with suspicion. "Um...let's say the good news."

"Well, I think we've proved our succubus theory correct!" Nick chuckled to himself as he fished his phone out of his pocket. "The bad news, however...well, see for yourself."

Holding up his phone, Amara saw he had turned the camera inward, giving her a mirror. Her hair was a bit of a mess, and there were traces of spit and cum on her chin. Her eyes were also glowing, more than usual, but one feature stood out more than all the rest.

A few inches above each of her eyebrows, two small horns had appeared. Each one was roughly two inches long, protruding out from her head before angling back, following the curve of her skull. They were black, but had red undertones that became more apparent as light reflected off them. She ran her fingers over them, thankful that they didn't seem able to register touch; the only thing she noticed was the feeling in her fingers. Although smooth, there was a fair amount of variation on the surface, almost like tree bark.

"God dammit, these are going to be way harder to hide!" Amara grumbled as she tossed her backpack to the floor. After a few seconds of rummaging, she pulled out a red cable-knit beanie. "Thankfully it's already pretty chilly. If it were summer it would be easier to just drop out!"

Pulling out her own phone, she took a few minutes to tidy herself up. It was awkward styling around her new features, but thankfully the beanie covered them up quite well.

"Good enough?" she asked Nick, both of them starting up the stairs.

"It's like they're not even there!" Nick chuckled as he held the door open. Amara turned off the lights in the staircase, and the two of them backtracked their steps until they were leaving the library.

A quiet autumn breeze danced across campus as they headed toward the cafeteria. Amara thought back to previous years when the weather had turned cold; she had always been the first to pile on the extra layers, but now her sweater felt stuffy and restrictive. Her tail twitched as she repositioned it, and her walking slowed as a thought crossed her mind.

"Huh," she wondered aloud.

"What's up? Nick slowed his pace to match hers.

"Back in the staircase, I uh..." she looked around, checking if anyone was close, "I took *His* name in vain. Should I not do that?"

"That's...hmm. You raise a good point." Nick went quiet for a moment, his eyebrows furrowed as he cycled through thoughts. "Does your existence prove His existence?"

"I keep worrying about other students finding out, but maybe we should be worried about bigger things?" She shivered slightly, though not from the chill breeze.

"Hey, whatever happens, we'll face it together." He paused. "I should take a religious studies class, make you my final project. It'll be the easiest A I've ever gotten!" Nick laughed.

"If you out me just to boost your GPA, I'll kill you myself so we can find out if the afterlife exists!" She grabbed his arm, digging her nails in before shaking him slightly.

The two of them burst out laughing, drawing a few looks from students who had wandered closer. Putting their existential dread to rest, they walked into the cafeteria to get dinner.

3
COLLEGIATE COMPLICATIONS

The smell of sulfur filled her senses, her hair catching the wind as she turned to find the source. Grasping her necklace, she muttered a prayer and felt her senses heighten. It seemed to be coming from the center of campus. Excusing herself from the group, she moved quicker as the smell grew stronger.

The sky darkened, ominous storm clouds forming much too quickly. They began to spiral in, the epicenter focused over the quad. Breaking out into a run, she knew she was the only one who could stop this, if she could just get there in time. Turning the last corner, she froze, her eyes growing wide with terror.

The quad was on fire.

Students were running, colliding with one another as they tried to escape. In the center of the field, a large runic circle flared to life, its red glow filling the sky as the storm clouds choked out the sun. The fire kept spreading, but she had to push forward.

Flames licked at her heels as she ran, and she avoided their unnatural energies as best she could. She pushed closer to the center of this mad ceremony, then muttered another prayer to ask for more assistance. A blade appeared in her hand, its radiant glow pushing back the flames. With a path cleared, she saw her target.

Just a few feet in front of her, a demonic woman stood in the center of the runes. Several bodies lay nearby, their blood spilled to power their hellish intentions. The demon's back was turned, hopefully distracted by the pending completion of its ritual.

She gripped her blade, running forward as she tried to stab the demon in the back, hopefully piercing its heart. The demon proved too fast, spinning in place and knocking the blade to the ground. Clawed hands grabbed her throat, drawing blood as she was lifted off her feet.

The demon grinned, its black horns wreathed in hellfire. Its terrible hands closed tighter, blackened claws digging into her neck. With one last smirk, the demon's eyes flared, her bright amber irises glowing, and everything went black.

—

She woke with a start, her breathing heavy and erratic. She had kicked the covers to the floor again, and the sheets were covered in sweat. She slid her legs off the bed, reaching for the glass of water on her nightstand. As she emptied it, she noted the clock: 5:37 AM.

"These dreams are gonna be the death of me," she muttered to herself.

Knowing it was pointless to try to go back to sleep, she started her morning routine. A cold shower to shock the system awake, followed by a small snack in preparation for her morning run.

Her route around campus was quiet, as usual. Other than the occasional drunk college student on Sunday mornings, the campus felt like it belonged to her at these early hours. Today, she was off to the Science Building, where her favorite spot on campus awaited her.

She crossed the quad—a beautiful space when it wasn't on fire—and approached the long stairs leading to the south end of campus. She skipped up the steps, pausing before she continued her run. Turning around, she slid down the railing, and jumped for joy when she made it the whole length without falling; her balance was getting better. Returning to the top, it was only a few short minutes to get to the trees surrounding the large, mirrored building. She paused when she arrived, taking a moment to study the tallest oak in the area.

"Alright: deep breaths, find your path," she muttered.

With a burst of speed, she vaulted up the trunk and grabbed a branch, swinging onto it. Her footing secure, she climbed higher, a smile growing on her face. Sweat formed on her brow, and before long she had reached her goal: the highest branch that could safely hold her weight.

Many months ago, she had secretly trimmed the branches to create a small window, only visible from this spot. She settled in, catching her breath, and looked out over the quad. The many paths crisscrossing the open field made it look like a piece of abstract art. Some paths were paved, some worn into the grass from the footfalls of thousands of students, all of them weaving in between the many trees that scattered the area.

The buildings that surrounded the quad were calm, their lights off, their still-ness emphasizing the subtle sway of the trees. Each building was unique, the older ones betraying the true age of the university, but all of them were beautiful. The newer buildings were made mostly of glass, and as such, were incredibly reflective. Their sleek design stood in stark contrast to the brown bricks and arches of the more historical buildings, and it was on these glassy monuments to minimalism that she finally saw the first flickers of dawn.

As the minutes passed, more and more light flooded the campus. Deep reds and oranges painted the buildings, the light reflecting into her tree and illuminating the similarly colored leaves around her. Next, the morning rays hit the trees in the quad, the dew sparkling as their colors joined the painting in front of her. She took a deep breath, crisp air filling her lungs, and drank in the beauty of the world around her.

Off in the distance, a car horn sounded, shattering the illusion. The world was stirring, and it was time to return to her life.

"Almost got a whole twenty minutes today. Same time tomorrow?" She smirked as she patted the branch underneath her, then descended out of her personal paradise.

She resumed her jog, taking a more direct route home; she had no interest in getting caught in the first wave of students trudging to class. A block away from her apartment, her phone went off. She pulled it out, curious who else would be up this early.

Mom: Mailed out your book yesterday! We're so proud of you :)

She froze, her key in the door, rereading the text over and over. Reloading the conversation didn't help: the words refused to change. When she finally respond-ed, she did so more out of obligation than anything else. She tossed her phone on the couch, looking at her surroundings.

"I'm home!" she called out, knowing full well no one could hear her.

She absentmindedly made herself breakfast, the book looming in her thoughts. It had been easy to lose herself in school, to pretend she was nothing more than a simple college student, but that would change once it arrived. She would need a few days to run some tests, and then her mission would begin.

Not my mission. **Their** *mission.*

She ate her breakfast slowly, alone in the house her parents paid for. Her tuition was graciously donated by the Church, all to support a life in Their service.

She sighed.

No longer hungry, she got dressed for the day and headed out.

"Gonna need a lot of coffee today," she mumbled, pulling a scarf around her neck as she locked up.

Thankfully, she had lighter classes today; most of the heavy stuff was front-loaded early in the week. They went by quickly, though there wasn't much to do other than show up and collect the homework. The one bright spot on today's schedule was choir: Music always cheered her up. She had been singing for as long as she could remember. After many years of lessons, she'd grown quite talented; her teachers always used to say she had the voice of an angel.

If only they knew how true that was.

Amara pulled her beanie down tight, the cold air billowing around her. The wind wasn't that strong, but she didn't want to take any chances. Next to her, Nick occasionally glanced around, always keeping an eye out for suspicious characters. At the moment, thankfully, the two of them were relatively isolated. She adjusted the strap of her camera bag, sighing in relief at the lack of company.

"So, Nick. I've been thinking about my dad," she started. After the conversation she'd had with Tessa's polycule earlier in the week, her family had been in her thoughts more and more.

"That's never a good sign," Nick muttered, slowing his pace to match hers.

"Well, it's different this time. Normally, thinking about him doesn't go any-where. I have no idea who he is, or even if he knows I exist." Amara sighed, her mind replaying past conversations.

Amara had gotten very little information about her father growing up, and eventually she had stopped asking. When she was old enough, her mother finally shared the slightly awkward truth; her father was just a drunken fling, a few nights of fun. He had left town long before Amara's mother learned she was pregnant. She cleared her throat.

"Now, with everything we've learned this last week, I can't help but wonder, if he were a succubus—"

"Incubus," Nick whispered.

"—Right, incubus, whatever. If he were an incubus, isn't this exactly what would happen? He shows up, impregnates an unsuspecting woman, and then vanishes. She's left to raise a kid on her own, and has no idea the kid's a demon."

"Well, when you put it that way, is it worth asking Evelyn about this again? If she remembers anything strange?" Nick suggested.

"Right, because that's a normal thing to ask a parent: 'Hey, was Dad, like, a little weird? Maybe a little demonic? Cuz I have horns now and I'm *really* confused'." Amara chuckled as she imagined the conversation.

"Well, I was thinking you could ask with a bit more tact, but clearly that's expecting too much," Nick laughed, jumping aside to dodge Amara's punch.

"You know what I mean!" she huffed. "I tell my mom pretty much everything; it would be obvious if I were tiptoeing around the truth."

Nick moved closer again, nudging her. "What if you *did* tell her?"

Amara went quiet, staring at the sidewalk passing beneath her feet. Her mind raced with possibilities.

"I...I don't know. She would be supportive, curious, and probably a little freaked out, but I'm not scared she would be upset. Like, she was never very religious, at least to my knowledge." Amara looked at Nick again. "I just don't think I'm ready yet. The thought of telling someone, even Mom, about this..."

The two of them walked in silence, leaves billowing around them as the autumn winds picked up. In the distance, cheering could be heard from the stadium, the game already underway. Nick pulled out his phone, silently texting for a moment, then pocketed it again.

"Vee says everyone is already there," he said, "and that she's mad we're late."

Amara laughed. "I'm not afraid of her! I'll be late if I want to!" She raised her arms over her head, arching her back as she stretched. She made a face as she did, clearly not getting the relief she wanted.

"Everything okay? You pull something?" Nick asked.

"No, it's this Go—" Amara stopped herself, biting her tongue, "this fucking tail. You ever get leg cramps? When you sit a weird way for too long, and you have to walk around to shake it out? My tail does that constantly in this sweater, and it sucks."

She looked around, wondering if she could find somewhere to hide. She grabbed Nick, dragging him to a nearby building before opening the doors. As she darted inside, she turned to him and held up her hand.

"Stay here; holler if anyone gets close. I'll just be a minute!" She closed the door, now mostly alone in a narrow staircase. Other than a few small bulbs, the only light was sunlight filtering in through the window in the door. Here, safe from prying eyes, she uncurled her tail from her waist and set it free.

She sighed with relief, and walked around as she stretched. She moved her tail in large, dramatic flourishes as she tried to shake it back to life. She flexed, raising it high before pulling it into her hands to massage it. Finally, she gave it a quick whip through the air, satisfied she'd worked all the kinks out.

"Back in the sweater you go," she mumbled, still not sure how to feel about it. As she left, she caught Nick looking back at her, but his eyes quickly darted to his phone as she reached the door.

"Nicholas! Were you watching me?" Amara asked, feigning indignancy.

"Hey, I'm just curious. You live with it, but most of this week we've been out in public, and I've barely seen it." He tucked his phone away again as they started walking.

"Well, don't let me catch you again, or I'll suspect you're developing a new fetish!" she smirked, bumping into Nick. "Girls with tails; that must be hard to find porn of."

Nick shrugged. "Eh, I'm pretty sure I'm not a furry, so I'm not too worried."

"What's a furry?" Amara asked, her head tilted.

"You *can't* be serious," Nick gawked. "You've never heard of furries?"

She shook her head, certain she was about to learn whether she wanted to or not.

"Wow. Where do I even start? Furries are like...did you ever see Disney's *Robin Hood*? Or *Zootopia*?"

Nick continued, his impromptu lecture taking up the rest of their walk to the game.

The campus stadium was full of life, though it wasn't at full capacity. It could technically hold close to 10,000 people, but it only reached those numbers a few times a year. The college football season had started about a month ago, and attendance had evened out after the first few games. Other than football, the stadium made an ideal spot for all kinds of large events, and it wasn't uncommon to see the field repurposed during the off season.

The team's big homecoming game was last weekend, and school spirit had been riding high ever since. Of course, of all the excitement over the event, roughly a third of it was focused purely on the unofficial celebration. Homecoming weekend always hosted some of the year's best parties, which had been Tessa's biggest selling point for convincing Amara to finally join the girls for a night out.

Thankfully, since today's game had already started, most of the students were comfortably settled into their seats. Amara hadn't been late on purpose, but the convenience couldn't be ignored; she'd been terrified of crowds ever since growing her tail, and this made it easier to navigate safely.

Walking into the open field, a raucous cascade of cheers erupted from the bleachers as another play finished. Amara didn't completely understand football, but always enjoyed the energy of the crowd when she came. On the field, several of the football players were shouting in encouragement, while cheerleaders on the side of the field were waving excitedly to the students in the bleachers. Both groups sported the school colors, purple and white, as they celebrated the play.

Nick helped Amara navigate through the crowd, giving her space to keep her tail hidden, and it wasn't long before they found their friends.

Tessa was sitting above everyone else, cupping a large thermos in her hands. Her eyeliner was as extravagant as ever, but the effort she put into her makeup wasn't reflected in the rest of her outfit. Her clothes were baggy, mismatched, and likely hadn't been washed in a while.

Vee sat on the bench in front of Tessa, her appearance much more polished. Her blonde hair had been partially braided behind her head, and what little makeup she wore was barely noticeable. She was leaning back against the bench behind her, resting her elbows next to Tessa as they talked.

Chloé, the last of Amara's friends present, sat off to the side. A long, deep blue coat hid her relatively small body, and a journal sat in her lap. A matching scarf hung off her neck, and she routinely fidgeted with the few strands of hair that weren't up in a bun. Thin glasses sat on the bridge of her nose, and her green eyes lit up with excitement as she spotted Nick and Amara approaching.

"—so that mostly makes sense, but why is there so much porn? What does that have to do with cute animal people?" Amara asked, scoping out a seat as she approached the girls.

"What's this about too much porn? Have you been holding back on me?" Tessa grinned as she jumped up. "Actually, I don't care. Amara! Get over here!"

Amara eagerly accepted the hug, but made sure that Tessa's arms stayed away from her waist. She repeated this with the other girls, excitedly greeting everyone before sitting down.

"We were just telling Chloé here about how boring you are," Tessa said, settling back down on her perch. "I mean, seriously, you leave your first ever party because you just got a little tired? You're such a grandma."

"Look, it was my first time, and it was a little overwhelming!" Amara glanced at her feet, hoping they would accept her answer; better they thought she was boring than find out about her and Nick.

Vee moved closer, stealing a seat next to Nick before talking. "Oh, lighten up, Tessa. At least she's smart enough to take care of herself. How hungover were you on Sunday?"

"No more than usual, but that's what coffee is for!" Tessa held up her thermos, then raised it to her lips and drank. As she lowered it, Amara noticed the heavy bags under her eyes.

"How much coffee have you had today?" Amara asked, eager to change the topic away from the party. Now that she was settled in, she opened up her bag and started assembling her camera.

"I dunno, five or six drinks? What do you care?" Tessa stuck out her tongue before noticing Amara's disapproving stare, "Look, I've just been sleeping like shit, okay?"

"Caffeine tends to be less effective in larger quantities; you really should cut back," Chloé said. Her eyes were focused on her journal, and she continued drawing as she spoke. "I bet you'd sleep better too."

Tessa groaned, rolling her eyes as she threw her head back. "You guys suck. Normally I love when it's three on one." She put her coffee down, then pivoted to lay across the bleacher. "Ah well, maybe I can put together a *real* foursome for the Halloween party. Wouldn't that be a treat!"

Amara bit her tongue hearing Tessa's comment. She was used to her friend being vulgar, but it felt different given her recent discoveries. "Speaking of Halloween, do we have a plan?"

"That depends on what we want to do," Chloé started, flipping to the back pages of her journal. "Officially, the school has a few events they put on. They always have a movie night in the quad, and normally several fraternity halls partner with the event committee to turn their places into haunted houses. Unofficially, however, there are several notable parties being planned for the weekend. The most prominent is at the Jade Palace."

Vee leaned forward, trying to catch a glimpse of Chloé's journal. "Do you always write stuff like this down? I thought your journal was just for drawings and class notes."

Chloé closed her book, pulling it into her chest again. "W-well, last year Tessa complained that we didn't do enough..."

Hearing this, Tessa sat up again, spinning to face Chloé. "You did all that for me? Seriously?" She leaned in, hugging Chloé tight. "You're adorable! Okay, let me see what our options are. We've got exactly three weeks to plan the best Halloween ever!"

Tessa moved down next to Chloé, pulling Amara close as all three of them looked over the holiday schedule. They pulled out their phones, trying to put together a plan for the coming weekend.

They spent the better part of the next fifteen minutes comparing schedules, but eventually grew distracted by idle gossip. Even though Amara had left the party early, she still had a few fun stories to tell, and continued to stress that she had enjoyed her time there, despite her early departure. The whole time she talked, she periodically adjusted the settings on her camera and took a picture. While she wasn't here officially—she never had any interest in the school newspaper—she enjoyed taking action shots. She also occasionally got requests from other students for small photoshoots.

Her phone went off, and she opened it to find a text from another student named Kate. She was in the school's color guard and had asked Amara to take pictures of her during her routine. Amara excused herself from her friends, walked down to the side of the field, and found the girl she was looking for.

Something that Amara always found curious about her school was its choice of mascot. While most schools picked animals, Aurelius University had chosen an Aurora Borealis. She occasionally heard athletes complain about it, wishing they had a more aggressive mascot, but Amara loved the visual. Auroras were beautiful, and because they were the mascot, the school was significantly more proud of their color guard. They had their own dedicated area on the sidelines, and were expertly twirling flags that depicted a cascading series of colors.

It was here that Amara found Kate, a pretty girl with long brown hair that had been tightly packed into a decorative hair piece. Her colorful outfit and large flag sparkled slightly, and she greeted Amara with a smile as they discussed the upcoming show.

With the details confirmed, and Amara checking that the payment was successful, she happily spent the next fifteen minutes taking a series of sharp, dynamic photos that highlighted the best moments of the routine. She didn't consider them her best work, it was hard to completely focus when she was paranoid about people bumping into her tail, but they were still miles above anything Kate likely already had.

As Amara finished up, and finalized Kate's contact information so she could send over the finished photos, she was even approached by another student. This one was an impossibly gorgeous redhead on the cheerleading team. Her name was Kylie, and having seen Amara offering her photography services, she was interested in getting photos as well. Amara gave her usual spiel, quoted her prices, and exchanged contact information with the cheerleader before they parted ways.

With Amara's side hustle now complete, she happily returned to her friends and began packing up her camera. It had been nice to lose herself in a simple, mundane activity. While she was still nervous about her tail and horns, it was reassuring that her transformation hadn't cost her quality time with her friends.

While Amara excused herself to go take pictures of the halftime show, Vee took advantage of her absence to slide closer to Nick. He'd been sticking pretty close to Amara for most of the game, and Vee was excited to finally have a chance to talk with him.

"So, furry porn? What was all that about?" Vee asked, smirking at him.

After a brief moment of confusion, Nick remembered the conversation he was having when he arrived at the game. "Amara didn't know what furries were, so I thought I'd...well, it doesn't matter. How's your week going?" Nick leaned back, breathing deep.

"A bit stressful, but that's college, right? I booked some tough classes this semester, and they've been wearing me thin. What about yourself? You and Amara both seem a little frayed, if I'm being honest." Vee glanced over to the side of the field where Amara was kneeling with her camera. She always enjoyed watching Amara lose herself in her photography. It helped remind her that school was so much more than studying.

"That's awfully perceptive of you. The party was a little more than she was expecting, to be honest."

"She certainly seems eager to go again, so it can't have been all bad!" Vee smiled, her eyes lingering on Nick's for longer than she'd intended.

"I think it'll be easier next time, now that she's got some experience under her belt." Nick caught Vee's glance, pausing as they looked at each other. "Hopefully, I'll have more chances to mingle; spend time with other people?"

Vee felt her cheeks redden, and she pulled her gaze away from him. "Well, lucky them, whoever it ends up being." A small smile appeared as she pushed her hair out of her eyes.

The halftime show came to a dramatic end, and the crowds applauded the performers as they left the field. The football team and cheerleaders now ran back, preparing to set up for the second half of the game.

Vee did her best to spend as much time with Nick as possible. He kept a busy schedule, and was sometimes hard to pin down. It didn't help that he knew so many people, either. He had been an athlete in high school, and while he didn't play anymore, he regularly joined in athletic outings of all kinds.

Their conversation was even interrupted a few times by some of Nick's friends, and Vee couldn't help but let her mind wander as she watched Nick make more plans.

Maybe I could tag along sometime? It would be a great way to spend more time with Nick, but it also wouldn't be as high pressure as asking him out directly. I should ask Alex or Mike what they're planning, I see them hanging out with Nick often enough.

The game continued, both teams occasionally scoring goals as the different sides of the stadium took turns cheering and booing. While Vee was mostly here to spend time with Amara, Tessa, Chloé, and Nick, she found time to chat with other casual acquaintances of her own. The peaceful atmosphere broke, however, when Tessa reached out and grabbed her arm.

"Careful: Derek is on the prowl again," she whispered, pulling Vee close.

The smile on Vee's face vanished, and she did her best to look small. It was too little, too late, however; Derek had seen her, and was closing the distance.

"Look who it is!" Derek moved in, resting a leg next to Vee as he leaned forward. "It's funny, if I didn't know any better, I'd swear you were avoiding me, Vee."

"It's not that, Derek; I'm just busy. I'm taking some pretty heavy classes this semester." A fake smile curved her lips.

"Too busy to answer a text? Weird, cuz you seem pretty free now. How about we lose the girl squad and find someplace quiet to talk?" Derek's eyes made his intentions obvious, focusing more on Vee's body than anything else.

"Look, I promised my friends I'd spend today with them," she replied with a stern look. "Besides, I've told you before: I'm not interested in dating right now." She did her best to stay calm, but she had no idea how this interaction would end; Derek was notoriously stubborn. Hopefully, the other people present would deter him from pushing too hard.

"Who said anything about dating? Maybe I just want to get to know you, and if we happen to hit it off...well, use your imagination. Come on, I know the perfect spot." Derek reached for Vee's arm, and she heard Nick jump to his feet in response.

A hand suddenly grabbed Derek's wrist, holding him back. She was shocked to see that it wasn't Nick, but Amara who had intervened. Nick's hands moved to Vee's shoulders, pulling her back as Amara stepped up to Derek.

"Hey! You heard her: She's not interested." Amara spoke with unusual confidence, given that Derek was nearly twice her size. She pushed his wrist away, standing firm as she moved in between him and Vee.

"Amara, you don't have to—"

Vee was cut off by Derek's increasingly frustrated voice. "Who the fuck are you? Does it look like I'm talking to you?" He made a show of his stature, clearly trying to intimidate Amara. "How about you sit yourself back down before we have a problem."

Vee watched as Amara stepped even closer to Derek, matching his confidence with her own. "What kind of problem? You want to beat up a girl in front of all these people?" The crowd nearby had grown quiet, and Vee could tell that Derek was keenly aware of the extra attention on him.

After a few moments, the standoff broke, Derek huffing and turning away. "Bitch. Was just leaving anyways."

Everyone watched as he sauntered off, his pride hopefully wounded as he left the bleachers.

As Amara turned back to the group, Vee looked up at her in awe. "Amara, that was incredible!" She stood, wrapping her arms around her friend's shoulders to say thanks. "You truly didn't have to do that, but thank you." As she pulled back, she noticed that Amara's breathing was erratic, her body stiff and her knuckles white.

"I-I'm glad you're safe, Vee."

Amara's eyes met Vee's, though they were unfocused. For a moment, Vee wondered if she had started wearing contacts; her eyes seemed to catch the light differently today.

"I'm not...I think I need to leave," Amara muttered.

Vee pulled back, letting Amara go as Nick stepped in. They whispered a few words to each other, then Nick turned to the group.

"We need to head out, sorry. Vee, I'm happy you're safe. It was great seeing everyone." As he finished talking, Amara grabbed his hand and pulled him away. The two disappeared from view quickly, leaving Vee, Chloé, and Tessa to themselves.

"Well, that was certainly something," Tessa mumbled, breaking the silence. "I don't think I've ever seen her that worked up. She's normally just as timid as you, Chloé."

"Can you blame her? I could never stand up to Derek like that; I can't imagine how scary that would be." Vee sat back down, pulling out her phone. "I never thought he would be this bold."

"He's been getting worse, actually." Chloé adjusted her glasses. "I've heard from quite a few student leaders that his behavior has grown increasingly erratic, to put it mildly."

"As long as we're all safe, I won't complain. Thankfully she's got Nick. He'll get her home safe." Vee sent a quick text, then leaned back and sighed.

Tessa sat next to her, pulling her in for a hug. "I wish I had a friend like that. I still can't believe they're not a thing."

The three girls laughed, settling in as they waited for the game to finish.

Amara grabbed Nick's jacket, pushing him hard against the wall. He seemed surprised at her strength, but before he could say anything, Amara's lips had found his. He pulled his jacket off, which prompted Amara to do the same. As their kiss broke, Nick took a moment to try and catch his bearings.

"Should we talk about this first? You seem different, and I can't tell if that's good or not," Nick asked as he kicked his shoes off.

"Did you see the way he looked at her? Like she was just some prize to win?" Her breath was still erratic, and she continued fuming as she walked past Nick toward her bedroom. "Fucking asshole!"

"Look, I'm glad you stepped in, but what if something had happened?" He followed her to the bedroom. By the time he got there, her shirt was already on the floor. "Guys like that tend to be the first to call a bluff. You should have let me handle it."

Amara fell backward on her bed, her feet in the air as she wrestled with her pants. "You don't understand, Nick: I wanted him to. I was itching for an excuse to hurt him."

"Did you see how jacked he was? He would've torn you apart!" Nick's belt fell to the floor, along with his pants.

"I didn't say I understood it! I just…it's like something inside me snapped." She stood, grabbing Nick's arm and throwing him to the bed. "And now I can barely think straight, so you're gonna fuck some sense into me, and we can talk later!"

Amara straddled him, pinning his shoulders to the mattress as she leaned in, her lips finding his neck. She inhaled his scent, eagerly reaching down to massage his cock through his boxers. Soon she replaced her hand with her pussy, moaning as he started meeting her thrusts with his own. Baring her teeth, she bit down on Nick's neck, eliciting a loud moan.

"Fuck! No marks, okay?" Nick gasped, his hands eagerly massaging her ass.

Hearing that, Amara pulled back, her eyes brighter than ever as she glared at Nick. "Yeah? What are you gonna do about it?" She ground against him as she bit her lip.

Curiosity on his face, Nick moved a hand to her neck, testing the waters. "There's a lot I could do, honestly."

Amara pulled his hand away from her neck, her other hand meeting his, and pinned his arms above his head. "Didn't you hear me earlier, idiot?" She leaned in, whispering into his ear, "I said I wanted a fight."

All hesitation vanished from Nick as he fought back, reversing Amara's grip on his hands. Combined with a quick hip thrust, he managed to push Amara onto her side, her tail hitting the wall with a soft thud. From there, he moved behind her, wrapping his legs behind hers to stop her from gaining leverage. With the advantage now his, he moved on top of her, flipping her onto her stomach, her hands pinned just like his were earlier.

Amara grunted as they wrestled, well aware that she'd never overpowered Nick before. Her hips writhed and twisted as she tried to break free, but it was no use. He was bigger, stronger, and her teasing had stripped away all pleasantries between the two of them.

She only had one advantage over him: an extra limb. Her tail was still free, and it moved to his hands to try and break his grip. Nick flinched as her tail found his wrist, wrapping tightly around it, and his grip loosened more from surprise than anything else. She bought herself a moment of freedom, planting a hand on the bed to try to push him off.

With one hand, he pulled Amara's wrist behind her back, then the other hand slipped out of her tail. He grabbed her loose wrist and pulled it to meet the other, able to hold both with a single grip. He pinned them tight while his other hand grabbed at her tail. It thrashed wildly, but soon he was able to wrap it around his arm, his hand holding the base.

Amara was now completely immobilized, and she craned her neck to look at Nick. "Please...I need it..." Her pussy had soaked through her panties, and her hips were twitching.

It was Nick's turn to lean in. "You need what?" he whispered.

"I need your fucking cock!" Amara's grunts of frustration turned to pitiful moans, her body begging for release.

He pulled Amara back, positioning her on her knees, her face still on the bed. A smile crossed his face as he spoke. "Be good, and I'll give it to you."

Nick moved his hand off Amara's tail, leaving it wrapped around his arm as he reached between the two of them. He pushed her panties aside and slowly teased her folds with his finger, a loud moan escaping her lips. Pulling away, he freed his cock and lined himself up, eager to give Amara what she wanted.

"The safe word is fursuit, by the way." Nick smirked as he spoke.

"Really? That's the best you've go—FUCK!" Amara screamed in surprise as Nick pushed into her, bottoming out in one quick motion.

Her body lit up, every nerve firing as pleasure surged through her. She had no idea why confronting that asshole had turned her on so much, but right now she didn't care. Nick's cock felt amazing; she was shocked she hadn't cum when he entered her. She twitched and moaned, still held tight in his hands.

She felt him pull back slowly, and he stopped just before leaving completely. He paused there, holding perfectly still, letting Amara struggle to try and push herself against him. Her efforts were in vain, as his grip refused to budge.

"Nick...please," Amara pleaded, her voice muffled by the bedsheets around her.

He finally took pity, giving her another powerful thrust. Her moans grew more guttural this time, reveling in the experience. Another thrust, another deep moan, and soon Nick was fucking her in long, hard strokes.

She still couldn't move herself, but Nick's strong grip continued to pull her back and forth. As he picked up speed, he made her do the same, and soon his moaning joined hers. She did everything she could to fuck him back, her tail squeezing his arm tight. She pushed her face into the bed, biting the sheets as their fucking grew more intense.

"You love being bent over, don't you?" Nick asked, punctuating his words with his hips. "Being pinned down while I fuck you senseless?"

Amara tried to respond, but each time she had something to say, another thrust would replace her words with moans of pleasure. She'd never felt this powerless before, especially around Nick, and the feeling was intoxicating.

She felt his hand leave the base of her tail, moving to her head and gathering her hair. He pulled back again, this time his grip causing her shoulders to leave the bed.

She heard something rip as he pulled her back, but she didn't dare distract herself from the fucking.

Amara's body shook with pleasure, and she cried out as her orgasm started. Her tail, now freed, wrapped around Nick's torso and held him close as her hips twitched. Wave after wave of ecstasy flooded through her, overpowering the anger that had built up earlier. For a moment, she swore she felt her orgasm transcend her body, but the feeling faded as quickly as it arrived.

As her pleasure started to fade, Nick's body picked up momentum. With another powerful thrust, he pushed Amara to the bed, her tail pulling him with her. He continued fucking her, his movements growing erratic, and soon she felt him succumb. His cock throbbed inside of her, shooting thick loads of cum deep into her body.

Amara gasped as she felt his teeth on her shoulder, biting down hard as his cock emptied itself. Feeling him cum was incredible; the warmth of his seed radiated throughout her body. She felt full, not just because of the thick shaft buried in her pussy, but also as if she'd just finished an amazing meal.

As Nick's pace slowed, then eventually stopped, Amara felt both their breathing calm as well. His body weighed down on hers, his cock growing soft before he pulled out. He released her hair, then her wrists, and finally collapsed off to one side.

"Fucking hell, Amara!" he gasped.

"You can say that again!" Amara chuckled as she turned to face him. "Where on Earth did that come from?"

Her tail moved to his chest, drawing little circles as they talked.

"Maybe we both have anger issues to work out?" he laughed as he watched her tail dance across him.

The two of them lay there together, slowly catching their breath as the minutes passed. Nick took advantage of this time to pull her tail closer, looking it over and satiating his curiosity. Occasionally, Amara would pull away and smack him with it, mostly to gauge if her control was improving.

"Oh! Quick!" Amara bolted upright, jumping off the bed and spinning around slowly. "Limb check! Anything new?"

Nick moved to the edge of the bed, carefully examining her. "Hmm...not seeing anything this time. How do you feel?" He held out a hand, motioning for Amara to sit next to him again.

"Fine? The anger is definitely gone, which is good." She leaned into Nick as she fidgeted with her tail. "I'm wondering if protecting Vee activated some kind of demonic fight or flight instinct. But, since I'm a succubus, my instincts are also sexual? I'll need to be careful about getting angry in public again, that's for sure."

"Well, I doubt it's a fight or flight instinct," Nick said, holding his chin as he thought about it. Amara leaned in, wondering where he was going with this. "It's probably closer to a fight or fuck instinct."

His serious face gave way to a mischievous smirk before he chuckled quietly to himself.

"Oh, grow up!" Amara pushed him back on the bed, then moved over to her dresser to grab some fresh clothes. She pulled out new panties, slipping them on, then quickly piled her old clothes in the hamper.

As she closed it, her heartbeat quickened, and she felt her eyes flare. A powerful feeling swelled inside her, and in that moment she knew there was something she needed to do. She spun around, eyes darting around the room.

"Nick, something's...off." She moved out to her living room as she tried to explore the feeling.

"What do you mean? Like, you feel something?' Nick was quickly following her, his pants half on as he walked.

"I don't entirely know. I think I need to do something. Or go somewhere?" She reached for her front door, her hand twisting the knob.

"Wait!" Nick leapt in front of her, his hand pushing the door, preventing it from opening. "You're still not dressed! What if someone saw you?" His breathing quieted as she moved away from the door.

Amara looked around one last time, realizing the feeling had vanished. "Weird, it's gone now." She slowly walked back to her bedroom. "Plus, I know what would've happened; my neighbors would have been too distracted by my tits to even notice my tail!"

Nick followed her again, buckling his pants. "Now who needs to grow up?" he chuckled, catching his shirt as she threw it at him.

Amara slowly got dressed, her lips pursed and her brow furrowed as she mulled over that strange sensation. Where had it come from? Why had she been so desperate to follow it? She reached for her bra, then noticed that it was caught on her bedding. When she went to untangle them, she found a large rip in her sheets.

"Fuck! We ripped my sheets!" she groaned, looking at Nick.

"Oh, yeah, it may have gotten caught on your horns," he mumbled, diverting his eyes as he finished buttoning his shirt.

Amara flicked her tail at him, hitting his thigh as she moved past. She grabbed a spare set of sheets, then returned to the bedroom and tossed half the linens to Nick.

"New rule: If we break anything during sex, you have to help me fix it, okay?" She began pulling her old sheets off.

"That's more than fair," Nick smirked as he helped make her bed. "But if you try to milk a new TV out of me, I'm signing up for that Religious Studies class!"

The two spent the rest of the evening together, getting dinner, doing laundry, and studying, before finally calling it a night.

4
A WEEK OFF

Amara yawned as she slowly marched across the quad. She'd just finished her morning classes, and planned to spend some time with Chloé before getting lunch. For some reason, however, she'd been sleeping terribly the last couple of days, and the simple walk across campus instead felt like a marathon. It also didn't help that Nick had taken a spontaneous week off school.

He'd been pretty vague about the reason, but it seemed like some family business had come up, and he needed to visit his grandparents' house to help out for a bit.

Initially, Amara hadn't been worried. After all, it had been just over a week and a half since her horns had appeared, and nothing else seemed to be changing. Her initial panic over her demonic transformation had calmed down somewhat, and the real challenge was just keeping her tail and horns hidden while attending classes. Even though Nick was the only one who knew about her recent changes, they'd been separated hundreds of times throughout their friendship, and Amara assumed this would be no different.

Unfortunately, she'd overlooked one crucial detail. Her libido had been growing ever since her tail appeared, but Nick had always been there to keep her urges in check. Now, without him to quell her desires, they had grown even more persistent.

Her body screamed for sex. The first few days had been tolerable, if a little frustrating, and she had been able to distract herself with schoolwork. After that, sadly, her libido had evolved from an annoying itch to a cavernous void. She could no longer focus on classes, and instead spent her time daydreaming about attractive students sitting nearby. She was once again thankful it was autumn, and people had stopped wearing revealing outfits outside.

Just like the day after the party, her toys had been useless, despite her many attempts. After classes had let out yesterday, she'd spent nearly four hours desperately cycling through every toy she owned, hoping that one of them would hold the secret to her release, but nothing had worked.

She once again cursed the existence of her tail. Under normal circumstances, a college girl like her would likely have free reign to set up all sorts of random hook ups, but the demonic limb under her sweater made that impossible. What choice did she have other than waiting for Nick to return? Tie someone to a bed, blindfold them, then ride them senseless? That particular idea had originated as a joke, but the more she thought about it, the more she was tempted to take it seriously.

Amara pulled out her phone and texted Nick again.

Amara: When are you getting baaaaack

Amara: Demon libidos SUCK

Nick: I fly back tonight, and we'll have all day tomorrow to cause trouble :P

With a loud groan, followed by another heavy yawn, Amara looked up. Despite her current exhaustion, she figured she was close enough to Chloé's dorm to text her as well.

By the time Amara made it to the front entrance, Chloé was already waiting to open the door.

"Amara! How are you? Morning classes treating you alright?" Chloé said, excitedly leading the way upstairs.

"Uh, they're fine. Nothing special, I guess." Amara clutched the railing tight as she walked, her eyes briefly lingering on Chloé's cute backside. She could feel her roiling libido acting up again, and shook her head to clear her thoughts. After reaching the first landing, Amara looked up to see that Chloé was easily twice as high up. "Hey, can you wait up a sec? I think I need to sit down."

Chloé apologized profusely as she ran back down the stairs. "I'm sorry! I didn't realize you'd fallen behind. Are you okay? Like, are you sick or something?"

"I'm just exhausted," Amara said. "I haven't been sleeping well, nothing crazy."

"Well, take all the time you need! We still have an hour 'til lunch, and I think you can make it up two more flights of stairs by then."

"Ugh. Have you always lived on the third floor?" Amara asked.

"Yup!"

The girls both giggled, then Amara rested her head against the wall behind her. She was breathing heavily, and felt silly for needing a break like this. After a few minutes, she grabbed the railing and tried to pull herself up.

"Do you want any help?" Chloé asked, reaching for Amara's waist.

"Don't touch me!" Amara snapped. The last thing she needed was Chloé accidentally finding her tail. In her panic, however, her words had come out harsher than intended. She looked up to find Chloé recoiling, clearly shocked by the outburst. "Fuck, I'm sorry, I didn't mean that. I'd just like to do this on my own, if that's okay."

"Y-yeah, that's cool," Chloé muttered.

Way to go, Amara. Yell at the nicest friend you have, that'll totally make everything better.

It took nearly ten minutes for Amara to finish climbing the stairs, and by the end, Chloé thankfully seemed to be in better spirits. She was always quick to forgive, which Amara appreciated, though she hated that it had been necessary.

She walked inside Chloé's apartment, kicked off her shoes, and happily collapsed into her friend's bed. She wrapped a blanket around her waist, just to be safe, and cuddled into a massive pile of plushies. "How are all your drawings coming along, by the way? I saw you working on them at the game the other week."

"Oh, they're alright. I mean, they're nothing special, it's just a hobby." Chloé pushed a loose strand of hair behind her ear as she talked.

"C'mon, give yourself some credit! I think your drawings always look fantastic. Can I see what you're working on?"

"Okay, but just remember that I'm not finished yet! Some of them don't have color, and for a couple I was trying out new things." Chloé pulled her notebook off her desk and then crawled on the bed next to Amara. With her tail buried under a sweater and a blanket, Amara felt more comfortable leaning in to look.

Chloé opened her notebook and continued. "Most of these are just character ideas I've had for tabletop role-playing games. So, like, this one is a wizard, but I gave her more of a nature look since she's an elf. This one is a merfolk paladin, and I tried to make her look more like a deep-sea creature rather than a stereotypical mermaid. This one is a tiefling rogue, and then down here I've got an air elemental monk. My newest idea is—"

Amara reached out, stopping Chloé from turning the page. "Wait, hold on, what's this?" She pointed at one character in particular, the one Chloé had called a rogue. The drawing was in black and white, and showed a tall woman wearing tight leather with a collection of knives strapped to her thighs. Amara didn't care about those features, and instead focused on the character's long, dramatic tail and sweeping horns.

"She's a tiefling! Have you never played D&D before?"

"You know I'm not much of a gamer, Chloé. Why has she got a tail and horns? Is she a demon?"

"Not quite. Tieflings are more-or-less human, but they've got a tiny bit of demon blood in them. It gives them their demonic features, and sometimes they have red skin too. She turned to crime after being ostracized her whole life, and now she tries to steal from the rich and stuff."

"She was ostracized? Why?" Amara asked, completely enraptured by this character.

"Well, in-universe, people don't trust tieflings. They look like demons, and demons are bad news. They're beings of pure chaos that try to sow misery and steal souls everywhere they go."

Amara paused, her eyes tracing and retracing the horns and tail on the character. Ever since she learned she was a succubus, the implications of her existence had been spinning around in her head. She was real, so wouldn't souls be as well? "In the, um, game, what happens when people lose their souls?"

"Oh, that really depends on who's running the game. Some people keep it simple and say that, without your soul, you basically just die, but I've always thought that was a little boring. I think the more interesting interpretation is that your soul is the source of your morality and your emotions. Losing a soul doesn't necessarily turn you into a bad person, but it removes your filter. Personally, I think it would be neat to play a character like that. Do they become cold and logical? Turn to external vices as they attempt to feel something? So many possibilities!"

Nick said he didn't feel any different, and he was still as nice as ever at the library. Everything I read said that sleeping with a succubus, even once, was enough to permanently change someone, but he seems fine. That's a good sign, right?

Before Amara could ask any follow-up questions, Chloé's phone went off. "Oh, shoot! I'm so sorry, Amara, I have to take this. It'll just be a second, I promise!"

Amara didn't mind waiting. She was still enraptured by the character in the sketchbook, and she occupied herself by scanning over every interaction she'd had with Nick ever since they started sleeping together. Thankfully, Chloé was true to her word, and the conversation was over in barely a minute.

"Everything alright?" Amara asked.

"Yeah! I volunteer at a local church, and I guess they had to change some hours this coming weekend, so they were calling to let me know."

"Huh, I never would have picked you as the religious type."

"I mean, it's not that cut and dry. Some places, like my hometown, use religion as a weapon against change, but they're not all like that. The good churches do everything they can to offer services to the underprivileged, and this one is also incredibly queer-friendly. I once made some recommendations regarding trans-inclusive language, and they actually listened!"

"Chloé, that's awesome!" Amara eagerly pulled her friend in for a hug, doing her best to hype her up.

"It was nothing big, I mostly just appreciated that they listened to me," Chloé muttered. She was still looking at her phone, only this time, Amara caught her face turning red.

"What is it this time?" Amara asked. "I doubt you're blushing because of the church."

"No!" Chloé stammered. "It's... well, I kinda met this guy in one of my classes..."

Amara immediately spun to face Chloé directly. "No way! Are you dating? Do you have a secret boyfriend you've been keeping from us?"

"It's not like that! We just got assigned to a project together, and at first I didn't expect much from it. Like, he's an athlete and really good looking, so presumably we don't have anything in common. But then I learned that he plays a lot of video games! We've been talking a bunch about some of our favorites, and he's just been really nice to me."

"Okay, you clearly like him, and it sounds like he feels the same way. Have you asked him out yet?"

"Of course not! He's probably just being friendly." Chloé pulled back from Amara, grabbing a ram plushie and burying her face in its soft fur. "Besides, the chances of him being into someone like me..."

"Chloé. Girl." Amara waited until Chloé looked up. "There's literally no harm in asking. If he says yes, then you've got a cute boy you can start kissing! If he says no, then you don't have to spend weeks wondering if he likes you or not, and you can focus on just having a cool new friend. Or, maybe he doesn't even realize that dating you is an option, guys can be silly like that sometimes."

Chloé didn't say anything, and instead started picking at her nails while she buried her face even deeper into her plushie. Amara sighed, then decided to stop pushing. She didn't want to force the issue and make Chloé do anything she wasn't comfortable with, so she decided to change the subject. "What games have you been talking about with him? Any that I've seen you play?"

The chance to talk about video games turned Chloé into an entirely different person. She was suddenly loud and energetic, even booting up a console to show Amara the game in question. Amara let Chloé rant about anything and everything she wanted, always happy to see her in her element, but eventually it was time to shut things down and head out for lunch.

This time, Amara made sure to budget extra time for travel due to her strange weakness. Chloé didn't offer to help again, which Amara still felt bad about, but it was certainly the better alternative to explaining why she had a tail.

Thankfully, the walk to the cafeteria was shorter than the walk to Chloé's dorm. It still took an impressively long time, and Amara needed several breaks, but soon enough they'd arrived.

The line in the cafeteria was longer today, and the wait for lunch was made worse by Amara's grumbling stomach. She occasionally caught sniffs of something delicious, but when she got her food, she was dismayed to learn the smell was coming from something else. With their food in tow, the two girls found an empty table and set down their backpacks.

"Ugh, I swear the food here gets blander every day," she complained, lazily dragging her fork across the food in front of her.

"Really? I've been enjoying it, but I might just be happy to have something to eat," Chloé chuckled.

Amara dug through her bag, trying to distract herself from the lackluster food in front of her. She checked some of her folders, making sure today's homework was ready, and eventually pulled out two matching notebooks. She set them up, then picked at her food as she analyzed the tables inside.

"What is all this? Class stuff?" Chloé was leaning in, scanning the notebooks to try and figure them out. "They look like calendars."

"This is my big project for the year! It's for my Marketing class: they want a practical application of skills rather than a written final." Amara pushed her food aside, then spun her notebooks to face Chloé. "You're right, they're calendars; I'm trying to piece together a posting schedule that doesn't overwhelm me."

"A...posting schedule?" Chloé tilted her head, her face scrunched up in confusion. "Come to think of it, I don't actually know what you're studying for."

Amara looked off into the distance briefly, digging through past conversations. "I guess I don't talk about it much, do I?"

Chloé shook her head.

"Well, long story short, I'm trying to specialize in Social Media Management. The goal is to understand how people engage with content online, and offer advice to anyone looking to up their marketing game."

"So, like...you're really good at Facebook?" Chloé asked, giggling.

"Kinda, yeah! All the different social media websites have their own cultures, and you have to post different types of content depending on where you are. Ideally, I would help people understand when to post, what to post, and how to engage with different online communities. For larger companies, I might offer to run their social media accounts, but for individuals I can help them improve their own abilities."

"That's really cool!" Chloé pulled the notebooks closer and flipped through them. "I bet there's a lot of ways to put those skills to use; so much stuff is online these days. What is your actual project?"

"I want to prove I can appeal to different online cultures, so I'm going to start two new social media personas. Each will have a unique handle, I won't cross-post anything, and each will aim to appeal to a different audience."

"So, what are your two personas?" Chloé pushed the notebooks back to Amara, returning to her meal.

"I'm still hammering out the details on that. I've been talking it over with Nick, but since he's been gone, it's been slow-moving." Amara forced another few bites down as she put her notebooks away.

"That explains why I haven't seen him around," Chloé muttered. "Where is he?"

"I don't know all the details, but I guess some family stuff came up? He's been at his grandparents' place all week," Amara grumbled. She tried to change the topic, eager for a distraction. "What about you? Any big projects this semester?"

"Well, it's not as impressive as yours, but I'm trying to start a charity platform." Chloé's voice grew quiet, her eyes falling to her lap.

"Not impressive? Chloé, that's incredible!" Amara leaned forward, trying to infect her friend with excitement. "Are you just trying to raise money for a specific cause?"

"Well, I do have a few causes I'm really passionate about. I donate to the Trevor Project every Christmas, for example, but the goal for now is to make people feel better about donating. I'm working together with some friends to make a new fundraising platform—one that makes it easy to donate, while encouraging transparency. We're going to have an app and everything!"

Chloé's eyes lit up as she talked, though not as literally as Amara's.

"That's honestly amazing. You should be super proud of yourself, Chloé!" Amara smiled, and caught Chloé blushing as she talked. "Maybe we should team up sometime! I might be able to help with exposure."

Chloé said nothing in response, but nodded enthusiastically as she finally looked up. Her gaze quickly left Amara, and she waved at someone entering the cafeteria.

Within seconds, the delicious smell from earlier filled Amara's senses. She turned her head and watched as Tessa walked up to the table. As she sat down, Amara eagerly looked at Tessa's lunch, only to find the same uninspired food that Amara had on her own plate.

"Hey, girls! Sorry I'm late; I had some trouble getting out of bed today." Tessa smirked as she popped open her thermos, chugging some more coffee.

"That's okay; Amara and I were just talking about our projects for the year." Chloé moved slightly to give Tessa more space. "Are you working on anything?"

"Me? Hell, no! I make sure to avoid classes that ask for big projects. I just want to show up, take my test, and leave. I've got more important things to do." Tessa eagerly started eating, making no effort to hide how hungry she was.

Chloé and Tessa started catching up, but Amara found it difficult to include herself in the conversation. She had to fight not to stare at Tessa, as she was trying to figure out where that smell was coming from. Whatever it was, it was igniting Amara's libido, and she squeezed her legs together as she fought to keep her eyes from wandering over Tessa's body.

It's not her food, obviously, but maybe perfume? Who am I kidding? Tessa doesn't wear perfume. Even if she did, it wouldn't smell like this.

Amara kept eating, occasionally joining in the conversation, but her mind was elsewhere.

Coffee? No, I've tried her drinks before. Maybe a new body wash? That wouldn't explain why the smell is so strong, though...

As she cycled through her thoughts, she also noticed that Tessa had an unusual glow to her. Her skin, hair, eyes, all seemed to be bursting with vigor, as if she were exuding an unnatural aura of vitality. She looked incredible, and Amara caught herself wondering what Tessa's skin might feel like under her lips. Before Amara realized it, Tessa was staring back at her.

"Hey, I got something on my face? Or are you just lost in my beauty?" Tessa asked, playfully throwing her hair back.

Amara flinched, realizing she'd been caught staring. "No, I, uh...you just seem a little excited today. You're more animated than usual, and I'm used to you fighting to stay awake." She tried to inject some attitude into her voice, hoping to deflect the conversation away from herself.

"Well, let's just say this isn't my first time eating out today." Tessa winked at Amara, but when she looked over to Chloé, it was obvious the innuendo hadn't landed. "I woke up with my partner straddling my face, and they returned the favor once I'd finished the job. Couldn't ask for a better way to wake up, am I right?"

Amara's eyes went wide as she pieced everything together: The smell, the unusual glow; she was sensing that Tessa had just had sex. Out of curiosity, she looked around the cafeteria, and realized she was able to identify quite a few students who had similar auras around them. They all looked different, and now that she knew what to look for, it was easier to piece together what she was seeing.

Amara spent the rest of lunch people watching, trying to figure out what all the different auras meant. She found it was easy to see a difference between people who had recently had sex, and people who were simply horny. She found a few students who had both auras, which made her chuckle.

One table over, she saw two of Nick's friends: Alex and Kellen. They were both laughing and smiling as they ate, but Amara could tell that Alex had likely gotten laid last night. His aura was more vibrant than other students', but more subdued than Tessa's.

In the corner sat a slightly smaller girl with a tight black braid. Amara vaguely recognized her from her U.S. History class, her name was Dana, and she was incredibly horny. Her aura was pulsating, which Amara assumed to mean she was texting someone or reading something exciting. As she kept watching, Dana bit her lip and shifted in her seat.

When Amara directed her gaze downward, looking at herself, she didn't see anything unusual.

Maybe I can't see my own aura? I guess, if succubi are supposed to be sexual predators, our own state of arousal would be irrelevant...

Eventually, as it approached the next hour, a sizable portion of the cafeteria stood up to leave for class. Tessa seemed to be in no rush to go, but she stood up anyway to give her friends a proper goodbye.

As Amara went in for a hug, she felt Tessa's aura wash over her. She basked in it for a second, fighting the urge to linger even longer, then pulled away. She joined Chloé in leaving the cafeteria, the two hugging before going their separate ways.

The rest of the day passed quickly, and Amara was eager to start the weekend. Nick's impending return lingered in her thoughts, and she was trying to decide what naughty fun she would get up to tomorrow.

Maybe I'll find a good porno for inspiration. Or we could watch some together! I wonder what he likes...

She chuckled, trying to guess what Nick's taste in porn might be. They had never shied away from talking about sex in the past, but they frequently left the dirty details to the imagination.

I'll bet he's into amateur stuff. "Oh, I just love how intimate it feels, it's so much more passionate."

She giggled as she made fun of him, and made a note to ask him tomorrow.

She continued her slow walk across campus, her pace just as sluggish as earlier, when a strange feeling came over her. Just like last week, after the game, Amara suddenly felt like she needed to be somewhere. The feeling had actually come and gone a few times since then, but always at inopportune times. Now, she had nothing but free time, and was determined to follow it.

She moved southward, crossing the quad. After a long trek up the stairs, she found herself facing the Science Building.

The feeling seemed to be pushing her inside, so she walked in and started exploring. She did her best to act natural, realizing she had no idea when classes stopped in this building. Oddly enough, the more she looked around, the more she knew she needed to be on a lower level.

Does this building even have a basement?

Amara wandered the first floor, and eventually answered her own question. A flight of stairs led to a sublevel. As she entered it, she was surprised to see it was much older than the sleek building above. In fact, it reminded her of the old staircase from the library.

They must have left the original basement when they rebuilt; weird.

Leaving the stairs, she now stood in a dimly lit hallway that branched out in two directions. She seemed to be standing in a corner of the structure, the hallway turning where it met the staircase. A quick exploration to her right revealed a dead end, with only a single locked door. She doubled back and headed the opposite direction.

The rooms closer to the staircase looked like they'd been slightly refurbished, and now served as utility housing. A series of water pipes and electrical wires ran up into the ceiling, presumably supplying the building with everything it needed. She poked around the room for a minute before shrugging, seeing nothing of interest.

Leaving the utility room, Amara continued following the hallway. The next few rooms were locked, but the windows in the doors were clear enough to see through them. They seemed to be equipment storage, but it was hard to tell if people still used them. Everything inside looked old-fashioned: chairs, desks, lab tables, and the occasional ancient microscope.

She pulled away from the locked doors and kept walking. The hallway suddenly opened up. The space ahead of her was much larger, seeming to occupy the rest of the basement.

Instead of smooth brick walls and the occasional door, the empty space resembled an ancient maze of plumbing. Pipes of every shape and size wove through the space; it felt like being in the belly of an ancient steamship, especially with the giant rusting boiler nearby.

Her gut told her she was close.

Amara walked deeper into the mess of plumbing. After nervously touching some of the pipes around her, she confirmed that they weren't in use anymore. She began ducking and climbing through the pipes, still unsure what she was looking for. It took her the better part of the next fifteen minutes to search the area thoroughly, not including the several breaks she needed to take as she lost her breath.

As she crawled underneath a large pipe, she found herself facing the back of the basement. Here, following the barren walls, she managed to find a small room tucked in the corner of the basement.

There was no door, just a gap in the wall; the dark brickwork had made it nearly impossible to spot from further away. She pulled out her phone and turned on its flashlight, ignoring the 'No Service' pop-up.

She expected to find more plumbing, and was surprised to see a relatively empty space. Stranger still, it looked like someone had been here recently. On the far side of the room was a small table covered with books and scattered papers. In front of it sat a small folding chair, and the floor nearby had a collection of jars and vials.

She found a light switch and flipped it. A dull, warm light filled the area, so Amara pocketed her phone.

The feeling had faded somewhat, and Amara wasn't quite sure what to do next. She wandered across the room, tracing her hand over the walls in search of anything strange. As she neared the table, she noticed unusual symbols drawn on the many pieces of paper. Unable to understand them, she started digging through the books for possible hints.

Most of the books were quite old, and even more were unlabeled. Their spines were heavily worn, and when she turned through them, she was again confronted with strange symbols she couldn't understand.

She turned away from the table, tossing the book back.

That's when she noticed the drawings.

The floor in the center of the room was covered with the same symbols she had seen in the books. They were all drawn with dull red paint. Many of them were connected with lines, but Amara couldn't make sense of the patterns they made. When she looked up, she saw the symbols had been drawn on the ceiling as well.

As she examined the strange scene, the feeling from earlier returned. It started small, but quickly grew into an intense curiosity. Although she couldn't read the symbols, she thought the patterns might be easier to decipher from the center of the room.

She stepped forward, her feet landing on the empty concrete in the center. A strange feeling swept over her, almost like a quick change in atmospheric pressure, then faded just as quickly. She spun around, looking at all the symbols, but still nothing made sense.

She sighed.

Well, this was a bust. Maybe I'll bring Nick down here tomorrow; he might recognize some of this.

Amara turned to the entrance of the room, but when she tried to step forward, her body collided with something. After catching herself, she pushed a hand forward and flinched when it touched something solid. A strange glow pulsed from the area she touched, which grew brighter when she pushed her hand against it. She traced the invisible object with her hands, and found that it was curving around her.

Her breathing quickened, a terrible thought crossing her mind. After a minute, she confirmed her theory: This strange wall completely surrounded her. It stayed invisible unless touched, and the harder she pushed against it, the stronger it glowed.

Panic set in, and she pulled out her phone. The pop-up from earlier appeared again: 'No Service'. She tried searching for Wi-Fi, but found none.

She started hitting this strange force field, punching it, driving her shoulder into it, but nothing worked. The more she exerted herself, the more she felt the gnawing hunger in her gut. She was still weak and tired, and these escape attempts were worsening that.

Amara collapsed to the ground, tears forming in her eyes, as she looked around the room. She was alone, trapped under the Science Building, and classes had likely just ended for the weekend. She called out, desperate to catch someone's attention, and her voice echoed through the empty basement.

"Hello?"

5

ALONE IN THE BASEMENT

Sulfur infiltrated her senses, and she turned as her feet hit the pavement. The clouds darkened, circling the quad as flames consumed the trees. She ran faster, weaving between students as she raced toward the demon responsible for this. Her blade appeared, dispersing the flames, and she leapt forward.

Her sword clattered to the ground, the demon's clawed hands grabbing her throat. She tried to break free, but its hold was too strong. Its grip tightened, claws drawing blood as her strength gave in. Her vision faded, the demon's amber eyes seared into her mind, and her breathing stopped.

—

Her hands were gripping the sheets when she woke, her lungs gasping for air. It took a moment for the nightmare to fade, the tension refusing to leave her body. When it did, she slowly sat up and steadied herself. The cold air in her apartment swept over her, and she closed her eyes to focus on calming her breathing.

The demon's eyes stared back at her, glowing in the darkness.

Startled, she fell off the bed, pulling the rest of the sheets with her. She sat quietly, scared to close her eyes, as the glow of her clock filled her vision.

5:23 AM.

"At this rate, I won't be sleeping at all come winter," she sighed.

Leaning forward, she grabbed the water off her nightstand. It relaxed her throat, strained from the heavy breathing. It also made the caffeine pill go down easier.

She showered quickly, but had to trade her running clothes for something warmer; there was no longer time to exercise. Instead, she grabbed her backpack and locked up the house.

Stealing a look toward the Science Building, she sighed, walking east instead as she pulled up a map of the campus on her phone. A loose grid had been superimposed onto it, and red X's filled many of the sections on the east side. She was almost finished with her first column, and was heading north this morning.

As she walked, she made sure no one was nearby, then uttered a small prayer under her breath. Holding out her palm, she focused, muttering the prayer again. It came slowly, but soon enough a ball of light hovered over her fingers.

Sweat danced across her brow, and she could only hold the light for a few seconds. Still, when the book had first arrived, she'd struggled to make anything at all. She had spent hours poring over its pages, relearning the language inside as she tried to connect with her magic once again.

She let the light disperse, relaxing as it faded. She hadn't expected everything to come back easily, but it was still frustrating that she could do so little. Spontaneous magic was always difficult, but thankfully she didn't need it at the moment.

Looking up, she realized she'd arrived at the library. She gave the front doors a push, and wasn't surprised to find them locked. A quick lap around the building revealed no easy way in, so she settled for an outside corner facing away from campus. Her backpack came off, and she pulled out her book.

It was large, with an ancient-looking faded brown cover. At one point in time, the sides of the pages had been lined with gold, and the edges of the hard cover lined with decorative symbols, but such flourishes had been worn away over decades of use.

She whispered a prayer, willing the book to open, and it did as she asked.

The language inside would be impossible to read for most people, partially due to its complexity, partially due to the innate power the words held. Even if one managed to decipher the written symbols, the meaning would still be lost without a divine spark to aid in the proper translation.

Enochian was the language of the angels, after all.

With her magical abilities still limited, she needed to rely on the rituals in this book to do her work. Turning to the page she wanted, she began reciting the prayer inside.

Power suffused her voice, the graceful words resembling a beautiful melody as she asked the divine for assistance. Today, just as she had done every day this week, she was casting a divination spell to locate demonic activity. As the prayer ended, the angelic overtones fading, she hoped for a predictable answer.

Instead, the magic pulsed with recognition.

Her eyes went wide, shock appearing on her face as she focused on the confirmation.

Shoot. Guess it was foolish to think a Patron would be wrong.

The magic told her to go inside the library, and she knew just what to do. Turning to another page, she gathered her backpack and moved to a side door. Enochian danced from her lips once more, and she asked for safe passage in the name of the Divine.

The door's lock clicked, then swung open for her.

Moving inside, she began following the magic of the location spell. It didn't lay out a path for her, and she was forced to navigate row after row of bookshelves while she looked. Eventually, she found a small door tucked away in a back corner.

"Never seen this before," she mumbled as she pushed it open.

The darkness inside taunted her inability to reliably create light; instead, she flicked a nearby switch.

The lights were old, and they revealed a staircase that had seen better days. She moved slowly, checking every nook and cranny as she descended. The location spell seemed strongest here.

Opening the book, she began reciting another prayer. Her words echoed off the old tile floors, surrounding her with graceful harmonies as she spoke.

While at first the goal had been to locate demonic activity, now she had to determine how big of a threat she was dealing with. If she were lucky, the demon would be a small imp or familiar of some kind; she'd actually banished an imp once in her youth, and felt confident she could do it again.

When the magic finished, her hopes were quickly dashed. Whatever had been active here was stronger, and likely humanoid. Oddly enough, the information from the spell seemed confused. Either this creature was rather weak for its class, or was powerful enough to hide its own aura.

The uncertainty didn't sit well with her. Her heartbeat quickened, and she closed her eyes to focus on her breathing.

Amber irises glared back at her.

"Fuck!" she gasped, dropping her Enochian Texts. "Pull yourself together! It's just...weaker than normal. Maybe it's a simple possession; that might explain this."

Another page, another spell, and soon she was placing a small ward in the staircase. Whatever this demon was, it would be in for an unpleasant surprise if it came here again.

She recast the tracking spell, focusing on the residual demonic energy as she willed the Divine to track the energy's path. This time, with a stronger foundation, she was able to see a slight trail that led to the library.

Following it took some time, as this spell demanded more energy from her. She found a lingering demonic presence at a small table, and traces of it scattered throughout nearby shelves. Eventually, she landed on a thick book shelved deep in a section on religion and folklore.

She dropped the spell, having already held it for quite some time. The dust on this book had been recently disturbed—another concerning discovery. She pulled it out carefully.

"*A Complete History of Demons and Demonology.* Hmm."

Weird. Why would a demon research itself?

She flipped through the book, hoping it might reveal what she was dealing with. As the spell was no longer active, she was instead looking for more mundane hints.

As she read, skimming quickly over the pages, she realized that one page in particular had been folded, dogeared to mark its place. She opened to that page and saw an ancient drawing of a beautiful woman, complete with horns, wings, and a tail.

"Shit. Shit shit shit!" She flipped to the front of the book, dismayed when she saw that no one had checked the book out recently.

A succubus! On a college campus! Crafty bitch—she'll have no shortage of eager victims...

She put the book back. With the Enochian Texts safely in her bag, she left the library, anxious as she began her journey home.

Every few minutes she would summon her light again; she could already feel her strength growing. Now that the threat had been revealed, she understood the stakes, and she was determined to be ready.

Presumably, she got here when the nightmares started. How many victims has she claimed already? She's going to get significantly stronger with every soul she consumes, so I need to act fast.

Arriving at home, she hid the Enochian Texts away and prepared for classes. Once she was ready, she stood at her front door and dared to close her eyes.

Once again, the amber eyes from her nightmare stared back.

"Your days are numbered, Hellspawn."

Amara sat on the floor, her backpack in her lap as she leaned against the barrier. She had stopped trying to push through long ago; she had quickly learned she wasn't strong enough. When she pressed lightly against the barrier, it felt soft and a little tingly, and it was easy to think breaking through was possible. The harder she tried to fight against it, however, the more the sensations became rigid and painful.

She moved her tail in small circles against the barrier, watching the ripples in the magic. Occasionally, she pulled it closer to fix her hair or scratch an itch.

Her stomach grumbled again, a headache setting in. She pulled some snacks out of her bag, hoping it might help, but she knew what her body really needed. She threw another wrapper on the floor before groaning.

Amara pulled her phone out of her backpack, where it was hooked up to a portable charger. She scowled as she saw how little battery she had left, then watched the clock change hours.

10 PM.

Four fucking hours in this dump. Nick's flight would have landed...two hours ago? Maybe three? Stupid time zones. I bet he's worried sick. How many calls have I missed by now?

A groan left her lips as she let her head fall against the barrier again, its unnatural energy tickling the back of her neck. She banged her head a few times before closing her eyes.

Of all the ways to find out magic is real... Guess it's not that surprising, all things considered.

It was easy to wish she could fall asleep, but that urge was tinged with fear. What if someone came to check the utilities while she was sleeping, and she wasn't awake to scream for help?

Endless questions repeated through her mind, and she continued waiting.

11 PM.

Amara spent most of this hour playing with her beanie. She would balance it on her tail, toss it up in the air, and try to catch it. She realized that this was one of the first times she'd really practiced her dexterity with it; at home, her tail was easy to forget about between homework, her friends, and her sex life.

12 AM.

Her phone clicked over to midnight, and Amara noticed the battery in her portable charger had finally depleted. All she had left was the phone battery, so she decided to turn it off. No sense in pointlessly burning it out while she had no service.

She put her phone back in her bag and looked at her class notes briefly, but decided she didn't have the energy to study. As she finished zipping up, she heard a distant noise. It echoed briefly, and almost sounded like the push bar on the basement door.

Amara stood up, pushing against the barrier.

"HEY! HELP! I'M TRAPPED BACK HERE!" Her throat ached, protesting the manic screaming, but she didn't care.

She continued shouting for another minute, then stopped to listen. Her heart leapt with joy when she realized she heard footsteps moving closer.

At the last second, Amara remembered to put her beanie back on and tuck her tail into her sweater. She also made sure no part of her was touching the barrier, just to limit how many strange things this person would see at once.

Finally, the stranger walked into view. He seemed understandably confused.

"Thank you! I'm so glad you heard me! I, uh...I'm kinda stuck." The tension in Amara's shoulders relaxed, and she smiled as he moved closer.

When he got closer to the light, she got a better look at his features. He had short brown hair, lightly tousled and shining slightly. His brows were furrowed in confusion as he looked at her. Strangely, Amara noticed a slight swell in his aura as he stepped closer. She figured it was a strange place to suddenly feel attracted to a stranger, but then again, men being horny was hardly ever surprising.

"How...why are you here?" he finally asked, looking behind her at the small table.

Shit. Of course he'd ask that.

"W-well, I'm really into urban exploration, and recently I've been interested in the older parts of campus, these little nooks and crannies that they tried to patch over." She bit her tongue, nervously hoping she was a convincing liar.

"And you say you're stuck? On what? You'll forgive me if I don't quite believe you." He gestured to the open room.

"Right, that's the weird part. If I try to move...well, see for yourself." She raised a hand, placing it lightly against the barrier. Magic danced around her hand as she pushed, and she looked up at the stranger again. "As weird as this might sound, I honestly think it's some kind of magic. I think all this weird writing is the source. I was hoping you could scratch it off for me?"

The stranger's face turned to the barrier, his eyes wide in surprise. For a second time, Amara sensed a pulse in his aura. "Stupid question, but can you break through it? Try ramming into it, with your shoulder," he suggested.

"No, I've tried that already. Nothing works: The harder I push against the barrier, the harder it fights back," Amara sighed.

She saw a look of confusion cross the man's face. He took a deep breath, then slowly started walking around Amara.

Why isn't he saying anything? He learns magic is real and just...doesn't care?

She watched as he circled her, avoiding the symbols as he moved. He was looking her up and down, and she saw his eyes linger on the wrappers littering the floor. Once he reached the table, he sighed heavily.

"Alright, let me level with you. These runes are all mine."

"They're...yours? You trapped me in here?" Amara asked.

"Well, yes and no. Not you specifically, at least. I'm something of an aspiring mage, and I've been coming down here to practice. That circle is a ward designed to trap anyone that's not me. Just a safety precaution."

Fuck. Does he think I'm after his stuff?

"I promise I'm just here by accident. I didn't even think magic was real until I got trapped in this!" Amara tapped on the barrier to accentuate her point. "I'll empty my bag too, if you want to make sure I haven't taken anything."

The man set his backpack down and turned to her, a smile on his face. "No need; I believe you. Now, letting you out is tricky. The runes won't break if I just scratch them off."

"Okay, so what can we do?" Amara asked.

"Think of the magic here like a firewall. I've told it to trap anyone that's not me, but I can alter the spell to let you pass too."

"That's great! The sooner the better; I've been stuck down here for hours."

An awkward silence filled the room as the stranger rummaged through the supplies on his desk. Eventually, he turned around, hands closed around several small objects.

"Alright, I think I've got everything I need. I'm Vince, by the way; pardon my manners. You are?" he asked, grinning awkwardly.

"I'm Amara! Sorry I triggered your trap; I hate to be a bother."

"Believe me, it's truly nothing. I must admit, it's not every day a beautiful woman wanders into my secret lair."

"Well, I hope you find better ways of meeting people in the future." Amara forced a smile, eager to stay on Vince's good side.

"Now, magic can be a little picky. I hate to say this, but in order to recalibrate the spell I'm going to need a bit of blood," Vince said.

Amara took a step back. "Blood? Is that really how magic works?"

"I'm afraid so. I used quite a bit to make this circle, if I'm being honest. However, since the spell has already been cast, I won't need a lot, just a small prick of the finger." Vince held up his hands, and she saw a small needle next to a clear vial.

Amara paused, her eyes locked on the needle.

This can't be a good idea, but do I really have a choice? He's the only one who knows I'm here. If he's telling the truth, it's my only way out.

She finally nodded slowly, holding out an arm.

Vince gently took her hand, turning her palm up. She noticed that his arms were now inside the barrier, and he seemed completely unfazed. Hopefully, that meant he was telling the truth about everything else.

He pricked the tip of her finger, then angled it so her blood flowed into the vial. True to his word, he only took a small amount before handing her some gauze. She pushed her finger into it and smiled meekly.

"Great! That should be everything I need." Vince grinned as he pulled away, heading back to his table. "So, how old are you?"

"I'm twenty?"

Vince chuckled quietly. "Okay, but how long have you been twenty?"

"Do you mean like, when's my birthday? Is that for the spell?" She shifted uncomfortably, not sure why he was asking these questions.

Vince turned back to her, his expression different. He looked colder now, and the smile had faded from his eyes. "You can drop the act, *Amara*. I'm not letting you out. Though I'll admit you almost had me—the candy wrappers were a nice touch. We both know demons don't eat anything other than souls."

Amara's eyes widened in shock. He knew she was a demon? How? She moved to the barrier and pushed against it, magic filling the air. "You're keeping me in here? Why?"

"Do you think I'm stupid? That barrier is the only thing keeping me alive. We both know you'd kill me in a heartbeat if you had a chance. Now stop talking; I'm trying to focus."

"Vince, I can't even kill the bugs in my house! Why on earth would you think I want to hurt you?" Amara's voice rose, anger bubbling up inside of her.

"Look, we both know you're a demon, so stop treating me like an idiot." Vince slammed a fist on the table before turning to face her. "Now why won't you listen to me?!"

"Why would I listen to the madman holding me hostage in a basement?"

"Because that's why you're here! The circle was supposed to summon a succubus and bind her to my will!"

Hearing this, Amara went quiet, her face frozen in shock. She moved to the back of her enclosure, leaning against it before sliding down to the floor. Her breathing quickened, and she closed her eyes as his words echoed in her head.

I'm nothing to him! He thinks I'm some monster, and he never planned on listening to a word I was saying...

"Honestly, I'm amazed you gave me some of your blood, but hopefully that will be enough to take control. Just have to figure out the runes..." Vince continued flipping through books on his table, his back to Amara once more.

This is only going to get worse, Amara. If you don't figure something out, he'll find a way to break your will and make you his puppet.

She looked around briefly, already intimately familiar with everything in the room, and pulled her beanie down over her eyes. She pulled her knees up to her face, trying to hold herself together.

Why couldn't I have any helpful demonic powers? What use is a tail now?

Vince continued looking through books, scribbling notes and muttering to himself as he did. He briefly looked back at Amara, huddled in fear, and rolled his eyes before returning to his work.

You can't just wallow in self-pity, Amara. You have to do something, now!

Amara closed her eyes, focusing on her breathing. In for two, out for four. There had to be something she could do, a way to turn this to her advantage. Her tail and horns weren't helpful, and she was extra weak because of the lack of sex, so what were her options?

Sex! I get my strength back by fucking, and there's a horny idiot right in front of me!

Her mind raced with possibilities, trying to piece together a plan. He clearly didn't trust her, and thought she was only acting like a helpless student to trick him.

Aren't I majoring in marketing? Vince is your audience: Figure out what he wants, overcome his hesitations, and sell him the product.

He had gone to great lengths to summon her here; the blood on the floor and the ceiling attested to that. He also didn't want any random demon, he wanted a succubus, and it was easy to guess why.

So, let's assume he's turned on by demons. Maybe my horns and tail aren't so useless after all!

A plan started forming in Amara's mind, and she no longer felt helpless. It was time to give him the demon he so badly wanted.

"Ugh, you're no fun," she said, standing up.

Hearing this, Vince turned around, a cocky grin on his face. "There we are. I was wondering how long you'd play the helpless schoolgirl."

"Can you blame me? I guess that's my fault for assuming you had a heart. It's a shame: Amara would have been so happy to get out of there, I bet she would have sucked you off."

Vince's aura pulsed, ever so slightly, but it wasn't enough. She had to keep pushing.

"I'm not the monster here; I'm just smart enough not to trust you," he replied.

"Well, if it's alright with you, *Master Vince*, I think I'll lose the sad girl sweater; it's getting a little stuffy."

Amara pulled her sweater off, taking the beanie with it, tossing them both to the floor. Underneath, a tank top hugged her curves, her cleavage prominent. Her horns were also on full display now, and she let her tail slowly explore the space.

Vince's eyes widened, and Amara saw an instant change in his aura; it pulsed with excitement now that she was fully on display. She traced her tail along the edge of the barrier, sparking a trail of magic as she spun around.

"That's better! It's so frustrating hiding my tail away like that." Amara playfully accentuated her words, taking care to appear extra flirty. "She's a beauty, isn't she? Long, powerful, firm..."

She smacked the barrier with her tail, flourishing it about as she did. She watched Vince's eyes follow it around, occasionally darting to her horns or her cleavage. Surprisingly, she found herself enjoying the attention, especially as it was focused on her demonic attributes.

Vince finally caught himself staring and turned back to the table. "I know what you're doing, and it's not going to work."

His aura told her otherwise; it was still growing.

"Oh? I wasn't aware I had an evil plan. You should tell me what it is!"

Vince stayed quiet, though he seemed to be working slower now.

"Aww, now I'm being ignored!" Amara pouted. "Well, might as well take advantage of that. It's been ages since I last got fucked; I think it's time to rub one out."

His hands stopped moving entirely, and she noticed him turn to look at her out of the corner of his eye.

"Do you know how hard it is?" Amara moved to her knees, leaning against the barrier as she pushed her hands underneath her shirt. She pushed it over her bra, her cleavage even more visible now. "Going so long without sex?"

She squeezed her breasts, letting out a soft, sensual moan. Her eyes closed, and she focused on putting on a good show. After a minute, she slid a hand down her stomach and unbuttoned her pants, spreading her legs slightly.

When she opened her eyes, she saw Vince now staring openly again. Even without reading his aura, his erection made his arousal more than obvious. His gaze reminded her why she was here, and she moved her tail in front of her again.

It traced her cleavage before moving down, pushing into her pants to find her pussy. The flared tip pushed against her sensitive clit, and she moaned again. Large, dramatic movements accentuated the teasing, and she saw Vince's aura grow even brighter.

"It's a shame there's no one here who wants to fuck me, to fill my holes with cum." She closed her eyes again, letting herself enjoy the pleasure.

"T-that's...I," Vince stammered. "You know why I can't. If we fuck, I'm handing over my soul on a silver platter."

Hearing this, Amara crawled closer, pushing her hands against the barrier, her tail on display again. "Oh, but Vince...*Master Vince*...surely we can figure something out? Find some middle ground where you feed me your delicious cum?"

She licked her lips, then leaned in and ran her tongue up the barrier. It tingled slightly, and felt like she was licking static electricity off a glass pane.

"Don't tell me you've never fantasized about giving a succubus a facial before?" She ran her fingers down her face as she spoke.

Vince shivered, and his aura was so vibrant she could taste it. She eagerly watched the conflict in his eyes, sure he would give in soon.

"I guess it would be rude to keep a pet without feeding her..." Vince started fumbling with his pants, and soon he was pulling out his cock. It was slightly smaller than Nick's, but Amara didn't care; she was one step closer to regaining her strength.

"I'll be such a good pet for you, Master. Do I get a pretty collar too?" she moaned, her tail pushing into her pants again.

"Only once I've broken you, but for now...I've fucking earned this." He stroked his cock slowly, precum already forming.

Amara pulled back from the barrier, pulling her shirt completely off before doing the same with her bra. She grabbed her breasts again, pinching her nipples and moaning loudly. Her tail continued massaging her pussy, and after a moment she brought it to her lips to taste it. Her tongue lingered on the tip of her tail, then pulled it inside. She locked eyes with Vince, her tail starting to push in and out of her mouth.

"Of course you get off to this, fucking slut." He began stroking faster, taking a step closer as he spoke. His cock was barely an inch away from the barrier, but he seemed determined not to cross it.

In response, Amara's tail pushed deeper into her mouth. She let herself gag loudly, spit running down her chin as she did. This repeated a few more times before she pulled her tail out, rubbing the tip on her face while she gasped for air.

"I just wish I had something else to suck on...something with a tasty snack in it!" Amara pushed her tits against the barrier, followed by her tongue. She licked as close to his cock as she could, but it was still just out of reach. Locking eyes with Vince, she knew he wouldn't last much longer. Her hands moved back to her tits, and she kept playing with them as she pushed her tail into her mouth again. This time, she timed her thrusts to match Vince's stroking, gagging loudly in time with him.

Before long, she finally got what she wanted. His aura grew brighter than she'd ever seen before, overwhelming her senses as he came. Amara barely had time to pull her tail from her mouth before it happened.

"Fuck! Get ready, pet!" Vince said.

Thick ropes of cum landed on her nose, her cheeks, and her tongue. Vince's moaning overtook hers, filling the room as his aura reached its zenith.

His orgasm took over, and Amara felt her energy returning. She breathed in the scent of his arousal, watching his aura as it released its pent-up energy. For a moment, she thought she saw it move closer, connecting with her as she fed from it.

Stronger. I need to be stronger.

Amara remembered that, contrary to Vince's wishes, she wasn't here to fuck. Her eyes roamed his body, and she saw the vial he'd used earlier in a side pocket of his jacket. Her hands, still pressed against the barrier, dug into it as she tested her restored strength. She could already feel a difference, and was pretty sure she could break through.

With a quick movement, she pulled a hand back and punched through the barrier, its magic sending shockwaves of pain down her arm. Vince was still recovering from his orgasm, and didn't have time to react as she grabbed the vial from his pocket. Just as her hands wrapped around it, the barrier's magic pulsed, sending her flying to the other side.

Her breath was knocked from her as she collided with the far wall of the barrier, but she managed to catch herself before she collapsed entirely.

"Fucking bitch!" Vince shouted, frantically zipping up his pants. "You lying whore! Give that back!"

Amara looked up at him, a devilish grin on her face as she tucked the vial into her backpack. She could feel her eyes glowing, and she felt surprisingly energetic.

"Or what? You'll trap me in a basement? Try to turn me into a sex slave? Face it, idiot: You've blown your load in more ways than one."

"You have no idea what I'm capable of! I'll make you regret this!" Vince snarled.

He gathered up his backpack, then walked past Amara to the entrance. He glared at her one last time before leaving, his steps slowly getting farther away.

Watching him leave, Amara grabbed her clothes and started getting dressed again. She eagerly cleaned off her face, pulling the rest of his cum into her mouth as she pulled even more energy from it.

Having regained her strength, she decided it was time to test the barrier again. Last time she'd been focused on grabbing the vial of blood, but perhaps she was strong enough to break herself out. A quick flick of her tail confirmed that the barrier was still active, and as strong as ever, so Amara jumped to her feet and prepared to get started.

Before she had the chance, however, she heard a new voice echo throughout the basement.

"Brandon? What the fuck is happening down here?"

"Nothing! I just...I had a little accident with the runes."

"Don't bullshit me—I can practically smell the magic pouring out of that back room! Who were you talking to?"

"No one! I mean, myself! I talk to myself all the time! Hey, don't go back there!"

Amara panicked, putting on the rest of her clothes as fast as she could. She tucked her tail into her sweater, her horns underneath her hat, and took a deep breath to try to dim her eyes.

Vince ran back into the room, looking Amara over briefly before pivoting to face this other person. He was clearly posturing to keep them out, but Amara could tell how nervous he was.

"Okay, just before you come in, I promise I can explain!" he stammered.

"Oh, I doubt that. Out of my way, idiot."

Amara tensed as this new stranger entered the room. She watched as a woman with short black hair stepped into view, her face covered with intricate eyeliner and multiple piercings. She was holding a short switchblade, casually spinning it in one hand, but she stopped when she looked away from Vince.

"Amara?" Tessa asked, her eyes wide.

In her own shock, Amara couldn't think of anything to say.

Tessa spun to face Vince, her face full of rage. As Amara watched, the tattoos on the side of her head began to glow, and she held a hand toward him. With a flick of the wrist, Vince was suddenly lifted into the air, his feet scrambling as fear filled his eyes. Tessa turned to Amara, who ducked as her captor went flying overhead.

The table against the back wall cracked in half as Vince collided with it. He fell into a pile of papers and books, his body limp as the impact rendered him unconscious.

Amara turned back to Tessa, not sure if she should be relieved or scared.

"Amara, Nick has been worried sick about you!" Tessa said, moving closer. "You're not answering our calls, we're looking all over campus for you, and you've been down here with this idiot?!"

"I-I..."

Tessa grabbed Amara's arm, trying to pull her toward the entrance. "Whatever—you can explain on the way."

"Tessa, I can't leave!" Amara said.

"Don't tell me you fell for his bullshit—you're better than that! What did he promise you? Money? Power?"

"No, you don't understand!" Amara pulled out of Tessa's grip. "I literally can't leave!"

Amara pushed a hand against the barrier, the magic reappearing. She watched as Tessa's eyes grew wide, then she fell quiet. Tessa walked around the circle, examining the markings over the floor and ceiling.

"Amara, that's...not possible. I gave all these runes to him, and most of them were fake." Tessa knelt down, looking at one rune in particular. "The few real ones I gave him were far too weak to do anything, and even with these additions he made..."

Amara shuffled anxiously, worried about where this conversation was heading. Tessa stood up, taking a few steps back.

"No human would be trapped in there."

Silence filled the room again, the words escaping Amara as she tried to speak. She saw Tessa glance at the exit, taking another step back.

"Wait!" Amara said. "Promise you won't freak out?"

"Amara, I just threw a grown man across a room. *Without touching him.*"

"Point taken. Um, okay, well..."

Amara took a deep breath, closing her eyes, then uncoiled her tail from her waist. It moved to her head, where it pushed underneath her beanie and pulled it off. Her horns now exposed, she opened her eyes again, urging them to flare. Looking at Tessa nervously, she forced a smile.

Tessa's eyes roamed her body, and Amara could feel sweat gathering on her brow. Moments felt like hours as they passed, the silence ringing in her ears. She wanted to be relieved, happy that someone else knew about this, but Tessa clearly knew more about what was happening, and she had no idea how she would react.

Has she met demons before? Are they...are we common? What if she doesn't trust me? Should she? What if I'm doomed to turn into a sex-craved murder machine and I just don't know it? For fuck's sake, Tessa, just say something!

"Huh," Tessa said. "So...a demon?"

Amara nodded. "A succubus, actually."

"How long have you known?"

"Like, two weeks. I'm still in the 'What the fuck is happening to me' stage? Look, I'll tell you everything, but can we please get out of here?"

"Oh, shit, yeah." Tessa stepped forward, positioning a heel against one of the larger symbols. She paused briefly, then looked up at Amara. "You promise you're still you? The same Amara who refused to party for over a year?"

Amara pulled her tail close, squeezing it as she locked eyes with Tessa. She smiled softly, sensing how important this question seemed to be.

"I promise."

With a brief nod, Tessa pulled her boot back, scraping the symbol off the ground. Amara felt the energy of the barrier dissipate, and she nervously pushed a hand forward. When it felt nothing but open air, she eagerly jumped out of the circle to hug Tessa. She picked her up, spinning around in glee as she laughed in celebration.

Was Tessa always this light?

When she put her down, she saw that Tessa's eyes were wide, and her tattoos were glowing slightly. Amara smiled, but sheepishly stepped back as she cleared her throat. She turned to look at the circle, stepping forward to grab her backpack.

As she threw it on, she stared at Vince's body, crumpled under a pile of books and papers.

"You wanna go kick him a bit?" Tessa asked.

"What? No!" Amara moved to the entrance, eager to leave. "I mean, a little, but more than anything I just want to fucking leave. I've been stuck in this room since classes ended."

Neither girl said much as they left the basement, weaving through the old plumbing. Amara pulled her phone out, turning it back on before tucking it in her back pocket. There was so much she didn't understand, so much she wanted to ask Tessa, and she didn't know where to start.

For now, she would settle with letting her other friends know she was safe.

Once they reached the staircase upstairs, her phone exploded. She had dozens of missed calls and texts, at first just from Nick, then from Tessa, Vee, and Chloé. She took time to text everyone, telling them she was safe and that she would meet them back at her place.

Fresh night air washed over her as they left the building. Amara paused, focusing on the breeze as it danced across her skin. She looked across the darkened campus, unexpected emotions rising to the surface as she did.

I almost lost this. He would have locked me up forever.

She turned to Tessa, then collapsed forward, tears forming in her eyes. She hugged her tight, and was surprised to feel her return the gesture.

"That asshole...the way he looked at me, he thought I was just something to break and use for his own twisted pleasure," Amara said.

"Honestly, I knew Brandon was a little fucked, but I never thought he'd go this far."

"Brandon? He told me his name was Vince."

"Well, you're not supposed to trust demons, typically."

Amara pulled back, the two looking at each other. She saw how nervous Tessa was, though she was trying to hide it.

"Tessa, I need you to be honest with me." She paused, hoping her friend would take this seriously. "You know magic, apparently, and I want to talk about that, but are you scared of me? Should I be scared of what I'm becoming?"

It was Tessa's turn to pull away, and she averted her eyes to stare at the ground instead.

"Look, objectively? Demons are fucking terrifying. Every instinct in my body is telling me to run, that I shouldn't have freed you, but...but at the same time, I can tell it's you." Tessa paused, breathing deep. "I think it'll be easier once I understand everything, what's happening, how this all started."

Tessa turned to walk, starting toward the quad, and Amara joined her.

"Oh, that's easy: It was at the party. Our theory is that, once I lost my virginity, my succubus ancestry finally activated. I've been adding limbs and gaining weird abilities ever since then."

"Wait, WHAT?!" Tessa turned and grabbed her arm. "You finally got laid? And what do you mean 'our' theory? Who the fuck else knows about this?"

Amara smirked, knowing exactly how Tessa would respond. "I...I've been sleeping with Nick, and he was there when my tail first appeared. He's been helping me research things and figure out what's happening."

Tessa began punching her arm, performative rage guiding her strikes. "Nick?! Why? How?"

The two of them started talking about the party again, this time with all the details out in the open. Amara described being at the party, her libido taking over, and not knowing who else to trust. She went over the appearance of her tail, then her horns, and finally the events leading up to her imprisonment under the Science Building.

Before long, they arrived at Amara's apartment, where Nick saw her and ran out of the house. He squeezed her tight, whispering in her ear.

"How serious was this? Is this about...you know what?" he asked.

"Almost very bad, but I'm safe. Tessa knows; we'll talk later."

Nick looked at her, nodding slowly before letting her go.

Inside, she made up a story to tell Vee and Chloé, and everyone decided to turn the night into an impromptu sleepover.

6

TURBULENCE

The sleepover had mostly been a practical solution; everyone was already out late, in the same place, and no one felt like walking home. Regardless, it proved to be a great idea, and they all stayed up much later than intended as they enjoyed each other's company.

The morning was close to over by the time everyone had woken up. Vee left first, muttering apologies about needing to study, and Chloé wasn't far behind. Tessa feigned a headache to stick around, but Amara suspected it wasn't entirely fake.

As Amara made the three of them coffee, she finally explained to Nick what had happened. She went over the week prior, discovering that sex had become a very literal need for her, and the weakness that ensued. She explained the strange impulse, following it to the Science Building, and getting trapped in the basement. It was difficult to explain her encounter with Brandon, and she glossed over some of the details, but eventually got everyone caught up.

"I think it's time we heard from you," Nick said, setting his coffee down and turning to Tessa. "I'm gonna need a damn good explanation why you helped that pervert make a demon trap."

"Hey! I admit it wasn't a great idea, but how was I supposed to know that one of my best friends had just become a succubus? Besides, it wouldn't have mattered if you'd been here," Tessa snapped.

"Will you both shut it!" Amara stood, slamming the couch with her tail. "I don't care whose fault it is! This happened because we were all missing a piece of the puzzle, so let's focus on fixing that."

She sat back down, huffing. Once settled, she gestured silently to Tessa.

"Well, I'm a witch. Everything kinda starts there," Tessa said quietly. She gestured toward Nick's mug, her tattoos lit up, and the cup floated into the air. "Brandon had a huge crush on me, and was stalking me for a while. Because of that, he found out, and was a huge ass about it. At first he wanted to learn magic, but when I said no, he tried to blackmail me into sleeping with him. To keep him busy, I decided to just play along; I told him that I could teach him how to summon a succubus."

"But you said most of what you taught him was fake, right?" Amara asked.

"That's right. Despite his enthusiasm, he's not very bright. I was able to draw up a whole slew of runes that looked demonic, and sprinkled in a few real ones to make it believable. When I found Amara, I realized that he'd added some runes without telling me, but the circle he made was still rather weak. It never would have been strong enough to reach into Hell."

"Let me guess: It was just strong enough to create a mysterious impulse in any succubi that happened to be nearby?" Nick spoke up, grabbing his coffee out of the air.

"That's my guess. Amara happened to be here, and felt drawn to explore it. You were smart to grab that vial of blood—he could have made things a lot worse."

"Oh! That's right!" Amara jumped up and ran to her backpack, pulling out the vial. She went to the kitchen, dumping its contents down the drain before rinsing it out.

"You're sure that's all of it?" Tessa asked.

"Positive. He only had a few minutes with it before I...well, y'know. He was just flipping through his books that whole time."

Amara vaulted the couch, landing next to Tessa before settling in again. She noticed Tessa staring at her tail, and she moved it closer so her friend could feel it. Tessa ran her fingers over it softly, but Amara could still see some anxiety behind her eyes.

Of course, that wasn't the only thing Amara noticed; as Tessa slowly explored her tail, there was also a noticeable pulse in her aura. Was the tail turning her on? Was this just residual attraction from all the time Tessa had spent hitting on her?

Amara had so many questions, about this, about magic, but she decided to wait. She could tell Tessa needed some time.

Realizing that Nick had been rather quiet, Amara looked over and saw him lost in thought. She knew from experience that he was going over everything he'd just learned, and was trying to think of what he wanted to ask next.

"What happens if Amara gets discovered?" he finally asked. "Men in black suits abduct her in the night and wipe our memories? Priests show up and attempt an exorcism?"

"That depends on who discovers her. Most witches, and the church, would probably assume she's from Hell and try to banish her. Many people would want to enslave her in a grab for power, but many others would be equally excited to do the opposite."

"The opposite? Like, pledge their allegiance to me?" Amara asked. "Why would anyone do that?"

"Power, sex, fame—all the usual stuff. It might not be soon, but if you live long enough, you'll find people who think you can grant their every wish if they're willing to forfeit their soul."

Amara shuddered. She'd only recently accepted that souls were actually real, and the thought of someone trying to barter theirs for power sounded awful.

"We need to assume nothing good comes from being discovered, then. What steps can we take to keep Amara safe? Are there spells we can cast? Wards we can put down? What if we—"

"Nick, how about we give Tessa some space?" Amara said, cutting him off. "She deserves time to process this."

Nick bit his tongue, nodding before grabbing his coffee again. Amara looked back at Tessa, who was still holding her tail, and kept speaking.

"Do you want to go home? Unless you think we're in imminent danger, I think we can fend for ourselves a while longer. Go spend some time with your partners, maybe...take a bubble bath or something, I don't know."

"A bubble bath? Seriously?"

"You know what I mean!"

Tessa smirked as she returned Amara's tail. Finishing her coffee, she stood up and collected her things, then said goodbye to Nick. Amara walked her out, keeping quiet as they approached the front entrance. Tessa seemed to have something on her mind, trying and failing to speak as they walked. Once they'd left the building, she finally moved in for a hug.

"Thanks, Amara," she whispered.

"Hey, you practically saved my life last night. You let me know if there's anything I can do to help," Amara said, pulling her in tight.

"Actually, are you free later?" Tessa asked. "I think I've got just the thing in mind."

"I'll be there with bells on; just text me the time and place!" Amara waved goodbye as she started down the hallway again.

"I prefer to leave the bells in the bedroom, honestly!" Tessa shouted at her.

Amara laughed, happy that Tessa already seemed a little better.

Once she got home, she found Nick cleaning up the remains of last night's festivities. She jumped in, eager to have something to do.

"You think it's okay letting her go? There's still so much we don't know," Nick asked, clearing plates off the table and moving them to the dishwasher.

"Nick, I've never seen her like this before. She wasn't cracking jokes, or bragging about her sex life: She was really scared. I didn't mention it earlier, but she hesitated when I asked her to free me."

Hearing this, Nick paused. A moment passed before he spoke, his voice quieter. "I guess I was lucky I was there when this started. I've never questioned if you were really you, but she didn't get that luxury. Especially since you're a succubus. You could have been a random demon disguised as her friend and there'd be no way to tell."

"Ugh, shapeshifting, yet another thing I can't do." Amara collapsed on the couch, pulling a pillow over her face.

"Another thing? What aren't you telling me?" Nick moved closer, sitting next to her.

"Nothing; it's stupid," Amara said. She immediately felt Nick's judgmental stare boring through the pillow and pulled it away. "Ugh, fine, it's just...I felt so helpless down in that basement. I'm a demon! Aren't I supposed to be a terrifying force of nature? Where are my magic powers? Why can't I lift cars? Or fly? All those books we read said that succubi are supposed to be able to charm people, but when I was trapped down there, it didn't feel like I had any control over what Brandon felt. It felt like I was just seducing him the normal, human way: by flashing my tits."

"Hey, slow down; it's only been a few weeks. Aren't you the one calling this a second puberty? You don't grow a beard or double Ds in a month."

"I said it was stupid, didn't I?" She leaned against Nick. "Tessa has cool witchy mind powers, and what can I do? Sense when someone's horny? Wow, lucky me."

"Wait, can you do that?" he asked.

"Did I leave that part out?"

Nick nodded.

"Shoot, my bad. Yeah, when people are horny, or have just gotten laid, I can tell. It's like a weird aura that surrounds them? But I can smell it too—it's delicious."

"Huh. Interesting." He paused. "Hey, you said you barely ate this week—want to get lunch?"

"That's probably a good idea; I have no clue what my body's up to anymore. Do you think I could survive on nothing but sex?"

"Even if you could, I'm not letting you find out today." He stood up, grabbing his things.

"But think of all the money I could save! What if I could stop sleeping? I'd have so much time to do stuff!" Amara pulled her shoes on before checking her beanie.

"Alright, say you suddenly have an extra eight hours a day, what would you even do?" he asked.

"I could catch up on all my shows?"

Nick stared at her, unamused.

"Okay, fine—I don't know. But there's a good idea here somewhere!"

The two of them locked up, then headed to the cafeteria. As they walked, Nick asked if she could sense anything from nearby students. She quietly pointed out everything she saw, even turning it into a game for Nick. She would find someone with an aura, then make him guess if they were horny or well fucked.

The impromptu game kept them amused all through lunch, and they sat around snacking until Tessa reached out, asking to meet up.

Lysander Hall was the oldest building on campus, and sat just north of the quad. Students wandering its corridors would find lecture halls, offices for the most prestigious professors, and many art installations celebrating the school's history. Most prominent was the bust of Arthur Lysander, the founder of the school, which stood on display across from the main entrance.

Once Amara was inside the building, she found Tessa at a small cafe near the central staircases. Walking close, she was greeted by the smell of grilled sandwiches and coffee, but that smell was soon overpowered by Tessa, who had apparently skipped lunch for more exciting activities.

"Where's Nick?" she asked.

"I invited him, but he said he wanted to look into something else? I guess this means he trusts you, which is good."

Tessa threw her backpack over her shoulder, then picked up her coffee. "Great! I won't have to put up with all his questions!"

The two hugged as Tessa stood up, and Amara could feel that some tension had already been lost.

"I take it you're feeling better?" Amara asked, pulling back from the embrace.

Tessa started walking, leading Amara through the building as they talked. "For the most part. I think I just needed some time to clear my head. It was a lot to take in, to be honest."

"Yeah? Is that what you said earlier today? Or were you the top this time?" Amara smirked, trying to keep the conversation from getting too heavy.

"Shit, is it that obvious? I showered afterward and everything!"

Amara laughed, grabbing Tessa's arm. "Don't worry, I doubt anyone other than me could notice. I can tell when people are horny, and see their afterglow."

Tessa paused for a moment, lost in thought. "That makes a lot of sense, honestly. I can't think of a more helpful tool for someone trying to weaponize seduction. Well, maybe charm magic. Can you do that?"

"Like, compel people to fall in love with me? Not that I'm aware of, unless you count showing off my cleavage."

The girls laughed as they turned a corner, now facing a hallway lined with statues. Walking past a few classrooms, they finally stopped at a small door tucked away in a corner.

Tessa pulled the door open, heading inside and turning on a light. "Okay, so, that creepy basement you were locked in? Old architecture like that exists all over campus."

As they closed the door, Amara felt a sense of déjà vu wash over her. She was standing in a staircase just like the one in the library, only these stairs were a little wider.

"Like the archives under the library?" she asked.

"Exactly! That actually gets the most use out of all these old spaces. They're all holdovers from the original buildings."

"So why are we here?" Amara started down the stairs.

"Well, I really appreciate you opening up about everything. I realize you didn't have much of a choice but, still, I'm happy you trusted me. I want to do the same."

At the bottom of the stairs lay another basement level, this one much better lit. It looked like someone had tried to redecorate at some point in the mid-seventies, and those efforts had unfortunately never been reversed.

"Speaking of opening up, can I let my tail out? It cramps like hell when I tuck it away."

Tessa nodded, and Amara eagerly uncurled her tail. She went through her usual motions to shake it back to life, all while stuffing her beanie into her backpack. For some reason, she liked having her horns out, though she was still trying to figure out why.

"Now, as a witch, I'm extra sensitive to shifts in magical energy. Magic exists everywhere, almost like water currents in the ocean, and by reading them, we can learn interesting things about the world around us. We call these leylines, and recently, there have been some strange shifts in the magic on campus."

"Let me guess: The shifts are causing problems?"

"Yes and no. Right now, there aren't any problems, but if this pattern continues, the changes could start affecting stuff around campus."

"Affecting stuff how?" Amara asked.

"Well, it depends on what exactly is causing the changes. Things from other worlds might get pulled over, or latent magic could start causing random problems. You know places that get famous for being really haunted? More often than not, those places sit on converging leylines. Anyways, it would be best to take care of this now before my coven catches wind."

Amara ran in front of Tessa. "Hold on, you're in a coven? That's so cool! What's it like?"

A flash of regret appeared on Tessa's face. "It's, um... look, maybe I'll tell you later, okay?"

Nervous that she'd found a sore spot, Amara happily let Tessa change the topic. She gestured for her friend to continue.

"Anyways," Tessa said, "when I started investigating, I found this."

Tessa had reached a dead end in the hallway. She closed her eyes, and Amara watched as her tattoos lit up. Moments later, a similar glow appeared on the wall in front of them, forming into runes. The wall shimmered, then faded until it vanished completely.

"Wow, Tessa, that's incredible! Did you set that up?" Amara moved closer, pushing her hand through the space that had previously been a brick wall.

"Illusions aren't really my thing, sadly. This was already set up; I just found a way past it, kind of like picking a lock. What's important, though, is what it was hiding."

In front of Amara, the hallway now extended another twenty feet or so. There was a dramatic shift in decor as well; the space beyond the illusion had clearly been spared during the last redecoration. Instead of carpet, flat concrete extended from wall to wall, with simple white brickwork connecting the floor to the ceiling.

In the center of the space, a large circle of some kind had been carefully drawn and filled with myriad different runic symbols. Despite knowing nothing about magic, Amara could tell it was quite different than the one that had held her captive. There was no empty space in the middle, for one thing, but Amara still took care to avoid stepping on it.

"It's another magic circle?" Amara asked, confused.

"Yup! This circle is fascinating for a million different reasons, but mostly because of how old it is. Whatever it is, it's been here for ages, possibly even since the school was founded."

"So, what does it do?"

"Well, if your offer still stands, I'm hoping you can help me figure that out."

Amara carefully moved around the room, keeping as much distance as she could from the circle. "I'm flattered, truly, but how am I supposed to help? I'm not a witch; this is all gibberish to me."

"Well, I'm not sure." Tessa sighed, leaning against a wall before sliding down to the floor. "I don't really know what you can do, but two minds have to be better than one, right?"

Amara finished circling the room and sat down next to Tessa. "I'll do my best, but don't get your hopes up. What have you learned so far about it?"

"The most obvious is the temperature. I'm sure you've noticed how cold it is down here?"

Amara pushed her hand forward, feeling the air before moving it to the ground. "I didn't, actually. Aren't basements always cold?"

"I mean, a little, but not to this extent." Tessa looked at her, her eyes wide with surprise. "You seriously don't feel it?"

Amara shook her head, resting her hand on the concrete beneath her. Now that she was looking for it, she could feel a deep chill inside the concrete, but it felt distant. Rather than creeping into her body, like she was used to, the change in temperature registered more like a strange texture or sensation. It was something she could feel, but only on the outside of her body.

"It's weird, I can feel it, but it also feels like my body is resisting it." Amara reached over to Tessa, resting a hand on her forehead out of curiosity. "So, you think this is coming from the circle?"

Tessa flinched as Amara's hand made contact, but relaxed just as quickly. "It's the simplest answer. A lot of magic relies on summoning energies or creatures from other places, so it would make sense if this circle were somehow connected to another place, somewhere much colder." Tessa ran her hands over Amara's. "Wow, you feel like you've been basking in the sun for hours."

Tessa moved closer, putting both her hands on Amara's neck as she absorbed her warmth. They stopped talking for a moment, Amara enjoying the touch, when she felt Tessa's hands move to her shoulders. They bumped against the straps of her tank, accidentally pulling one off.

Amara grabbed her hands, realizing how cold they were, and the two girls locked eyes. As she looked at Tessa, she saw a softness that she'd never seen before. It was like a mask had slipped off, and she was finally seeing the person underneath.

Suddenly, the look in Tessa's eyes changed, snapping back into focus. She pulled back, averting her gaze back to the circle.

"Um, so, the circle?" Tessa muttered.

"Right, yeah, it's definitely cold." Amara readjusted her top. "Do we know anything else?"

"I know it's not a trap of any kind. The runes used here are pretty strange, but they're definitely not built to release any kind of magic. I've walked over it dozens of times. Other than that, nothing really." Tessa paused, looking back at her. "You said you can see sexual auras—can you see anything else?"

"I'm assuming you mean anything out of the ordinary? Not that I'm aware of."

"What do you see when you look at the circle? Describe it to me."

Amara did just that, taking a few minutes to talk through her vision of the strange circle. The more she talked, the more obvious it became that she was seeing exactly the same things as Tessa.

"No luck there; dang. Maybe we're looking at this from the wrong angle. I should play to your strengths, instead of hoping you can do what I need. What else can you do?"

Amara paused, her tail curling around her arm as she thought of what to say. "Tessa, I can't really do anything. I've got my horns, my tail, my weird horny radar, and a million unanswered questions about what's happening to me." She pulled back, shrinking into herself.

"What have you tried? According to myths, succubi can summon fire, enthrall mortals, even shapeshift. Maybe we could—"

"I can't do anything! Not everyone has cool powers like you, okay? Can we just drop it?" Amara hissed.

Tessa bit her lip, then diverted her eyes. The girls sat in silence for a minute, the faint hum of the lights ringing throughout the space.

"Amara, I didn't...I wasn't trying to...look, I'm sorry. I didn't mean to make you uncomfortable. I've never met a demon before, I wasn't implying..." Tessa muttered, pulling her hands into her sweater.

"Well, I've never turned into a demon before." Amara pulled her phone out and texted Nick. "Look, I'll keep you company, but I'm just gonna work on my homework or something. Sorry I couldn't help."

Amara opened her backpack and rummaged through her schoolwork. She could feel Tessa's eyes on her, but she couldn't bring herself to look up and meet them.

Soon enough, Tessa pulled out some books of her own and started poring over the strange symbols inside. Occasionally, she would shift to a different spot on the floor, but it looked more like nervous fidgeting than actual research.

Amara had a feeling that neither of them were getting much done.

They stayed there for a while, but when Nick finally responded, Amara jumped at the excuse to leave.

Tessa summoned the illusory wall again before they left, and they marched up the stairs in silence. They passed the cafe, the bust of the founder, then walked outside.

It was already getting dark, and Amara pulled her beanie down tight out of habit. The quad stretched out in front of her, lights turning on to illuminate it. She turned to her friend, who clearly wanted to say something, but was holding back.

"Tessa, I've just...this is really hard for me. What's happening is scary, but that's no excuse to take it out on you. I'm happy you showed me this part of your life. If you'll have me, I'll gladly keep you company."

She pulled Tessa in for a hug.

"I didn't mean to push you, and I'm sorry too. I'll come up with a better plan for next time. I'm just happy to have someone I can share this with," Tessa said.

After a minute, the girls broke off their hug. They each went their separate ways, and Amara was happy she'd fought past her frustration enough to apologize.

Amara met up with Nick outside his dorm. He was being suspiciously quiet about his plans for the night, but he had told her to wear running clothes.

"So, what did Tessa want?" he asked, leading the way.

"I guess she's been investigating weird magic stuff? She wanted my help but...I kinda snapped at her."

Nick gave her a questioning look.

"She kept asking about what I could do, what my demon powers are, and after everything with Brandon..."

"I'm sure she understands. She's normally the hothead, right?" Nick smirked. "You'll both be back to normal before you know it."

"Doesn't mean I don't feel bad about it, but thanks." Amara pushed him affectionately. "What's the plan tonight?"

As they walked, she realized Nick was taking them further east. They weren't heading to the stadium, but this side of campus mostly existed for all the sports programs.

"So glad you asked! I've got a lot of friends from back in my wrestling days, and I called in a favor." Nick pulled a hand out of his pocket, holding up a small key. "I'm now the proud owner of a key to the gymnastics building."

"Gymnastics? What scheme is this?"

"Scheming? Me? I don't know the meaning of the word. I've just got a theory I want to test."

Soon enough, they made it to the gymnastics building. Nick guided her to a side entrance, checked for onlookers, then opened the door.

It was eerie being inside such a large gym with no lights, but thankfully Nick knew how to turn them on. The building hummed back to life, and Amara looked around at the equipment all around her.

She had no idea what anything was called, but she wandered around curiously as she examined everything. She recognized the balance beams, but there were also big rings hanging from the ceiling, pits filled with squishy colorful cubes, and quite a bit more.

There was also a viewing area on one side of the room. A white brick wall about fifteen feet tall supported a series of built-in bleachers, with the only separation being the railing at the edge. A small staircase that connected the two areas had been tucked away in a corner.

Nick approached her, pulling off his sweatpants and sweater to reveal his gym clothes underneath. Loose-fitting blue shorts hung just past his knees, but his gray shirt was much tighter. His athletic form was on full display underneath the thin fabric, and Amara happily stole a look.

"So, not that it's a secret anymore, but I think we need to run some tests," Nick said.

"For what? We're not looking for new powers, are we? That's the last thing I want to do right now."

"It's not that, I promise. Have you noticed how much your body has changed recently?" Nick commented.

Amara stared daggers at Nick.

"Okay, I phrased that poorly. I meant outside of the horns and the tail. Your form is more athletic, and your muscles have more definition."

Intrigued, Amara followed Nick's example and pulled off her sweats. Underneath, she was wearing deep crimson red shorts with a matching sports bra. They both hugged her form tightly, and she looked down to examine her stomach.

"Holy shit, are these abs?!" Amara pulled out her phone, setting it down and using it as a mirror as she examined herself.

"Do you never look at yourself in the mirror?" Nick asked, gathering their clothes and putting them aside.

"No, I do that all the time! But recently I've been pretty focused on my demon bits." Amara spun around to look at her back. "Plus, I normally judge my body by what clothes I can wear, but the tail forces me into those baggy sweaters."

With their clothing now safely out of the way, Nick moved closer and started doing some stretching. "So, I've been thinking a lot about—well, everything. Yesterday changes a lot, and we can't assume this is the last time something goes wrong."

Amara joined in, copying Nick's movements despite not fully understanding what he was doing. He continued talking as he warmed up, moving slower so Amara could copy him.

"We need to accept that I'm not always going to be around. When this happens again, you need to know what your body is capable of."

"So, we're just here to...work out? Nick, I've never been good at this stuff."

"That's why we're starting slow; just keep copying me."

Nick walked her through his warmup routine, explaining why each part mattered. After a half hour of stretching and cardio, he finally brought her over to some equipment.

Her first task was a balance beam. She felt silly crawling on top of it, but with Nick's help she was able to stand up without falling.

"Alright, this one's easy. Just walk to the other side," he said.

Taking a deep breath, Amara took her first steps. She raised her arms as she walked, trying to stay balanced, but each step proved more difficult than the last. Before she could make it halfway across, she lost control and slipped off the side.

"Fuck!" She fell quickly, and thankfully landed in Nick's arms. "I thought you said this was easy?"

"I also said I was testing a theory, so thank you for proving me right!" He put her down softly, a smug grin on his face.

"What did I do?" Amara asked.

"What *didn't* you do?" he asked in return. He moved closer, boosting her up to the beam again.

Once she was steady, she sighed and looked down at Nick. "I didn't...not fall?"

"Amara, you have a tail. It was stiff and lifeless the whole time."

Amara stared at Nick, the gears in her head clicking into place. Taking a deep breath, she looked back at her tail, then started walking again.

Though her arms were still outstretched, she tried to let her tail adjust to her shifts in balance first. It felt surprisingly natural to use her tail like this; she found she was able to let it correct her balance without much effort or thought.

She lowered her arms and walked slightly faster. The steps came easier, and before she knew it, she had reached the end of the balance beam.

A smile grew on her face, and she walked back to the beginning even quicker. She moved with confidence, suddenly seeing her tail in a new light.

"Nick! You were right: That was so much easier!" She jumped for joy, forgetting she was still on the balance beam, and felt herself falling. Nick ran forward, and Amara braced for impact, but her fall stopped unexpectedly.

In her panic, she had tried to reach for something. While there was nothing for her hands to grab, her tail had moved down and wrapped around the balance beam, pulling her back. She now stood at a slight angle, and it felt like she was hovering over the ground.

She looked back at her tail, then to Nick, her eyes wide. "This is SO COOL!"

Using her tail, she pulled herself upright again, then took another few laps across the beam.

"So, now you like it? Last week you couldn't stop complaining about how in the way it was." Nick smirked, watching her prance back and forth.

"I didn't realize I could do things with it!" Amara paused, realizing how silly she sounded. "That's why you brought me here, isn't it?"

Nick jumped up onto the beam, sitting down and inviting Amara to do the same. "Look, I know you're frustrated you don't have any flashy powers, but your transformation has been a physical one, not magical. The tail, the horns, the stronger musculature: They all serve to make you faster, more agile. You've never been much of an athlete, so I had a feeling you couldn't see the possibilities in front of you."

Amara leaned in, hugging Nick tight as she sat next to him. "So, what's next, teacher?"

With an excited smirk, Nick walked Amara through a series of exercises, each designed to test or condition something new. The more she exercised, the more she understood just how different her body was. She was stronger, faster, and definitely had more endurance. Nick set up a series of obstacle courses, and she cleared them with ease. She learned that her tail lowered her center of gravity and made an incredible counterweight; when she ran, she was able to stay closer to the ground, which kept her fast and maneuverable.

They also tried getting up off the floor using a set of uneven high bars. She started small, checking how many pull-ups she could do. From there, she practiced swinging back and forth, testing how she could manipulate her movement with her tail.

When her arms got tired, she switched to hanging from her legs. She tested her core strength for a while before trying something a little riskier; she wrapped her tail around the bar, asked Nick to get himself ready, and released her legs. The two of them were pleasantly surprised to see that her tail could easily hold her up on its own. She again practiced swinging back and forth, this time managing to switch bars by grabbing the lower one with her hands.

Fresh off of that discovery, Nick decided to switch gears and stacked a set of tumbling mats against a wall. He showed Amara the basics of throwing a punch, using the mats as a makeshift punching bag. He also walked her through the basics of how to navigate a close-quarters fight.

Amara found that her tail gave her an advantage here as well. Not only was she able to put the extra weight behind her punches, but she could also use it to more easily dodge and reposition.

Out of curiosity, Nick moved the mats off the wall and held them up by himself. He then asked Amara to practice hitting again, this time to try to gauge how hard she could hit. In addition to practicing her punching, she tried kicking, and striking with her tail. The kicking felt quite natural, no doubt because of her lower center of gravity, but attacking with her tail took a bit of adjustment. At first, she stood still and just practiced the movement, but eventually she tried adding weight and movement to her strikes.

To her surprise, and Nick's, the tail strikes seemed to hit the hardest.

When they took their first break, they theorized about how her tail might be used in a fight. They had a few ideas, but it was difficult to know which ones would actually hold up.

After clearing out Nick's snacks, he decided it was time for a mock fight. He set up more mats, on the floor this time, and invited Amara to join him. Together, they slowly worked through different methods of gaining advantage over an opponent, while also testing how those ideas could be adapted to suit her tail.

After nearly an hour of testing various strikes, parries, and grapples, the two of them slowed down. Amara had started to feel the wear and tear of their exercise; no doubt she would be sporting a fresh collection of bruises in the morning.

"So, what's next?" Amara asked. She had just gotten back into position after their last test, but she was also huffing from exertion.

"Honestly, I'm kinda running out of ideas," Nick said. "At this point, it really just boils down to practice."

"C'mon, you've got nothing? I'm having so much fun!" Amara jumped around, punching the air excitedly.

"It's pretty late, Amara. We should probably think about turning in for the night."

"Ugh, you're no fun." Amara sighed dramatically, then leaned back as her tail supported her weight. She stretched her arms over her head, breathing deep as she did. When she looked back at Nick, she caught him quickly averting his eyes from her body. She also noticed that his aura had started pulsing.

"Actually," Amara said, "I know one thing we haven't tried yet!" She moved closer to Nick, a smile on her face.

"Yeah? I guess I've got time for one more test." Nick moved back in front of her, bracing himself once more. "What are you thinking?"

Amara turned away, pretending to walk to her starting spot, but instead lashed out with her tail. It wrapped around Nick's ankle, pulling hard and sending him crashing to the floor.

"Fuck!" Nick managed to catch himself, and he shot Amara a look of surprise. "What the hell?"

She moved in, not letting him recover as she pushed him down. With her hands on his shoulders, she held tight as she sat on top of him, her crotch grinding against his.

"Nick, I can read auras, remember? You can't hide what you're thinking anymore." Amara bit her lip as she moved her hands off his shoulders, instead letting them trace up her own curves. "I guess that's my fault, though—I did wear a pretty revealing outfit."

Nick's eyes grew wide in recognition, then a smile appeared on his face. He let himself stare at her body again. "It was pretty rude of you. You're lucky I was able to stay on task this long." His hands gripped her legs, moving higher until he was massaging her ass.

"What can I say? I guess I'm a terrible influence!" Amara leaned forward, gently biting Nick's neck as her hands pushed under his shirt.

"Lucky me: I actually get to fuck the devil on my shoulder." Nick let out a deep moan as she kissed further down, her hips still grinding against him.

She sat up again, pulling her bra over her head before tossing it aside. She felt a small breeze as she exposed her chest, a thin layer of sweat causing her breasts to glisten. Nick moved his hands to them, pinching her nipples and causing her to moan out.

He took advantage of her distraction to flip her onto her back. Leaning in, he bit her ear softly before whispering to her: "Our second time in public already; I'm starting to think you have a kink."

Amara eagerly pulled his shirt off. "Please, I hardly think this counts; there's basically no risk of getting caught."

Reaching into his shorts, she found his bulging underwear and massaged it, feeling it harden in her grasp. His moans were intoxicating, and he returned the favor by sliding his hand into her shorts. His fingers pushed against her clit, and she twitched as he started rubbing. It had been so long since they last fucked, her body had nearly forgotten how good another person's touch could be.

Nick moved down, his cock pulling out of her grasp, and he pulled her shorts off. She lifted her hips, eager to expose herself, and soon she was spreading her legs wide.

He kissed her legs, then her thighs, inching closer to her pussy. She felt his breath first, then finally his tongue started teasing her entrance. She wrapped a hand in his hair and pushed him down, his tongue pushing into her pussy.

"Fuck!" Amara moved her other hand down, holding Nick tighter. "If you ever leave again, you have to find a replacement. I'm not giving this up anymore."

She felt Nick grin as he kept eating her out, and they continued like this for another minute before he stood up. He pulled his shorts down, his cock already hard as he stroked it.

Amara stood as well, wrapping her hand around his as she moved in to kiss him. She thought about sinking to her knees to return the favor, but another thought crossed her mind.

"This way, *teacher*. I've got an idea!" Grabbing Nick's hands, she pulled him over to the high bars they'd been practicing on earlier.

With his help, she jumped up to the lower bar, then flipped upside down. At first, her legs were holding her up, but then she curled her tail around the bar and released them. Her tail was dexterous enough that she could slowly lower herself down, and soon she had matched Nick's height exactly. It was slightly difficult to hold this position, given how much she'd exerted herself during all their previous sparring practice, but the promise of some kinky fun made it more tolerable.

She grabbed his hips, pulling him closer, then kissed the tip of his cock. Her tongue explored the head, then up and down the shaft, and finally she pulled him into her mouth.

His moans were brief, as they were stifled by her legs finding his head. As her mouth started pleasuring his cock, her legs pulled his tongue back onto her pussy. They both pleasured each other now, their tongues moving in tandem as their moans echoed through their bodies.

Nick's hands explored Amara's body again, pinching her nipples before moving up to her waist. He grabbed her ass, squeezing tight as he pulled her closer, his tongue pushing deeper into her sex. Moving even further, he felt the base of her tail, tracing it up slightly as he marveled at its strength.

"Fuck!" Amara pulled back, spit dripping onto her face. "That's really fucking hot, but I think my tail might be ticklish, so watch yourself! If I fall, I'm taking you with me." She sucked Nick's cock into her mouth again as his hands moved away from the sensitive spots.

"You think I can't hold you up?" Nick dug his nails into Amara's thighs, teasing her.

She returned the favor, but instead of nails, she leaned in and bit his thigh. "Don't you fucking dare! You'll leave here with blue balls, mister!"

Nick wrapped his arms around her waist, then carefully tickled the base of Amara's tail. She began laughing and her tail twitched, losing its grip on the bar. Her laughter turned into a playful shriek as she plummeted an inch, but Nick was able to hold her up.

He teased her pussy again, licking her clit before carefully setting her down on the soft mat underneath them. She glared at him, her eyes incredibly bright as she summoned all the mock anger she could manage.

"You asshole! I'll call your bluff!" Amara watched as Nick laid down next to her, their lips just inches apart. He traced a finger down her cheek before grabbing her chin, pushing her face to the side.

"I know you won't," he whispered into her ear, "because I can go much longer without sex than you can."

Amara groaned in frustration. "Ugh, you're the worst!" She grabbed his cock and stroked it, eager to feel him again. "If you're done pushing all my buttons, can we please get back to the fucking?"

Without saying anything, he pulled Amara's chin closer and kissed her. He climbed between her legs and positioned himself, then entered her. As he pushed into her pussy, inch by inch, she moaned loud enough to hear her own echo in the empty gym.

It took a minute to fully adjust to the angle, as her tail made lying on her back slightly awkward. Once she was comfortable, she ran her hands behind Nick's back and held him tight, urging him to fuck her harder.

His cock bottomed out, and soon he was fucking her in long, purposeful strides. He grabbed her waist, holding her down as he picked up his pace. She could feel his body growing tense, and had a feeling his orgasm was close. Moving her hands to his hair, she pulled him close and whispered to him. "Give me your fucking cum, Nick. I want to feel your cock explode inside me!"

She felt him shudder, and his aura glowed brighter. It was strong enough now that she was able to connect with it, and she could feel Nick's sexual energy feeding her. It flowed through her, eliminating every ache and dispelling her exhaustion.

With one last powerful thrust, Nick's orgasm took over. He pulled Amara close, his body tensing as his cock emptied inside of her. While she had already been feeding on his arousal, that connection suddenly exploded tenfold, catching her off guard. She'd never felt this much energy before, and had no idea what her body would do with it.

With this burst of strength, she used her tail to push up, flipping Nick onto his back. He continued cumming, his cock twitching as Amara now sat on top of him. His load pushed into her, and she moaned out in pleasure. She started bouncing up and down, fucking him hard to get herself off.

It didn't take long, and soon she was screaming with pleasure. Her voice echoed through the building as she came, and her orgasm shook her body to its core. Every vein in her body felt like it was burning with passion, and it was intoxicating. She could feel her eyes flaring, stronger than ever, and she planted her hands on Nick's chest as she rode out her orgasm.

She focused on her pleasure, feeling it course through her, when a familiar feeling appeared. Just like the last time she fucked Nick, she could feel her own orgasm expand itself, and she briefly felt like she could connect with the world around her as if it were her own body.

Warm lights appeared behind her, washing over her, accompanied by a burst of heat pulsing out from her. She couldn't see the light directly, but she saw her shadow briefly grow stronger as she continued fucking Nick. It took several minutes for her to calm down, but soon enough her breathing grew quiet.

"Fuck, Nick. That was incredible!" She smiled as she leaned back, running her hands over her horns and through her hair.

Nick had been staring at the ceiling the whole time, likely lost in his own orgasm, and finally pulled together the strength to prop himself up on his elbows. As he pulled his focus back to Amara, his eyes went wide.

"Holy shit, Amara," he said.

"Was it as good for you? I hope so—I fucking lost it!" She smirked as she leaned in briefly to kiss him.

"No, I mean yes, but that's not...you'd think I would be used to this by now."

"Used to this? Wait! Did something happen?!" Amara's voice rose in excitement.

Nick was unable to respond, but his eyes were moving from side to side, seemingly looking at something behind her. Before she could turn her head, she noticed two large shadows on the floor next to him. They were extending out from her back, and she was able to move them up and down.

Amara jumped to her feet, her eyes wide. "Nick. Nick! NICK!" She was bouncing up and down, unable to hold back her excitement.

Nick stood up next, fumbling with his shorts as he got dressed. "Oh, I see them. They're honestly bigger than I expected."

Amara followed his lead, quickly pulling on her shorts before grabbing her sports bra. She stared at it awkwardly, realizing she didn't know if she could still put it on.

"Nick, could you, um..." She held up her bra, flexing her wings.

He smirked as he nodded, and the two of them managed to get her properly dressed again, though it took some creative thinking.

"They've got to be functional, right? They're huge! I wonder where I can..." Amara's voice trailed off, and soon she was staring at the observation deck that towered over the gymnastics area.

Nick followed her gaze, his own eyes growing wide with concern. "Absolutely not! You need to take this slow!"

She scrunched her face, glaring at Nick. She was at a crossroads, and one path was simply too enticing to pass up.

She lunged forward, dodging Nick as he tried to grab her, then ran for the staircase in the corner. At the top, she pivoted to face the open gym again, and watched as Nick stared up at her. He was breathing heavily; it looked like he had tried to run after her but didn't have the energy for it.

"Think about this, Amara. If you're not careful this could go really bad!" Nick shouted. "What if you break something? We have no idea if sex cures broken bones!"

"C'mon, where's your sense of adventure?" Amara climbed the railing, pivoting to the other side before steadying herself. Her tail wrapped tight around the middle bar, and she stretched her wings as far as she could.

The bones that formed the structure of her wings were black, while most of the skin in between was an incredibly dark red. The skin seemed to be thick; light barely passed through them.

They extended much further than her arms, and when she flexed them, she could feel how strong they were. They looked quite similar to bat wings, only they came to a much sharper point where the new bones all converged. When she pulled them in close, she realized the points were actually solid bone that extended from the skin, and were identical to her horns, even just as sharp.

She opened them again, moving them up and down as she adjusted to how they felt. With a deep breath, she pushed them down hard, and almost threw herself backward over the railing.

A huge smile was frozen on Amara's face. She looked down at Nick, then surveyed the area in front of her. "Alright, Nick, what's the plan?"

Nick sighed in defeat. "If I can't talk you out of this, can you at least aim for the foam pit?" He pointed at the collection of colorful pointy cubes nearby, then moved toward it to get ready. "What if you just tried gliding first?"

Amara shuffled back and forth, then clapped her hands together. Her tail still holding tight, she continued testing her wings.

Okay, Amara, you can do this. You're just gonna learn how to fly real quick, no big deal. Keep your wings open: The bigger they are, the better.

She locked her eyes on the foam pit, slowly unwrapped her tail from the railing, and jumped.

Fear gripped her body as she surrendered control to her wings, and she fought the urge to pull her body into itself. She could sense the air around her, feel it as it pushed against her wings and kept her aloft. She looked down, watching the floor beneath her as she passed over it.

Dozens of new sensations flooded her brain; it was too much to process all at once. She felt like an advanced fighter jet, perfectly engineered to fly, but she had no idea how to translate the instruction manual.

She could tell that her wings were capable of making hundreds of small adjustments, but she couldn't tell them what to do. Her horns suddenly started buzzing, but the extra sensations only confused her further. With each second, she moved closer to the foam pit, and she had no idea how to direct herself downward.

"You're overshooting! Aim down!" Nick shouted, running behind the pit.

After another few seconds, Amara approached the edge of the pit. If she didn't stop now, she would be heading straight for the far wall, and she had no idea how much that would hurt. In a panic, she pulled her arms and her wings around herself, falling out of the air and crashing into the pit.

Nick circled around, leaning over the pit. "You alright?"

Amara's wings opened, scattering foam everywhere as she scrambled to get out. "Nick! Did you see? I FLEW!"

Helping her get out, Nick sighed in relief when she finally stood up. "I'm just glad you're safe. I really don't want to have to test if you have supernatural healing."

Amara ran past him, and soon she was standing in the middle of the spring floor. "Okay, I'm past the impulse to jump off high places. Let's figure out how these things work!"

Nick walked over, taking a moment to run his hands over her wings before the two of them started running more technical tests. She started small and tried to practice fine motor control. Nick would hold his hands out, and she would attempt to touch them with her wings as he moved his arms around.

She found that her wings could rotate quite a bit, and she practiced holding them at different angles to simulate different flight maneuvers. Though she felt a little silly, she also ran circles around the gym to practice using her wings while in motion.

Next, Nick suggested that she practice jumping. Again, they started small, testing how high she could jump without her wings, and slowly moved up from there. She continually put more and more force into her jumps, pairing them with stronger wing thrusts, and caught herself by surprise a few times. Though she never fell, she had to scramble to land after a few surprisingly high jumps.

Confident with her ability to get into the air, it was time to push into unknown territory. Standing over the foam pit, she took a deep breath, and launched herself as high as she could go, then tried to ascend a second time with another strong push.

Instead, she found herself flung downward, thankfully crashing into the foam. After she scrambled out, Nick pointed out that she hadn't retracted her wings to prepare for the second push, and they had caught too much air.

She kept trying, and it took a few dozen attempts to figure out the right movements, then commit them to muscle memory. Soon enough, she was able to reliably create a second round of lift with her wings. From here, it took another half hour to practice transitioning from ascending to gliding, but soon she felt confident enough for the main event.

Amara looked at Nick, then around the gym. "Alright, what's the plan?"

Nick joined her in looking around, examining the airspace. "Well, avoid anything hanging from the ceiling, and then...I dunno. We've moved way past my field of athletic expertise."

Nick moved away from the spring floor, clearing space for Amara. She identified her main threats—a series of hanging rings—then took a running start.

With a powerful thrust, she leapt into the air. She followed that up with another, and another, and continued to climb. She realized she was closer to the far wall than she wanted to be, and angled her wings back for another thrust.

Her forward momentum stopped, and she looked around as she hovered in midair. Looking down at Nick, she screamed with delight before changing direction. She started gliding around the gym, and she felt all the sensations from her first flight again, but this time she had the experience to navigate with them.

Her horns were resonating again, and she realized they were sensing the air currents around her. They stayed relatively quiet in certain corners, but in others she felt the familiar breeze of the building's air conditioning. Inside, this information was only so helpful, but the ability to sense subtle changes in air currents and temperatures would be invaluable if she ever flew outside.

After the first few circles, she cut through the center of the gym to change direction, and found she could use her tail as a rudder. Its extra weight allowed her to adjust her angle quickly and reliably, just like when she was running earlier.

To finish things off, she decided to test her speed. She climbed as high as possible, then dove down, pulling up at the last second. The feeling was incredible, the air beneath her wings blowing through her hair. The weight of this whole transformation felt like it had vanished in the last few hours, and in the air she felt more like herself than ever.

When she looked down, she caught Nick in the middle of a big yawn. She flew by the clock one more time, realized how late it was, and decided to call it a night.

Landing next to Nick, she ran in and gave him a huge hug. Her arms and wings wrapped around him, and she accidentally picked him up in her excitement.

"Nick! Thank you so much for tonight! You were absolutely right about everything; I can't believe how much better I feel."

He gasped as Amara put him down, and she realized she might have been squeezing a little too tight.

"Hey, I just hate seeing you bummed out. I'm glad you're feeling better!" He smirked as he put on his regular clothes again. "So, how's flying? I gotta admit, this is the first change I've been a little jealous of."

Amara gushed about what the experience had been like, and she shared every little detail about it while she got dressed. Her rambling stopped abruptly when she picked her shirt up.

"Did I just lose access to, like, half my wardrobe?" she asked, giving her shirt to Nick.

He helped squeeze her wings through it, which was thankfully still possible given its open shoulders. The sweater, however, proved to be more challenging. Raising her arms high, she wrapped her wings and her tail around her torso as tight as she could, then Nick pulled her sweater over her head.

He stepped back, then failed to hold back a laugh.

"Is it really that bad?" she asked.

"You look like you're wearing ten sweaters underneath some body armor." He moved closer, testing to see if she could reposition anything. "I honestly have no idea what to do about this. Maybe Tessa has some ideas?"

"I mean, we can ask, but she told me illusions aren't really her thing." Amara sighed, grabbing her bag before heading to the entrance.

Nick made one last lap around the gym, making sure everything had been reset, then turned off the lights. He locked the door as they left, and the two headed home.

As they left the building, Amara initially focused on how ridiculous she felt with her wings crammed into her sweater. If they ran into anyone, there would be no good explanation for this, but thankfully it was already well past midnight, and the campus was deathly quiet. A chill autumn wind picked up around them, scattering some leaves, and Amara breathed it in. She felt the breeze pass over her, when a curious thought appeared.

"Hey, take lookout for a sec?" she asked.

After Nick nodded in agreement, she pulled off her beanie and shook her hair loose, opening her horns to the world around her.

Ever since they'd appeared, she had never left the house with them uncovered. With everything she had felt flying, however, she was eager to feel what they could do.

As the breeze danced through her hair and over her horns, she discovered a connection with the wind she'd never felt before. She was acutely aware of its temperature, and she was able to sense slight changes in its speed and direction. These sensations, while they originated in her horns, were also traveling through her body, and she found herself instinctually making small adjustments with her tail and her wings.

When she looked away from the sky, she caught Nick smirking at her.

"Enjoying the weather?" he asked.

"It's so much more than that. I can feel the air, the wind...the sky is calling to me. Like I belong there."

"That's a beautiful sentiment, Amara, but think about the risks. Tessa warned us what could happen if the wrong people discovered you."

Nick pointed at some shapes turning a corner in front of them, and Amara quickly put her beanie back on. Once she'd fixed her hair, she pushed her hands into her pockets and sighed dramatically.

"Yeah, I know. I'll figure something out one day." She quietly daydreamed about soaring through the skies as they walked.

When they finally reached Amara's apartment, one last thought crossed her mind.

"Oh, by the way, what kind of porn do you like?" she asked, hugging him goodbye.

"Hmm, good question. I'm not too picky, but I think I tend to watch amateur stuff the most. It just feels a bit more real, more passionate. Why do you ask?"

"Oh, no reason. Just curious!" Amara laughed at his answer, and the two waved goodbye for the night.

7
OUT OF BODY

Amara kicked off her covers as she yawned, stretching her arms over her head. Before she could finish, a loud thud caught her attention, and she groaned with frustration. Looking at her nightstand, she saw that her left wing now sat where her phone had previously been charging.

She pocketed her phone before moving to the middle of the room, where she stretched open her wings. When she flexed them, her wings had just enough space to open, so long as she didn't face the short wall, and she did her best to avoid breaking anything else.

Thankfully, she'd figured out how to dress herself, but only if the clothing accommodated her wings. Racerback tanks were the most comfortable, and she'd already ordered a new set online.

Pushing out into the hallway, she carefully made her way to the living room. The walls were covered with fresh scratches, and a stack of partially broken frames sat on the floor. She walked at an angle, eyes darting between the walls and the ceiling, and she counted at least four new gouges before she cleared the hall.

"So long, security deposit..." Amara mumbled.

Her living room was fairly open, and it combined with the kitchen to make the largest room in the house. There was a small breakfast counter between the two spaces, technically, but Amara didn't feel like it counted. She made her morning coffee as she checked her messages.

Her wings had appeared late Saturday night, and Nick had stayed with her Sunday in hopes of finding a way to hide them. After hours of research, including a quick fuck, they'd decided it was no longer feasible for Amara to go to class.

Putting her coffee on the counter, she set up her laptop and emailed all her professors for the week, explaining that she was taking time off due to sickness. As replies slowly filtered in, she gave Nick a list of teachers that he needed to visit to get her homework. He was planning to swing by later this afternoon, and Tessa had offered to bring her lunch.

With nothing to do, Amara briefly considered taking a shower, but the memory of yesterday's attempt still haunted her. Hopefully the new shower curtain would be here soon.

Maybe I could sneak into a locker room? Who am I kidding—I can't sneak anywhere with these.

Amara hopped onto her couch and turned the TV on, wondering what she could do with her sudden vacation.

The next few hours passed slowly. At first the downtime had been nice, but before long she was itching to do something. She frequently found herself staring out the window, up at the sky, wondering what flying out there would feel like.

When Tessa showed up with bags of fast food, Amara was ecstatic for the distraction. She opened the door, hiding behind it to stay out of sight.

"Alright, let's see these bad boys! I'm used to people lying about their size, so don't let me down." Tessa smirked as she kicked the door closed, and her eyes went wide when she saw Amara. "Fucking hell, Amara, you weren't kidding."

'Right? Hang on, let me open them up!" Amara moved to the center of the living room, then extended her wings out to let Tessa inspect them.

"And you can actually fly? What's a girl gotta do to go for a ride?" Tessa walked slowly around her.

"I'll do it for free if you can guarantee no one sees us, but until then I get to be a hermit."

"I think you're worth a lot more than free, but you do you." Tessa laughed as she finished her circle. Her eyes darted from Amara's wings, to her tail, to her horns, and Amara noticed another swell in her friend's aura, more significant than the last time.

The two sat down, eagerly digging into their food as Amara shared all the details from her adventure in the gymnastics building. She was thrilled that the tension had vanished between them, and their lunch felt just as natural as always.

Tessa shared updates about her magical investigation. She had more theories she wanted to test, and the two agreed that Amara would make a great bodyguard should anything strange happen. Tessa had started worrying that the changes to the leylines might not be natural, which could mean other mages might be involved.

They agreed to meet up again Saturday, if Amara's physiology allowed it, then Tessa had to leave for classes. Hugging goodbye, Amara wrapped Tessa up in her wings and her tail, and she caught another pulse in Tessa's aura, which made her smirk.

The day dragged on, and Amara grew more restless with each passing hour. When Nick arrived with her homework, he caught her in the middle of trying different YouTube exercise routines. They spent a good chunk of the afternoon together, doing homework and making food, but he sadly had other plans for the evening.

The rest of the week continued in a similar fashion. Amara spent time trying to stay caught up with her classes, and many of her professors were kind enough to offer brief summaries of the week's syllabus. She supplemented her schoolwork with more demon research, but most of what she found was hypothetical.

Amara also made sure to keep in constant contact with Vee and Chloé. Unlike Nick and Tessa, it wasn't safe to let them come visit, and she missed them more with each passing day. She flooded them both with texts, eager to hear what they were doing, trying to nourish her fading connection to a normal, human lifestyle. It sounded like Vee was spending more time with Nick, which made Amara giggle excitedly, but Chloé still hadn't mustered up the strength to ask her mystery crush out. It was nice to stay in contact, but with each passing day, Amara grew more worried. Was this her life now? Was her transformation slowly going to push away everything she'd loved about being human?

Before she knew it, Friday evening had come, and she was no closer to finding a way to hide her wings. Nick had just arrived with food, and she opened the door to let him in.

"Niiiick, I'm so bored!" Amara groaned.

"Oh, hi, Nick! It's so good to see you! How was your day?" Nick walked inside, closing the door behind him as he mocked Amara. "It was great! I'm so glad you asked."

"Yeah? Should I ask about the weather too?"

"Hey, maybe I just want to feel appreciated sometimes." He set down his backpack before joining Amara at the counter.

"Appreciated? Is the constant sex not enough anymore? I knew it! You only like me for my personality!"

They stared at each other for a moment before breaking out into laughter. They started eating dinner, and Nick handed over her homework while catching her up on his day.

Unfortunately, Nick's research into her wings had also hit a dead end. The few theories he had were starting to pull from fiction, and Amara stopped caring at that point.

"I finally find the silver lining to this transformation, and immediately have to hide myself away. This sucks." Amara groaned as she pushed her empty plates away.

"Hey, we'll figure it out. Just the other day you were complaining about not being able to fly, but look at you now!"

"You're probably right. Doesn't make the waiting easier, though."

"Well, speaking of change, I've got something I kinda wanted to talk to you about?" Nick moved to the couch and gestured for Amara to join him.

"Should I be nervous?"

"Um, nothing has happened yet; I'm just trying to stay on top of things."

Amara got up and joined him, taking care not to hit him with her wings. "Alright, I'm a big girl, lay it on me."

Nick leaned forward, and Amara saw that he was more nervous than she'd initially realized. "So...I asked Vee out."

"AAH! Nick! Fucking finally!" She threw herself at Nick, squeezing him tight. "I thought you'd never do it! Tell me everything!"

"We've just been talking a lot more frequently, and since you've been locked up this week, we ended up spending more time together."

"So what's the plan? Fancy dinner? Crime spree?"

"Nothing crazy; we'll probably just get some cheap food and hang out. I guess she's got a lot on her plate right now, so we're gonna wait a week or two."

Nick cleared his throat, then kept talking. "But there's a lot I haven't talked about with her. If we start dating, I don't know what that means for you and me."

Amara grew quiet, the reality of the situation setting in. "I hadn't thought of that."

"Best-case scenario, she's cool with us continuing to hook up. However, if she asks this to stop, I'm gonna have a hard time explaining that you need sex the way you need sleep."

Amara pulled back from Nick, his words spinning in her head. She curled her tail around herself, pausing before speaking. "I need time to think about this. No rush, right?"

They looked at each other, each recognizing the uncertainty in the air.

"You know I'm always here for you, right?" Nick asked. "We're not dating, but I realize I kinda did this without asking."

"No, you're right. We're not dating, and you deserve an actual partner."

Despite their agreement, the tension refused to dissipate. After another few moments of silence, Amara stood up, excusing herself to the bathroom.

Did you really think nothing would ever change? That he wouldn't want something more than a fuck buddy?

She closed the bathroom door behind her, then turned on the faucet to fill the silence.

Vee's cool! Maybe she'll let you keep hooking up! If not, Tessa is poly, and clearly into you, so you have options; this isn't the end of the world.

Cold water splashed her face, but it did nothing to dislodge her thoughts. Despite her best efforts, it was tough to stay positive.

As she dried her face, a strange feeling swept across her body. It felt similar to the pulses of heat she felt the last time she and Nick fucked, but smaller, and more focused. Instead of feeling more connected with space around her, however, that connection turned inward.

She shivered, then opened the door to share this feeling with Nick. She tried to close the door behind her, but she couldn't feel her tail. She panicked, and a quick examination revealed that her wings and horns had also vanished.

"Uh, Nick? I think something happened!" She walked into the living room to rejoin him. As she did, she swore her clothes weren't fitting right anymore.

When he looked up, his eyes grew wide with shock. "Fuck!" He flinched in surprise, and his phone clattered to the floor. "Amara? Is that you?"

"Ha ha, very funny. Everything's gone! Is that good or bad?" She sat down next to him.

"I guess that's also true."

"Also?" Amara groaned, bracing herself for another surprise. "Great, what else? Is my skin red? Am I on fire?"

Nick opened and closed his mouth a few times, the words taking a minute to catch up. "No, you...you're Vee?"

"Shut the fuck up! I am not!" As she spoke, she realized that her voice was higher than usual.

Nick nodded slowly, unable to speak.

Amara stood up and ran to the bathroom, her pants almost falling off her hips as she moved. Sure enough, when Amara looked in the mirror, she saw shoulder-length blonde hair, piercing blue eyes, and an athletic figure several inches taller than normal. "Why am I Vee?!"

She returned to the living room, frantically pacing around her couch. "The point of hiding my demon bits was to get my life back! I can't go out like this!" Amara froze, strange blonde hair bouncing in front of her face. She collapsed next to Nick as she groaned. "Does this mean I can shapeshift now? It has to, right?"

Nick pulled her close, but his body felt stiff and awkward. Either things felt different in this new body, or Nick was trying to hide his own conflicting feelings. "Alright, this is certainly strange, but I think you're right. This is definitely shapeshifting. Now we just need to figure out how it works."

"Okay, well, what's worked in the past?" She started thinking back to when aspects had previously appeared. "I tend to gain more control when we, well..."

They looked at each other, both finishing the sentence in their minds. At the same time, they both pushed away from each other and moved to opposite ends of the couch.

"Absolutely not, nope, not gonna happen. Not while I'm literally Vee."

"I felt weird even thinking about it."

"What other options do we have then?" Amara asked.

"I...I don't know. It's interesting; normally your abilities show up right after we hook up, but we haven't done anything since yesterday. Does this mean your control over them is increasing?"

"Do I look like I'm in control?"

"Okay, fair point." Nick paused, running ideas around in his head. "We should just start trying shit. Try to turn back!"

Amara nodded in agreement, then stood up in the middle of the living room. She closed her eyes, focusing on the feeling from the bathroom. She thought about that sense of control, of connecting with both herself and the space around her, and tried to look inside.

She stood perfectly still for a minute before opening her eyes. "Anything?" she asked hopefully.

Nick shook his head.

She wasn't surprised; the connection she was looking for had never materialized. The two of them kept talking, and wound up spending the rest of the evening trying to re-activate her shapeshifting abilities.

They explored meditation, yoga, exercise, and nothing worked. Whatever feeling Amara had connected with refused to resurface, and eventually they ran out of time to experiment. Nick needed to get home, and was unavailable to run experiments with her tomorrow.

Amara went to bed in a sour mood. She had successfully traded one problem for another, and was no closer to getting her life back.

Waking up Saturday morning was disorienting. Amara stumbled to the bathroom, half-asleep, her new body completely out of mind. When she finally looked in the mirror in the middle of washing her face, she screamed in surprise.

The rest of the day proved to be one frustrating inconvenience after another. Vee's body was taller, but slightly less curvy, so Amara struggled to find clothes that fit comfortably. She also accumulated a series of bruises throughout the day as she kept running into drawers and counters.

While it was slightly relieving not to worry about her wings destroying her place, it was overshadowed by how much she missed her demonic traits. She'd gotten used to closing doors and drawers with her tail, and after her night at the gymnasium, even walking without it felt wrong.

If nothing else, she felt confident enough to do more investigating with Tessa. They had agreed to only go out during the night, though initially that had been because of her wings. Now, as long as Amara disguised herself walking around campus, it would be easy to stay out of the way in whatever basement Tessa wanted to explore next.

She pulled out her phone, desperate to get out of the house.

Amara: Up for some snooping tonight?

Tessa: got ur wings under control?

Amara: More or less. What's next on your to do list?

Tessa: tbh I think the science building again, wanna check a few things

Tessa: that cool?

After agreeing on a time, which was much later than Amara would have preferred, she spent a few hours trying to find a good outfit. She settled on a pair of loose cargo pants, a baggy hoodie full of school spirit, and another one of her beanies to hide her hair.

Hopefully, the disheveled wardrobe would help disguise her current body. As far as she could remember, Vee never wore anything this casual, so leaving the house didn't feel too scary.

She spent the rest of her day trying out various exercise programs again. Interestingly, it felt like she was just as athletic now as she was in her normal body, apart from the missing tail. Either her newfound strength was inherent to her, regardless of form, or Vee's body was ridiculously agile.

After a hearty dinner, Amara gathered her things and left the house for the first time in over a week. The open air felt incredible, and she stared longingly up at the sky as she walked.

She looked around, didn't see anyone, and felt brave enough to pull her beanie off. Without her horns, she noticed that she couldn't read the wind as easily as she had the week before. The lack of connection felt strangely isolating, especially given how little she'd bothered to think about her horns over the last few weeks. She'd gotten used to the idea that they were simply a cute decoration, and discovering they had uses had been a pleasant surprise.

Once she heard voices again, she pushed her hair back into her beanie and adjusted her posture. There weren't too many students out this late in the evening, and Amara had a feeling that most of them were already at parties for the night.

The sun had set hours ago, and the campus was now illuminated by a series of tall lamps scattered across the sidewalks. She took her time getting to Tessa, partially because she was trying to avoid other students, but also because she was thrilled to be outside again. She took every scenic route she could, wandering over fields and around trees, eager to explore the open world.

As she finally drew close, she saw Tessa leaning against a tree near the Science Building. She had a backpack slung across one shoulder, and a pair of bulky headphones hanging around her neck. She was idly tossing a switchblade around, and a look of surprise appeared as she realized who was approaching.

"Vee? Damn girl, I almost didn't recognize you! Going to a costume party or something?" she asked.

"Oh, this? I just felt like trying something new," Amara smirked. It felt strangely validating to see that her shapeshifting was this effective. She watched as Tessa pulled out her phone, typing quickly for a moment. Her own phone vibrated a second later, and she fought the urge to laugh as she checked her messages.

Tessa: Be careful, Vee is here

"So, what are you doing here? You're normally the party girl. Shouldn't you be at a frat house or something?" Amara said. She sent out a quick reply through her phone.

Amara: I'm super close!

"I was just waiting for a partner. I wanted to do stuff with Amara, but since she's been sick, I just moved my plans around," Tessa mumbled unconvincingly.

Wow, Tessa is not good at lying.

"Isn't that such a bummer? She's really seemed off her game recently. I hope everything is okay. Hey! Let's send her a pic!" Amara pulled her phone out, then moved behind Tessa and rested her head on her shoulder. While definitely on edge, Tessa went along with it, and the two smiled for a selfie.

"Though, if I'm being honest," Amara leaned in, lowering her voice, "hasn't Amara seemed a bit different? I swear she's like, way hotter now, and I can't figure out why."

Tessa coughed in surprise, obviously trying to hide how nervous she was. "I-I haven't noticed anything? Sometimes college just changes people, y'know?"

As they talked, Amara quickly drew something on the selfie they just took, then sent it to Tessa. When it arrived, small red horns had been drawn over Vee's head, and her eyes had been colored amber. Tessa looked at her phone, paused for a moment, then her eyes went wide with realization.

"You're such an asshole!" she yelled, hitting Amara. "When the fuck did this happen? Holy shit, you're like a perfect copy."

"Yesterday! Cards on the table, I can't really control it yet. I'm kinda stuck like this."

"But why Vee?"

"Fuck if I know," Amara shrugged. "But hey, at least I'm not you!"

Tessa glared at her. "You know, I think I liked you more before you turned into a demon. Now you're all confident and assertive and shit."

They headed toward the Science Building, and Amara saw Tessa's tattoos light up slightly underneath her hat. With a flick of her wrist, the door leading inside clicked open, and the two girls entered.

"Well, does it feel good knowing that you can shapeshift?" Tessa asked.

"Absolutely! I miss my demon bits like crazy, but I think I'll figure it out soon enough."

Most of the outer walls of the Science Building were made of glass, so the two of them had plenty of light to navigate with. After the first few turns, however, they approached the door to the basement, and were forced to pull out their phones. Their flashlights turned on just as the door closed, enveloping them in darkness.

"You need a phone for light? No spells for that?" Amara asked.

"That's not really how witchcraft works," Tessa said.

"Well, how does it work? I've been trying not to bombard you with questions, but I'm insanely curious."

Tessa pushed open the door at the bottom of the stairs, and they started walking through the hall toward the hidden room.

"How to keep this simple? So, magic can't create anything; it's mostly about channeling energy from other places."

Amara moved closer, eager to learn more.

"Our world has very little magic, and trying to draw from here would be tough. Instead, we use magic runes to connect to other, inherently magical planes, and borrow that energy for ourselves. Humans are innately non-magical, so this is our only option."

As they approached the tangled mess of ancient plumbing, they slowed their pace. While they made quicker progress than Amara had last time, it was still slow going.

"Okay, so, you're not creating anything, you're just moving it around. And the tattoos build a bridge to bring it over?"

"That's not the worst comparison. Most importantly, the runes also set the destination. If we put those runes on a structure, like what Brandon attempted, we're telling the magic to always go there. But, if we tattoo the symbols on ourselves, we can summon the magic to us, wherever we are."

Amara stepped over the last few pipes, then huffed in satisfaction. When she looked back, she saw Tessa still a minute behind her.

"So what are your tattoos? Where do they draw their magic from?"

"These are low-level telekinesis runes. Pretty much all witches have these. They connect with my own strength and transform it into psychic energy."

Tessa finally crawled out from the piping, then sighed in relief before stretching her arms out. "I mean, *technically* they take my energy and briefly phase it through—Look, it's complicated, alright? I'm paraphrasing a lot of this stuff."

Amara led the way into the hidden room, flicking on the light. It was strange being back here, staring at the familiar brickwork and runes. In many ways, it felt like this was where everything had pivoted; her transformation had suddenly stopped being entirely about her, and she was now aware that being a demon could attract unwanted attention from bad faith actors.

The table against the back wall was still there, cracked in half from Brandon's fall. All other signs of his presence had vanished, however. The scattered piles of books and papers were gone, leaving only Amara's bitter memories of her would-be owner. It also looked like many of the runes had been scratched off—at least partially.

"Hey," Tessa spoke up, "you gonna be alright? Being back here?"

Amara shook her head. "Y-yeah, I'm fine. What's the plan?"

Tessa moved forward, scuffing a few more of the runes as she walked. "I had a thought a while back, after freeing you. This room is a lot like the others, right? Out of the way, in an old basement, likely from the original university. Well, the other rooms had large magic circles, and I think there might be one here too."

"Like, a secret one? I spent a lot of time here, bored out of my mind, and I never saw anything like that."

"The first one I showed you was hidden behind an illusion, remember? Maybe there's another false wall, or they covered the circle up somehow."

Tessa explained all the different ways a magic circle might be hidden, and Amara tried to understand. In the end, they decided it would be best to split up their talents; Tessa would use magic to look around, and Amara would look for more mundane secrets.

It was a slow process, as neither girl had any solid lead on what they were looking for. Amara had never been the most perceptive person, but she did her best to check various nooks and crannies for anything abnormal. As she looked, she would sporadically ask more questions about magic, both out of curiosity and to help with the search.

Since the two of them were looking for an illusory wall, she focused on that topic. Tessa explained that, contrary to popular belief, illusions could easily take a solid form. They could look and feel like anything, but often had their own limits. Most illusions had trouble standing up to physical force, for example, but others could be limited by the creativity of the witch making them.

This led to Amara ramming her shoulder into the walls of the room, which made her feel incredibly silly.

After an hour of inspecting every surface, corner, and crevice, Tessa felt comfortable saying that there weren't any illusions present. The two took a break, collapsing against the broken table to think things over.

"This is bullshit! Stupid university founders and their stupid secret magic stupid circles," Tessa groaned as she pulled out her phone, then remembered this basement didn't have any service.

"How long did it take you to find the other circle?" Amara asked.

"I discovered the illusion pretty quickly, once I had gotten close enough. The trick was learning how to turn it off and on."

Amara moved closer, putting her arm around Tessa and pulling her in. "Well, maybe there just isn't a circle here. Or maybe it's hidden another way!"

"Hiding something like this without an illusion would be tricky, to say the least." Tessa looked up at Amara, then pulled away from the embrace. "Also, not gonna lie, little weird doing all this while you look like Vee."

Amara wanted to clarify if she meant the investigating or the cuddling, but decided against it. She stood up again, wandering the space while avoiding the center of Brandon's circle.

"Could it be hidden without magic? Like, maybe it's covered in dirt, or a carpet, or under the bricks?"

"I mean, I guess so? But covering up the runes would make it hard to summon anything." Tessa went quiet, her eyebrows furrowed, and soon her eyes went wide. "Unless they're not trying to!"

Tessa jumped up, excitement in her eyes, and scanned the floor as she talked.

"Building a bridge is only necessary to bring something over. But what if they wanted to build a wall?"

"Wouldn't that mean they wanted to keep something out?" Amara asked. She took a few steps back, giving Tessa space as she circled the room.

"It might! I really don't know; the circles I've found are incredibly complex." Tessa finally paused, then moved to her knees in the center of the circle. "Alright, tell me if you see anything—I've got an idea."

Amara watched as her friend closed her eyes, and soon after her tattoos lit up again. She kept her eyes glued on the floor, looking for any sign of activity.

Five seconds passed.

Ten seconds.

Thirty.

She was about to speak up, to tell Tessa to stop, when something finally happened. Faint lines started appearing on the floor, slowly expanding and growing brighter with each second.

After another minute, Amara now saw an entire circle of magical runes. It bore a considerable resemblance to the one under Lysander Hall, and she cleared her throat to get Tessa's attention.

"Whatever you're doing, it worked: there's a whole circle here!"

Tessa opened her eyes, and Amara noticed the strain on her friend's face.

"Quick, grab a picture, I can't hold this for long." Tessa spoke quickly, her breathing labored as she concentrated on maintaining the magic.

Moving as fast as she could, Amara pulled out her phone and took a handful of pictures, all at different angles. "We're good! You can drop it!"

Tessa gasped, her posture collapsing as she released the magic. Her tattoos dulled, and it only took a few seconds for the entire circle to vanish. She kicked her feet out in front of her, then fell back on the floor, her chest heaving as she caught her breath.

Amara moved closer, kneeling as she put her phone down. "Need anything?"

"N-no. I...fuck. Just gimme a sec," Tessa gasped.

"Guess I'm surprised. I really thought you'd last longer our first time."

A middle finger shot up, and Amara's laughter filled the room.

It took another few minutes for Tessa to collect herself. When the color had finally returned to her face, she sat back up. "Alright, let's take a look!"

Amara grabbed her phone and moved to sit next to her friend. "I took a bunch, so hopefully we have everyth—What the fuck?" She stared at the first picture and saw nothing but dull concrete. "There's nothing here!" It only took a few moments to confirm that the rest of the photos were empty as well.

Tessa groaned before cursing under her breath, "They must have found a way to hide the symbols somehow? Maybe cameras count as scrying? There's magic that can prevent scrying." Her eyebrows furrowed, and she bit her lip ring while she thought.

"Regardless of how it works, don't you need to see the symbols to try to decipher them? What are we supposed to do now?" Amara said.

"I think we only have one option, sadly." Tessa pulled her backpack over. After a few seconds of silent rummaging, she pulled out a notebook and a pencil. "Ever take art class?"

"That's going to take forever! You could barely manage a minute or two! How am I supposed to draw the whole circle that fast?"

Tessa pushed the notebook to Amara. "I needed time to piece together how to reveal everything, but that only needs to happen the first time. Look, I won't bore you with the details. I should be able to do it faster, that's all I'm saying. We'll sketch a little, take a break, then rinse and repeat."

Grabbing the pencil and the notebook, Amara gave Tessa a concerned look. "Fine, but I'm not letting you wear yourself out. If I think you're stretching yourself too thin, I'm calling it quits."

"Oh, but Amara, I love stretching myself out!" She sat back in the middle of the circle and cracked her knuckles. "Now, I'm ready to go all night if you are. Think you can keep up?"

Amara rolled her eyes, but took her place next to Tessa anyway. "As long as you promise to be gentle—I'm still new at this." She elbowed Tessa as she readied herself.

The girls looked at each other, then broke out in laughter. With a mutual nod, Tessa closed her eyes and started focusing. True to her word, the symbols appeared much quicker than last time, and Amara did her best to start copying them over.

Sulfur poisoned the wind, screams following soon after. A bloodstained ritual, helmed by a maniacal succubus. She watched again as the ritual completed, her body weak from the losing battle. Blood stained her face, and claws punctured her throat.

Amber eyes, piercing through the darkness.

—

She shot forward, sitting up in a panic as the nightmare finally ended. Labored gasps filled her bedroom and sweat poured down her face. With a guttural shout, she slammed a fist into the wall next to her.

"Fuck!"

A small indent remained, a specter of where her impact had landed. It wasn't alone.

Once her breathing had calmed down, she grabbed the glass on her nightstand and swallowed another few caffeine pills. The clock read 4:58. She had finally broken 5 AM; yet another twisted accomplishment she could attribute to her nightmares.

Making her way to the bathroom, she summoned a ball of light to give herself vision. It hovered over her fingers, flickering slightly as she started the shower.

Inside, as the freezing water cascaded down her body, she thought about everything she needed to do. She still hadn't found any more leads on the succubus, and she was close to finishing her initial survey of the main campus. Perhaps it was time to start placing tracking runes? If she tagged the exits and entrances of the major buildings, she might be able to chart its movements.

She sighed.

I can't keep going like this. Maybe...maybe a small break, just this once.

The thought filled her with a brief moment of stolen joy, and she eagerly finished her shower so she could get dressed. She pulled out her running clothes, pocketed her phone, and left the house.

Starting down the familiar route, she forced herself to leave her worries behind. Breathing in the morning air, she found a familiar pace and kept running. Off in the distance, she saw the steeple of a church located a few blocks away from campus. She chuckled to herself, imagining all the families and students that attended service there, looking for purpose, unaware an angel was living just minutes away. She'd never visited the church herself, it felt redundant given everything she knew. Besides, the Church that had trained her bore little resemblance to any organized religious structure.

She shook her head. This wasn't the time to think about that. Skirting around the cafeteria, she soon hit the quad and made for the tall stairs at the south end.

She noticed that she had more energy, and her steps felt lighter than usual. That wasn't surprising, given how much she'd been practicing her magic. Channeling divine energy wasn't easy, and the more she practiced, the more her body adapted to the stress of the magic. She reached the top of the stairs quicker than usual and looked back in surprise before continuing.

Soon enough, she found a familiar tree and started climbing its branches. This, too, was much easier, and she reached the top in mere moments.

The sun hadn't hit the campus yet, which was perfect. She settled in, took a deep breath, then exhaled.

The view hadn't changed, though some of the branches had started crowding her window. She let them be, her eyes wandering the buildings surrounding the quad. It felt like it had been ages since she'd come here last, yet the view was always the same. Lysander Hall lorded over the quad, its noble architecture setting it apart from the other buildings. She'd always thought it felt like a crown sitting atop the center of campus.

As she waited for sunrise, in no rush to return home, she summoned a small ball of light once again. It bounced slowly between her hands, and she practiced hovering it around the tree, enjoying the way its radiance illuminated the leaves.

As much as she'd previously tried to ignore her magic, she couldn't deny it had some perks.

A sudden noise pulled her back to reality—a nearby door opening. She snuffed out her light immediately, then turned to see someone leaving the building next to her.

Who would be in the Science Building at this hour?

She held her breath, watching as the figure looked up into her tree. Her light had definitely caught their attention, and as they turned toward her, she got a good look at their face.

The girl staring up into the tree had medium-length blonde hair and bright blue eyes. She was somewhat taller than average, seemed to be in decent shape, and was yawning lazily. Her clothes were quite baggy, and they seemed out of place only because Vee knew how that person usually dressed.

That...that's not possible. What the fuck is going on?

Vee was staring at an exact copy of herself.

The succubus!

A thousand thoughts flooded Vee's head. Fear gripped her, and she had no idea how to react. She couldn't risk confrontation, not like this. Even if she managed to summon a sword, there was no way she would win a straight fight with a demon.

She kept watching, and soon the demon shrugged. It continued walking away from the Science Building before jogging down the tall staircase.

Why here? Why now?

There had to be a reason for this. A fight was out of the question, but this might be a good time to figure out the demon's plans.

Once Vee knew she was alone, she dropped out of the tree. Approaching the glass doors nearby, she opened them with a quick prayer and moved in. The building was quiet, and she had no idea what she was looking for.

"What twisted game are you playing, Hellspawn?" she muttered.

Checking her phone, she realized she only had an hour or two before classes started. Though it wasn't the best idea, she tried to cast the tracking spell from memory.

Her eyes closed, quiet melodies escaping her lips. Her magic stirred, and she pulled from her own reserves rather than the Enochian Texts. Though incredibly taxing, she was able to hold the spell long enough to find a solid lead. It seemed as if the demon had been in the basement.

Vee dropped the tracking spell, opened the door to the basement, and pushed on. She summoned her light once more, illuminating the darkness as she checked every nook and cranny. Content that the stairs were clear, she moved on to the basement proper, and was pleased to see she wouldn't need much time. She only saw a small number of old classrooms, and the thick buildup of dust revealed that the demon had been elsewhere.

The last place to check was a strange maze of ancient plumbing. Vee groaned when she saw it, but took solace in the assumption that this was the last place to check.

Although it took longer than she had wanted, and she was now sporting some new bruises, she eventually found the other side. Following the darkened walls, she eventually found a small room tucked out of sight. It wasn't hidden, necessarily, but the placement certainly kept it out of the way.

Vee's eyes widened when she stepped inside. The floor and ceiling were covered in strange runes, clearly drawn in blood, and a table across the room lay in pieces on the floor. She kneeled down, inspecting the runes closely, and cursed the fact that she'd never bothered to learn more about witchcraft.

These almost look like summoning runes, though they've definitely been damaged.

Things still didn't add up, but Vee felt like she'd found another piece of the puzzle. Pulling out her phone, she snapped pictures of all the different runes.

After another quick search of the area, she decided there was nothing else to be found. She made her way back upstairs, stepping into the morning light as she left the building.

This has to be how the succubus arrived. Maybe someone summoned her, and she broke free? A fight would explain the broken table.

Vee jogged down the long staircase, an eerie sense of déjà vu washing over her. She had just watched her doppelganger do this same thing, and it felt wrong to walk in that thing's footsteps.

If another demon were to show up, they would either have to fight for control over the campus, or share the spoils, and no demon would want that. So, she returns to the circle, makes sure it can't be used again, and cements her hold here.

As she turned a corner outside the cafeteria, the smell of alcohol washed over her, followed by a loud crunch under her shoes. She looked down and saw a broken bottle, its contents spilled all over the sidewalk.

Rolling her eyes, glad she had missed whatever drunkard had been here last night, Vee sidestepped the glass shards and kept walking.

But why was the demon disguised as me? Is it just a disguise while she wanders campus? She clearly didn't know I was there with her...

As Vee arrived home, she greeted her empty apartment with a familiar groan. Despite seeing the actual demon, and finding how it arrived, she was still no closer to her goal. All she'd managed to do was lose yet another morning of peace.

It took Amara and Tessa quite a while to copy the whole circle. Tessa needed frequent breaks, each one longer than the last, but she was determined to get everything done in one night. By the time they finished, it was already close to five in the morning.

Eager to get some sleep, the girls packed everything up and started the trek home. Backtracking through the piping, they soon found themselves at the main entrance, but had to say their goodbyes there. They lived in opposite directions, and it was easier for Tessa to use a different exit. After a long hug, the two parted ways.

Walking outside, Amara immediately noticed the sunlight reflecting into a nearby tree. The sun hadn't quite risen over the buildings yet, but she assumed it was hitting some strange angles to be visible here already. She yawned slowly, waiting for the door behind her to close, then resumed her journey.

The walk home was quiet, and pretty much the entire campus was hers. She didn't bother putting her beanie on, as the wind in her hair felt amazing.

As the sunlight slowly filled the quad, Amara let herself wander around, tracing lines in the morning dew. She even considered climbing some of the trees, but realized that the earliest risers would likely be rousing soon. She opted to head straight home, deciding it would be best to get what little sleep she could at this hour.

Soon enough, she put the quad behind her and started the last leg of her trip. Walking down the long side of the cafeteria, she rounded a corner and accidentally bumped into someone.

"Oh! Sorry!" she mumbled, moving to avoid the stranger.

He turned around quickly, and Amara froze when she realized who she'd run into.

"Well, well, lookit what the cat dragged in," Derek said. His words slurred together, their unnatural cadence betraying why he was still awake at this hour. "What'r'you doing out? Coming from...from a party?"

Amara took a step back, her body tense. Her heart was racing, desperate to get away, but she couldn't muster the strength to turn and run. "N-nothing like that. I just need to get home, Derek."

Derek matched her steps with his own, then quickly overtook her. He pushed her back against the brick wall, one arm propped over her shoulder. "What's this...this fuckin' outfit? You're a hot little bitch, aren't you? But you know that, always teasing me, playing hard to get..."

His breath washed over Amara, heavy and poisoned with booze.

"Please, I just want to go home, I'm tired," Amara said. Her voice was shaking, and she was desperately looking for a chance to escape.

"Well, I don't. Y'know what I want? Some fuckin' company, but all the hot chicks're ignoring me." His other hand came into view, and he took a drink from the large bottle he was holding. "You wouldn't know anything about that, would you?"

Eyes wide, Amara noticed that the bottle was almost empty. Her mind raced, cycling through options as she tried to find a way out. The same thought came up, over and over; she'd just learned to fight, but without her tail she felt defenseless.

Derek was massive, and the bravado she had felt during their last encounter had vanished. She wondered if, being drunk, she'd be able to outrun him, and took a deep breath.

She ducked under his arm, attempting to stay low, but only managed to get a few steps in. His hand closed around her wrist, and he threw her back against the brick wall.

Her breath left her body, and her head started spinning from the impact.

"Don't you FUCKING run from me!" Derek shouted. He smashed the bottle against the wall, just shy of Amara's head, showering her with glass and alcohol. "I'm sick of your little games...so we're gonna play a new one."

Her ears were ringing, and her vision was still blurry from hitting the wall. She desperately scanned the area, looking for anyone who might be able to help.

She stopped moving her head when she felt cold glass on her neck. Derek was staring at her, eyes mad with power, holding the broken bottle against her throat.

"This game's called Stay. Fucking. Quiet." He was practically growling now, his mouth twisted into a horrific grin. His other hand moved down, his heavy fingers fumbling with his pants. "I've waited too long for this, Vee..."

Vee.

Derek's attention was slipping, and the bottle pushed even harder against her. Its jagged edges scratched her skin as she strained to keep away from it.

He thinks I'm Vee.

The thought snapped Amara out of her fear. Her thoughts raced and her panic turned to white-hot rage.

"No."

Amara grabbed the bottle against her neck and pushed it back.

"The fuck was that, bitch?" Derek pushed the bottle harder, but seemed surprised that he couldn't overpower Amara anymore.

"I said NO!" Amara pushed hard, moving Derek's hand further away from her neck.

Gritting his teeth, he pulled his other hand away from his pants, and tried to grab her throat. Amara met that hand with her own, and they stood in a stalemate as each attempted to overpower the other.

Amara's blood raced, boiling with anger as she fought back. Her rage was building, growing hotter with each second, desperate to burst out of her.

And then it did.

Flames appeared at her fingertips, lingering for a moment before roaring to life. Soon both her hands were completely ignited, their flames casting terrifying shadows on the bricks behind her. She watched as the fire grew hotter, its red glow developing shades of purple in a fraction of a second.

Derek panicked, screaming in surprise. The alcohol on his arm ignited, sparks and embers racing across his skin. His eyes wide, he surrendered control and fell to his knees, then doubled over.

Without thinking, Amara started running. Each step felt heavier than the last, but she had to get home. Her vision blurred again, not from blunt force, but from tears. They clouded her vision, yet when they left her eyes, they evaporated on contact with her skin.

She felt as if she'd been running for hours by the time she made it home. When she pulled out her keys, she tried to open the door, but dropped them immediately when she saw her hands. Flames still lingered on her skin, their pale light filling the hallway. She tried to pat the fire out on her pants, then grabbed her keys and opened the door. Once inside, she slammed it shut with her tail and fell to the floor, her back against the entrance.

Amara reached into her pocket, desperate to call Nick. She tried to breathe deeply, to count the way he had shown her, but she kept losing focus. Nick wasn't answering, and Amara tried again.

And again.

And again.

She had no idea how long her phone would survive the heat, and she swore the fire was getting hotter. Miraculously, Nick answered while her phone was still working.

"Amara? What's—"

"Nick, I'm on fire! I can't stop it!"

8

PLAYING WITH FIRE

When Nick finally arrived, Amara was standing in the middle of the living room, her hands held high. Fire surrounded her fingers and palms, and she was pretty sure she could feel heat emanating from her horns as well. Her phone lay on the floor next to her, its case blackened and warped.

"Niiiiick, this is really scary!" she shouted. Fear kept her perfectly still: She didn't want to risk setting the house on fire.

Nick's eyes were wide, his chest heaving from the sprint over here. He had clearly gotten dressed in a hurry, and was wearing what looked like very loose-fitting pajamas. "Okay: Cliff Notes—what happened?!"

"I was on my way home, and I ran into Derek, but he was super drunk and we kinda fought a bit, and then I got really angry and suddenly my hands were on fire and then he was on fire and he ran away and now I can't stop and I'm scared if I move I'll set something on fire and I don't know what to do!" Amara's words were bleeding together as she tried to stay calm.

Moving closer, Nick held up his hands to mirror hers. "Okay, wow, that's a lot to take in, but we can get through this. Eyes on me, match my breathing." He made a show of taking big breaths, trying to calm her down. "We can get this under control, alright?"

Amara nodded, her eyes locked on Nick's. She already felt better with him here, but the flames on her hands refused to go out. "Okay, deep breaths, I can do this, I can do this." She watched as he moved closer, and soon they were only a few feet apart. "How bad is it?"

He laughed nervously at the question, then took a minute to look her over. "Well, you're not Vee anymore. Your hands are on fire, and so are your horns, which also seem to have grown a fair amount. They've practically doubled in size. Wings are still gone, though."

"Okay, that's honestly better than I expected." She forced a laugh, trying to fill the silence. "So, options? What can we do about this?"

Nick furrowed his eyebrows, deep in thought. "Oh! Didn't Evelyn make you buy a fire extinguisher?"

"Yes! That's perfect! It's in the hall closet!" She pointed down the hall, then jumped when a small ember leapt off her finger and floated a few inches before vanishing. 'Fuck! Sorry!"

It took a few minutes for Nick to ready the extinguisher, and they moved to the hard floor in front of the main entrance.

"Hands first? I'd feel weird starting with your horns."

"What, you're not into facials?" Amara laughed again as she pushed her hands forward.

He rolled his eyes before pulling the trigger. A thick foam burst from the nozzle, covering Amara's hands as she jumped in surprise. They both froze for a moment, waiting to see what would happen, and after a few seconds the flames returned.

"You've got to be fucking kidding me!" she groaned in frustration.

"Hey, at least we've learned something. I had a feeling this wasn't normal fire; the purple tint makes no sense. It must be magically resistant somehow." He put the extinguisher down before grabbing a towel to clean up the foam on the floor.

"That's cool and all, but it doesn't help me right now. What else can we try?" She leaned against the kitchen counter as she waited for Nick to finish cleaning.

"Well, there might only be one option left." He sighed as he threw the towel aside. "The one thing that seems most effective with you."

They locked eyes, and a moment later Amara figured out what he meant.

"Seriously? Now?"

Nick shrugged. "Hey, you're the one with sex-fueled superpowers."

Amara grew quiet, admitting that Nick had a point. She looked at him and nodded in agreement. "Alright, it's worth a shot. How do we do this? I can't really use my hands."

"Some people would consider that a turn on, actually." Nick stepped closer, his aura stirring as he walked. "Ever thought about trying bondage?"

"It may have crossed my mind a few times. You?"

"Tried it once or twice. I think it's pretty fun!" He knelt down in front of her, his hands moving up her legs. "Not an option now, what with the fire hazard, but maybe something to try later."

He pushed her sweater up, exposing her toned stomach, and lightly kissed her. She bit her lip as he explored her waist, his hands pulling her pants down slowly. A cool breeze tickled her hips, but the tingling sensation was soon replaced by Nick's hands.

He grabbed her exposed hips, holding her tight as he tenderly bit them. She yelped impulsively, then giggled as he kept pushing her pants down.

"Mmm, fuck, when did you become a biter?" she asked.

"You seem to enjoy it. I thought I'd turn the tables since you can't use your hands." He smirked, then bit the other side of her hips. She jumped again, then felt her pants hit the floor. Nick helped her pull her shoes and socks off, and soon she was eagerly kicking her pants to the side.

When he returned his lips to her thighs, she moaned softly. He was taking his time, which was perfect. With each passing moment, each teasing kiss, the panic from earlier faded. The tension gradually left her body, replaced by an all too familiar demonic itch.

He continued to tease her, biting the sensitive skin inside her thighs. She wanted so badly to grab his head, to make him pleasure her more directly, but she knew she had to keep her hands safely in the air.

Instead, a different thought crossed her mind. Adjusting her stance, she moved her tail between her legs and reached for Nick. He was still kneeling on the floor, and her tail traced up his legs before finding a hard bulge in his pants. She massaged it slowly, exploring what she could do with her tail.

Nick responded by hooking fingers into her panties, pulling them down frustratingly slowly. He kissed each inch of skin that he exposed, and she moaned when she felt his lips on her sensitive clit.

"Yes, please taste me," she whispered, eager to feel more.

Amara twitched when his tongue ran over her pussy, her body tingling with excitement. He moved it back and forth, each time teasing her entrance as she pushed her hips into him.

Her tail moved up, pushing into his pants in an attempt to return the favor. It wrapped around his shaft, and she carefully started stroking him.

"Fuck, that's new!" Nick whispered, his breath hot against her sex.

Amara grinned at his surprise. "Good new, or bad new?"

He dug his nails into her hips to make her squirm again. "Very good! Just...surprising. It feels like a snake is giving me a handjob."

They both laughed, but Amara's voice quickly gave way to more moaning as Nick pushed a finger into her. He pushed deep, curling it the way he knew she loved. His free hand dug into her ass, pulling her close as a second finger entered her.

Moaning even louder, her tail squeezed his cock tight. "Mmmm, yes, that feels amazing!"

His fingers pulled back, almost leaving her, before pushing in hard. He started fucking her in long, slow strides, his fingers wet from her arousal. He kissed her clit again, teasing it with his tongue as he picked up the pace. Her body was tensing, an orgasm building as he kept fingering her.

Nick was focused on her pleasure much more than usual, and it was having an incredible effect. Before long, a slow, rumbling orgasm surged through her, catching her by surprise.

"Nick! Don't fucking stop!" she moaned, her body tensing around his fingers. He kept a steady pace as he continued, his tongue massaging her clit.

As she came, convulsing against the kitchen counter, she felt her senses expand once more. She connected with the space around her, and her apartment seemed more vivid than ever. The flames surrounding her hands and horns suddenly felt safe, as if they were just another extension of her body.

It took a minute for her orgasm to stop, and once it did, she looked down at Nick. He slowly pulled his fingers out, his eyes jumping to the fire in her hands.

"Fire's still going. Can you put it out now?" he asked.

"I think I've got a bit more control? But that's not how this works, Nick."

"What do you mean?"

"I'm a succubus: I need to feed on *your* arousal, your sex, not mine." She tensed her tail again, teasing his cock. "If masturbating could power my abilities, I'd be ruling Hell by now. How do you want me?"

"Let me lay down; I think that will be the safest." Nick pulled back, his cock leaving her tail's grasp, and started pulling his clothes off.

Once he was finally naked, Amara stood over him, her eyes glued on his cock. Using her tail, she carefully straddled him, lining up her entrance. She almost moved for a kiss before remembering that her horns were on fire too. Her arms were getting tired, and she hoped she would be able to get rid of all the fire after this.

Her tail, no longer supporting her weight, moved to his cock again. She wrapped around his shaft, testing all her different muscles as she teased him. His aura grew brighter as she stroked him, her flared tip playing with the head of his cock.

"Ready to be inside me, Nick?" she asked, taking full advantage of his love of dirty talk.

He nodded slowly, his body twitching as she kept stroking him with her tail. It finally loosened its grip, aiming his shaft at her entrance before she sat down completely. Moving her tail out of the way, she gasped as she started to ride Nick with purposely slow strokes, mimicking what he did to her just minutes earlier.

She watched his aura eagerly, adjusting her rhythm and angle to make it as bright as possible. Nick's moans grew louder as she did, his body thrusting deep into her.

"Fuck, Amara, you get better every time," he whispered.

"You love it, don't you? Having your own personal demonic sex toy?" Amara kept bouncing on his cock, her hands grabbing her horns as she rode him. "I'm such a slut for this cock. I'd do anything to keep feeding on you!"

Her words strengthened his aura further, and Nick's hands moved to her legs as she picked up the pace. She focused on her newfound sense of control, reaching out with her senses to connect with his aura, and began to draw strength from it. While it had no conventional taste, she felt as if she suddenly had ambrosia coursing through her veins.

She kept a comfortable pace, taking care not to push Nick too far as she fed on his sexual energy. She was amazed at how much insight she gained from his aura; it was incredibly easy to move him closer to, or further from, his orgasm.

"Don't think I can't see what you're doing; you're such a tease!" Nick whispered, his thrusts still meeting hers.

"Who, me? I'm just an innocent little college student..." She playfully bit a finger, flames dancing up the side of her face. Her eyes grew brighter, and this time she had a feeling their flare was more literal.

"Well, if you're not in control, then I think I'll take what I want!" Nick shifted his hands, holding Amara's hips slightly, and started fucking her faster.

She watched as his aura grew quickly, its intensity pushing more energy into her. She felt her own body start to betray her, to ask for another orgasm, and she had every intent of letting that happen.

"I'm close!" Nick gripped her legs tight, his body tensing. As his orgasm approached, Amara did everything she could to fuck Nick back, looking for another climax of her own.

She moved her hands off her horns, instead grabbing her sweater. Her tail joined in, wrapping around her torso as she started cumming hard, screaming out in ecstasy.

With one final thrust, Nick's orgasm joined hers, his cock emptying its load into her. Amara's hips twitched as she came, her senses overwhelmed with pleasure. Her tail burst into flame, joining with the fire on her hands to turn her torso into a small inferno.

Nick's hips continued bucking with pleasure as he finished cumming, but soon the moment started to pass. His body relaxed onto the floor, and it only took another few seconds until Amara felt her own tension ease as well.

As her breathing relaxed, she focused on the flames surrounding her body. She closed her eyes, connected with the fire, and tried to extinguish it. The flames dwindled, eventually dying out completely, but their potent energy lived on. Amara pulled it inside of herself, where it nestled comfortably.

When Nick opened his eyes, they immediately widened with panic. "Fucking hell, Amara!"

"Are you okay? I didn't hurt you, did I?!" Amara looked down, scared she might see burns on Nick's clothes.

"I'm fine, but I could feel how intense the fire got. And look at your sweater!"

Looking down, Amara saw her tail was still wrapped around her chest. When she uncurled it, she realized the parts of the sweater it had covered were burned away. She was effectively wearing an elaborate burnt ribbon for a shirt, and she was surprised it hadn't fallen apart yet.

"Well," Amara said, looking at Nick, "how does it feel to fuck the hottest girl on campus?"

Nick groaned, his head hitting the floor. "Can I assume the terrible joke means you're feeling better?"

Amara slowly got off Nick, his semi-hard cock leaving her body. She stood up, holding her hands out in front of her, and looked down at Nick. "You tell me! Any fire?"

He took his time getting up, making sure to pull his underwear back on, then looked Amara up and down. "Not a single spark! What do you feel like? Is there control? Or does it feel like the first shapeshift?"

"I can still feel the fire, but now it's inside of me? I think if I focus..." Amara paused, holding out a hand. She focused on the energy she'd moved earlier and tried to pull it into her palm.

Within moments, a flame appeared in her hand. She giggled as she watched it, running her fingers through the fire. The extent of her heat resistance finally hit her; she knew how hot the fire was but couldn't feel it at all.

"AHH, look at it! It's so cute!" Amara tested her control, bouncing the flame between her hands as Nick watched.

"Wow, that's incredible! Let's try to be careful with this, alright? We have no idea how this compares to regular fire." Nick's face was, comparatively, filled with caution. "How about we put it out for now and test something else. What about your wings?"

Amara nodded, recognizing Nick's wisdom. She put the fire out, pulling its energy inside herself again.

Next, she shifted her attention to her demonic body parts. She flexed her tail, pulling it in front of her. Content that it existed, she then tried to connect with her wings. While she couldn't flex and engage them the way she had with her tail, she could still sense their presence.

Curious, she tried to reach for them, to pull them forward the same way she'd done with the fire. With a dull flash of light, and a small scattering of fire, her wings suddenly reappeared on her back. As they did, she heard a ripping noise, and watched the charred remains of her sweater fall to the floor.

Amara jumped for joy, running to Nick and squeezing him tight. In her excitement, she even picked him up, spinning him around slightly.

"NICK! This is incredible, thank you so much!"

When she finally put him down, he gasped for air.

"Oh, uh, sorry. I don't think I know my own strength."

"Well, in your defense, it's been growing exponentially for the last few weeks." He coughed again while rolling out his shoulders. "Maybe we should start tracking it? Who knows, you might be throwing cars around by Christmas."

"Could you imagine?!" Amara jumped around the room for a moment before speaking again. "Okay, moment of truth: it's shapeshifting time. Who should I be?"

Nick moved to the nearby couch and took a seat. "You think that's a good idea? What if you get stuck again?"

"C'mon, Nick, I gotta try! Pick someone!"

"Alright, alright. You've already been Vee, so how about Tessa? If something goes wrong at least you'll be able to talk to her about it."

Amara nodded, then closed her eyes. Connecting with that energy, that inner fire, felt comfortable. It seemed to be the source of her abilities. It could manifest her wings, it could appear as a sweltering flame, but could it do more? Focusing on it, she pictured Tessa, then tried to turn that fire inward.

It took a few moments, but soon she felt a tingling sensation. It was warm, coursing through her body in a fraction of a second, and then she opened her eyes.

"Anything?" Amara immediately noticed that her voice was different, a little lower than usual.

"Oh, that's weird," Nick mumbled, his eyebrows furrowing in confusion.

"What? What'd I do?!"

"I've just never seen Tessa without any eyeliner or piercings before." Nick said with a smirk.

"Wait, seriously?" Amara sat down next to him, pulling out her phone and turning on the camera.

Sure enough, the body staring back convincingly resembled Tessa. She shimmied in excitement before looking herself over, marveling at the changes. "You're completely right, though; I barely look like Tessa at all. I've seen her once or twice without her makeup, but the piercings too? Wild!"

Before turning the camera off, Amara took a few selfies and sent them to Tessa. She giggled maliciously, then turned back to Nick. "Time to turn back!"

"You might want to stand up again—there's fire when you shift," Nick warned.

In the middle of the room again, Amara repeated her previous actions. She connected with her inner fire, aimed it at herself, and pictured...well, herself. The same sensation from earlier washed over her, and within seconds she knew it had worked. It felt a little strained this time, as if her strength were wearing thin, but her body was hers once again.

This time, however, she hadn't manifested her demonic features. She pushed her hands through her hair, confirmed the lack of horns, then did the same with her low back.

"Looks like you're getting pretty good at this!" Nick said. "Did you get rid of the tail and horns on purpose?"

"I did! This solves all my wardrobe problems!" She remembered she wasn't wearing her sweater anymore and picked it up off the floor. "Although, it seems like I need to be careful when I bring my wings out."

"Good thing the sweater was already destroyed, right?" Nick yawned, leaning back on the couch. "Now, no offense, Amara, but I don't normally get up this early. Can I crash here for a bit?"

"Now that you mention it..." Amara yawned herself, checking the time. "I was about to go to sleep when everything caught on fire, and the shapeshifting definitely took more energy than I anticipated. Maybe we should both get some sleep?"

The two nodded in agreement, hugging briefly before retiring to the bedroom and the couch, respectively. Nick set an alarm for both of them, mostly because he had other plans that afternoon, and soon the two had passed out from exhaustion.

By the time Vee was free to go, the sun was close to setting. She pulled her hood over her head, doing her best to avoid eye contact with anyone as she walked home. When she arrived, she caught herself staring at the front door, unable to picture herself walking through it. The thought of going inside, of being alone, sounded terrible. She pulled out her phone.

Vee: Hey, can I come over? Are you still sick?

Amara: I'm all better! I'll leave the door open :)

Vee happily left her porch, quickening her pace as she walked. Tears threatened to fall, but thankfully Amara lived close by. After only a few minutes, Vee was closing the door behind her and pulling off her shoes.

Amara ran over, giving her a soft hug. "What's happening, babe? It's been so long since we hung out!"

Vee couldn't respond. Her mind was racing, and all she could do was look at Amara. She could feel the emotions building up, the heat growing in her face.

"Vee? Talk to me, what's going on?" Amara's tone grew serious, and her hands landed on Vee's shoulders as she lowered her voice.

"I...I don't..." Attempting to speak broke what little control Vee had left. She fell forward, her arms wrapping around Amara as the tears started falling.

Minutes passed, neither saying anything as Vee buried her face in Amara's shirt. Her breathing was erratic, her body occasionally twitching as she released all the frustration of the day.

"It's...it's Derek," Vee managed to say.

"What did he do? Did he hurt you?!" Amara had a fire in her voice, as if she were ready to go to war.

"No, nothing like that," Vee said, wiping her nose on her sleeve. "He...he says I attacked him! That I set him on fire!"

Amara's face turned white with shock. "I...that's...that's absurd! You would never do that!"

I wouldn't. But a demon would.

Vee tried to shake her thoughts loose. "I saw him, briefly, at the station. Whatever happened, he's in bad shape."

Amara froze, her face betraying her confusion. "Wait, station? As in the police station?"

"He filed an official report. I was there all day, answering questions and shit..." Vee moved to the couch, shrinking into a corner as she sniffled.

"Okay, well, obviously you didn't do this. What do you think happened?" Amara sat down, draping one arm around Vee's shoulders. While the gesture was meant to be comforting, Vee could feel the tension in her friend's body.

I think the succubus knows I'm onto her.

The thought lingered, and Vee was unable to shake it loose this time. What other explanation was there? The succubus was trying to frame her, to warn her against continuing her hunt.

Despite Amara holding her, Vee felt hopelessly alone.

What if I told Amara everything? Would she believe me?

She leaned into Amara, wordlessly looking for what little comfort she could get.

It would be so easy! 'Hey, Amara, this is gonna sound weird, but I'm an angel! A soul-sucking demon is trying to frame me!'

Despite her desperation, Vee couldn't bring herself to say anything. The Church had warned her, time and time again, never to share her holy mission with humans. Either they don't believe you, or worse, they do. They become obsessed with divinity, the afterlife, worshipping you to gain favor and salvation.

Her friendship with Amara was genuine, one of the few things her divine lineage hadn't tainted, and she refused to give that up.

Minutes passed, the silence broken only by Vee's sniffling. She was glad Amara lived the closest of her friends; Tessa had a habit of being too flippant, and Chloé wasn't the most reliable in stressful situations. Amara had always been safe and comfortable, eager to help however she could.

"What happens now?" Amara asked eventually. "They obviously don't have any evidence, since you didn't do anything."

"I can't say for sure, but it seems like nothing is going to stick. Like you said, there aren't any witnesses, there's no evidence, and Derek was clearly drunk. They're probably only taking him seriously because...well, you know."

Amara nodded in acknowledgment.

"Even if nothing happens, with how popular Derek is, school is gonna be a living hell. He's going to make sure everyone thinks I attacked him in cold blood."

"Hey, whatever happens, we're here for you." Amara shifted to look Vee in the eyes. "I'm here for you. I swear I'll find a way to fix this."

There was unusual determination in Amara's voice. While Vee appreciated the concern, and had always known Amara to be protective, she was slightly taken aback by the reaction. It's not like Amara could actually do much about the situation.

"Thanks, Amara." Vee leaned closer, hugging her friend tight. "I knew I could count on you."

"No! Absolutely not!"

"Tessa, this is all my fault! What other choice do I have?"

"Uh, the sensible one? The one that keeps you safe?" Tessa paced back and forth, her hands gesturing wildly. "I can't believe you'd even consider it!"

"I told you, didn't I? That went fine." Amara crossed her arms, her tail twitching in frustration.

"I'm a witch, Amara! I already knew magic and demons were real! And even then, are you forgetting that I almost left you there? I was terrified!"

"I'm not saying it's going to be easy, but I have to try! What would you have me do? Nothing?"

Tessa moved closer, grabbing Amara's shoulders as her voice softened. "That's not what I'm saying. We just have to be careful about this."

Amara stayed quiet, moving her eyes to the floor to avoid looking at her friend.

"Look, this is a shit situation, I get it," Tessa continued, "but there's more at stake here. Our secrecy is what keeps us alive, in a very literal sense. You've heard of witch hunts, right?"

"Weren't those all made up by colonists to justify killing women they didn't like?" Amara asked.

"I mean, yeah, but the first one? The first one was legit. It got a lot of attention, and people realized that witch hunts drove communities apart, created a vacuum of power for whoever could control the narrative. Things are a lot better now, but that hatred can still be stoked under the right circumstances."

"Vee's our friend! She's one of the smartest, kindest people I know!"

"Her family is also super religious! Did you know she's got some kind of grant from her church? You think they're going to give out money to people who are down to fuck with witches and demons?"

"I...I didn't know that. Seriously?" Amara finally looked Tessa in the eyes, surprise in her voice.

"She doesn't like to talk about it, and I don't even know what it's for. I only found out because I was at her place when a payment came in."

Tessa moved her hands to Amara's face, keeping their eyes locked. "Look, I want to help Vee just as much as you, but there's a right way to do it. What's happening on this campus needs to stay a secret. From everybody."

"What about your coven? They already know about magic, can they help patch this up?"

"Trust me, that would cause more problems than it would solve." Tessa's voice was bitter, though Amara couldn't tell if her anger was directed at Amara or something else.

Ugh, that's the second time she's shot down my questions about her coven. What's up with her?

Amara couldn't find the words to respond, and instead kept looking into Tessa's eyes. The same vulnerability she had seen before had returned, only this time it was laced with fear. She had a suspicion that Tessa wasn't telling her everything, but her words seemed honest enough.

"Alright, fine. I won't tell her." Amara sighed in resignation. Who was she to doubt Tessa's wisdom? Amara had only known about her lineage for a few weeks, but Tessa seemed to be speaking from significant experience.

There was another small pause before Tessa spoke again. "What about you? Obviously everything about this is fucked, but you haven't talked about, y'know...Derek attacked you."

"I'm torn. It was terrifying, absolutely, but I also got out unscathed." Amara paused, taking a deep breath as she thought back to this morning. "You know what's weird? The thing that shook me to my senses was when he called me Vee. As far as he's concerned, he was trying to attack her, not me. My blood boils every time I think about it, but there's this tiny part of me that's almost glad this happened?"

"Amara, what the fuck are you on about? Do you even hear yourself right now?"

"I know how it sounds, and that's not what I mean. I keep coming back to the same thought, over and over. What if he'd found her instead? He's obviously the type to do this shit, and if it's going to happen, I'd rather it happens to me than her. I was able to fight him off, but Vee..."

Tessa clearly wanted to say something, but it took a few moments before she did. "Fuck. I hadn't thought about that." She pulled Amara in for a hug, squeezing her tight.

"I'll make this right. For Vee," Amara whispered. She squeezed back, doing her best not to hurt her friend.

She felt Tessa nod, then pull back from her. "So, you can actually summon fire now?"

Amara looked up at Tessa, shifting her focus. "Oh, yeah! It's pretty neat, if a little scary at times. Wanna see?"

Tessa nodded enthusiastically, turning off the flashlight on her phone as she pocketed it. "Uh, obviously! My phone is close to dying anyways."

Holding out her palm, Amara turned her focus inward. She was able to find the connection much quicker now, and soon a small flame sat in her hand. "Just be careful; it's not normal fire."

The firelight reflected in Tessa's eyes as she moved closer. There was caution in her steps, but it was clear she was fascinated. "Can I just say how jealous I am? You get stronger by fucking. Talk about getting lucky."

The flame moved higher, growing slightly brighter as Amara fed it more energy. She moved it around, watching as it illuminated the room around them.

The two girls were currently under the cafeteria, as they had been trying to find more magic circles. With only a brief investigation, they had discovered an old storage room filled with discarded kitchen hardware. Industrial fridges, freezer chests, deep fryers, all sorts of massive steel contraptions. Some of this equipment had been pinning down a large throw rug, and they had found a magic circle underneath.

The most peculiar thing about the room were the breaks in the floor. The entire place had cracks in the foundation, through which dozens of different plants were growing. Most of them were quite small, but the sheer variety on display was impressive. As the firelight grew, the amount of plant life in the room finally hit them both.

When Tessa finally pulled her eyes away from the flame, she looked around and whistled. "Damn, this place looks like it's seen a few apocalypses. How long can you keep that flame going? We need to start moving this shit so we can see the circle."

"Uh, maybe a bit? I just figured it out today, remember. You get started; I'll try to get the lights on." Amara walked back to the entrance, flipping the light switch up and down a few times.

I wonder if they purposely fucked with the lights to keep people out. Who would want to wander around in the dark room filled with half-broken freezers?

She kept searching, tracing the walls in hopes of finding another light switch, or maybe a breaker. As she walked further away from Tessa, she kept focusing on her connection with the flame. It floated roughly ten feet up in the air, and it grew more difficult to maintain as the distance increased. Although she didn't have any physical muscles flexing to support the fire, she could feel the strain building, and managed to find the breaker just before dropping the flame.

"We have light! How's the heavy lifting going?" Amara asked, returning to her friend.

"I moved some smaller stuff, but the rest of this crap isn't moving without both of us." She gestured to a few large appliances still sitting on the rug.

"You can't just, y'know, float them away?" Amara tapped the side of her head and wiggled her fingers.

"My telekinesis has limitations. Like I said last time, that energy has to come from somewhere."

"Alright, alright. This one first?" Amara pointed at an ancient soda fountain, and the two of them got to work. While Tessa's telekinesis was unable to lift the whole thing, she still used it for her half of the lifting. Amara chuckled as they worked; it looked like Tessa was lazily supervising while a ghost helped her do the dirty work. As they worked, she found herself wondering how long Tessa had been a witch.

Presumably a while? She's had her tattoos since at least freshman year, and they didn't seem very fresh then. Were her parents witches? Has she ever talked about them, even before all this? Ugh, I wish she'd stop dodging all my questions!

It took close to half an hour to finally clear the rug, at which point the two of them draped it over a nearby appliance. With the circle now uncovered, Tessa pulled out her notebook and looked around.

"So, have we learned anything yet? I feel like we've found quite a few circles, but I don't really know what you've been doing with them."

"The first step of science, Amara, is gathering data. I've been familiarizing myself with all the symbols, the connections, the ways the circles are built. So far, they've all been pretty consistent, but I'm getting better at telling them apart."

Amara jumped to sit on a nearby freezer, pulling out her phone as she settled in. "But this all started because you felt...what did you call them, shifts? Changes in the magic around campus? Any clues on that yet?"

"I have a few theories, but nothing concrete." Tessa chewed on her lip ring as she looked over her notes. "Although..." She shifted, moving closer to a spot on the edge of the circle.

She flipped through her book, hunting for a specific page. Amara drew closer, eager to see what she might have found.

"I knew it!" Tessa pointed at one particular symbol. "Someone's been fucking with the circles! Look, the rune here is newer, and the signature doesn't quite match."

"Signature? I'm still not a witch, Tessa."

"It's...how to put this? The context is wrong. Like, if we were talking and I suddenly said 'Thou art mistaken'. The language of magic has changed over time, which can help with identification."

"So, can you tell what it's for? The new bit?"

Tessa traced her hand over the symbol, comparing it to some writing in her journal. "It's a subtle change. Either it's trying to recalibrate the circle, or it's trying to weaken it. I bet if I..." She trailed off, mumbling to herself as the tattoos on her head lit up again.

Her fingers stopped moving on one specific rune. It pulsed slowly for a moment, but soon its glow spread to other parts of the circle. The whole thing now pulsed, several times in succession, before Amara felt a charge move through the air.

She braced herself, then watched as something burst out of the circle on the floor. It was moving fast, but Amara managed to spring backward over her perch to avoid it. The sound of scraping metal filled her ears, and she jumped back again to avoid a large fridge as it tipped over. By the time she made it to the far wall, the chaos seemed to have stopped, and she finally looked around.

The far corner of the storage room, where the circle had been, was now thickly covered with deep green vines. The smallest ones were only as wide as Amara's fingers, but many of them were much bigger. They had wrapped around most of the nearby appliances, and she could see that the nearby fridge wasn't the only one that had tipped over. The one thing she couldn't see was Tessa.

"Tessa! Are you okay? Where are you?" Amara paused, trying to listen for her friend. She soon heard a muffled response, too quiet to understand, but enough to start searching.

Moving closer to the vines, she tried touching one to check for movement or danger. It didn't seem to react, so Amara felt comfortable pushing further. She climbed over appliances and vines, looking for any sign of where Tessa had ended up.

"Keep talking! I can hear you, but it's faint."

Another muffled response told Amara she was closer.

After another few minutes of climbing, she closed in on the far corner of the room. The girls had pushed everything toward the center, which had left the walls open, and vines now eagerly clung to those walls. It was in this corner that she finally found Tessa. She was immobilized beneath a thick blanket of vines, though parts of her were still visible.

"Alright, I'm here. Let's see if we can get you out of this mess!" Amara moved closer, standing over Tessa as she reached for the vines covering her face. They were smaller, but she was caught off guard by how much they resisted her attempts to pull them off.

It took a few moments of heavy pulling, but soon Amara had freed most of her friend's face.

"Thank fuck, it was getting hard to breathe under that." Tessa looked around at the storage room, then at herself. "How the fuck did you avoid this shit?"

"I was further away from the circle, and I could tell something was about to happen. There was a weird shift in the air." Amara sat down on some nearby vines, looking for other ways of freeing Tessa.

"Well, lucky you! Now are you gonna get me out of here, or what?" Tessa was straining, doing her best to break free, but nothing seemed to be happening.

"I'm open to ideas if you have any. I was barely able to move those small vines off your face, and everything else looks to be twice as thick." Amara kept testing different vines, hoping to find ones that she could pull at. "I don't suppose we could reverse the circle? Put everything back?"

Tessa threw a dirty look at Amara. "No, the circle doesn't have a built-in 'undo' feature." Her words dripped with bitter sarcasm.

"Hey, I'll never know if I don't ask." Amara stuck her tongue out at Tessa.

The two girls looked at each other, each sighing with resignation. They were in for another long night.

9
TANGLED ASSUMPTIONS

As Vee walked out of the store, she shrugged to reposition the heavy water jugs on her shoulders. The cashier had given her some funny looks when she'd left, but quickly turned his attention elsewhere. No doubt he'd seen weirder things at five in the morning. A few bags of other miscellaneous purchases hung from her arms as she made her way home, which was only a few blocks away.

The weight was negligible, especially now that she'd gotten better at enhancing her body's strength with her divine magic. She smirked as she thought back on how much progress she'd made recently. In only a few weeks, she was close to surpassing many of her previous limits from the last time she'd seriously trained.

As she crossed the final intersection, she briefly stepped toward home, then paused.

This would be a great place for a rune. This path splits to a few different dorms.

Setting down the water, Vee pulled her backpack off and withdrew her Enochian Texts. Sure that no one was watching, she quickly asked for another tracking rune to form in the center of the path. It appeared, briefly pulsing with light, then vanished from sight.

I think that's seventeen? I haven't hit the auditorium yet...

Vee hoisted the heavy jugs over her shoulders again and resumed her walk home. Her thoughts wandered as she made a mental list of all the tracking runes she'd placed around campus. She'd tried to tag the main entrances to all the major buildings, and had already gotten a few hits. Unfortunately, unless she happened to be extremely close, a single activation of a rune only served as another data point to add to the map.

As she arrived home, she put down all her purchases and pulled out her notebook. Inside, she was recording the times of each rune activation, trying to find patterns in the demon's movements. Vee assumed the demon was masquerading as a student, but it was hard to know how often she did so.

Is she...going to classes? That's what the runes seem to say, but that feels like a huge waste of time for a demon. Wouldn't it be easier to just go to parties? Find some drunk idiots, take their souls, and be on your way.

She was happy that the runes around her dorm had never activated; it gave her a tiny sliver of peaceful sleep before the nightmares inevitably returned each night. It also occurred to her that she should place runes around all the major dorms on campus. If the demon was fully committed to being a student, she might be living in a dorm. Even if she weren't, it would be easy to convince another student to invite her over.

Vee started up some coffee, then checked her phone. She quickly navigated to local news sites and social media feeds, looking for possible clues.

Still no bodies, no missing people, nothing. How is she hiding her victims?

The lack of news concerned her. Although taking someone's soul wouldn't always kill them, most demons felt it was quicker to do so anyway. People who stayed alive after losing a soul often experienced personality shifts, some more alarming than others.

She pocketed her phone and made herself breakfast. There was something missing; there had to be. A campus with a demon running around shouldn't be this calm.

How does she find her victims? How does she hide them? Why is she bothering to go to classes?

Frustrated with the lack of answers, Vee turned her attention back to the water jugs. Placing one on the counter, she opened her Enochian Texts and started a familiar spell. Placing her hand on the side of the container, she asked the Divine to purify the water inside.

She did the same for the second container, then moved them into a corner with the rest of the holy water. She now had ten large containers, along with a few water bottles that she kept with her at all times. While she didn't know how it would all get used, she was happy to have a significant backstock.

Content that the water was ready, she unpacked the rest of her purchases. A few rosaries, some chalk, several bags of salt, even some water pistols that had made her feel quite childish. The last item was a small bag of sulfur.

The religious importance of rosaries, even cheap ones, meant that imbuing them with magic was easier than usual. Salt wasn't inherently religious, but its association with purification had made it a staple in various dispelling rituals throughout history. With a bit of magic, the salt would hopefully help slow down the demon's movements, likely even creating an impassable barrier. The chalk wouldn't be helpful in a fight, but it would make it easier to set up more elaborate circles should the need arise.

She took great care handling the bag of sulfur, fully aware of how bad it could smell even in small quantities. Moving to the bathroom, she poked a small hole in the bag before returning to the living room.

Vee sat on the floor, closing her eyes as she focused on her magic; her connection with the Divine. Enochian filled the room as she said another prayer, this time enhancing her senses as well as her strength. It took a minute to acclimate to the new sensations; the hum of the building's heating filled her ears, a low bass occasionally broken by the persistent dripping of her neighbor's bathroom faucet.

She opened her eyes, testing her enhanced vision by reading the nutritional information on the cereal boxes in the kitchen. Finally, she breathed in through her nose, looking for one smell in particular. The most easily identifiable sign of demonic activity: sulfur.

To try to name all the different types of demons would be an exercise in madness. Demons took every size and shape imaginable, and the overwhelming variety of abilities they could wield made hunting them extremely challenging. Thankfully, all demons were born of damnation, and thus shared one important trait. Any demon that drew on its natural magic would inevitably leave behind a trail of sulfur.

While faint, Vee was able to smell the sulfur she'd set up in the bathroom.

She smirked, glad that her test had worked, then jumped to her feet. Having enhanced senses was nice, but if she couldn't utilize them properly, she wouldn't stand a chance in a fight. She moved through a series of basic exercises, slowly adjusting to her new skillset. It started slowly, as her enhanced perception dramatically altered how she perceived her own body, but soon enough she felt everything start to click.

Her vestibular senses were flawless, and she found she now had perfect balance. With each new movement, she slowly retrained her muscle memory to accommodate her enhanced physique. Before long, she felt completely comfortable with her body, and it was time for one final test.

She was currently upside down, her weight supported entirely by one hand planted firmly on the carpet. One leg extended straight toward the ceiling, and the other was bent, its foot resting on her inside knee. She reached forward with her free hand, then closed her eyes and focused.

Her magic stirred, eager to respond, but it took a moment to focus it properly. Creation was exceptionally difficult, and Vee hadn't manifested anything in years.

Sweat fell from her temple, landing on the carpet. Her balance faltered, just for a second, as she started the necessary prayer. The heavenly overtones of Enochian filled her ears, resonating with her magic, and within moments she'd achieved her goal.

A glimmering sword appeared in her hand, radiant power emanating from its blade. She moved it around, listening as the steel literally sang with every flourish. It was a beautiful weapon, and she was surprised at how little it weighed; no doubt her strikes would be quick and precise. She continued testing its weight, adjusting her own movements to accommodate the weapon, and before she knew it, it was time to prepare for classes.

With her eyes still closed, she pushed off the floor. Her body sprang into the air, folding into a tight somersault as she inverted one last time. Her feet landed softly, barely making a noise as she flourished her sword in front of her.

Vee grinned, knowing she was ready for a fight.

Amara grunted as she grabbed another vine, pulling as hard as she could. It shifted slightly, but nowhere near enough to make a difference.

"Fuck, why are these things so tough?" she groaned, collapsing backward.

Tessa was still trapped, but over the course of the last hour or so, Amara had managed to move some of the smaller vines off her body. Parts of her legs could be seen, but most of her upper body remained enveloped.

"Look, pulling them off doesn't seem to be working. Can you try something else? I'd rather not die under these things." Tessa sighed, tired from the constant struggling.

"I don't see you suggesting anything." snapped Amara. "Actually, where's that knife you always play with?"

"Not anywhere helpful. It's in my backpack, which I'm currently on top of."

"Ugh, just our luck. I'll see if I can find one laying around." Amara turned toward the massive pile of vines, then paused briefly. "Look, I'm sorry. I know this is worse for you than it is for me. I'm just sick of not being able to help when it matters."

"Hey, of all the people to be tied up in front of, I'm glad it's you."

Amara smiled before starting her climb, picking her steps carefully as she pushed toward the bulk of the storage. She was at the highest point of the mound of vines when her friend spoke up again.

"Could you stay within earshot?" Tessa's voice grew quiet, almost in embarrassment. "I don't want to be alone."

"Believe me, I know what that's like. I'll stay close, I promise."

The girls nodded at each other before Amara disappeared over another bundle of vines. She spent the better part of half an hour digging through old cabinets and appliances, looking for anything that might be sharp enough to cut through the vines. The whole time, she kept talking with Tessa, eager to keep her comfortable as best she could. In the end, while the conversation was as lively as ever, she returned empty-handed.

"This place has nothing but scrap metal, and none of it is even remotely jagged." Amara pulled her phone out, holding it up to look for service. "Do these circles fuck with cell signal? I swear I never get any bars when I'm near them."

"It would definitely make sense, but it's hard to say for sure. Older witches tend to ignore modern innovation, so us younger folk have to figure out for ourselves how magic and technology interact. Hey, can I get some water?"

Amara nodded and sat next to her friend, grabbing a water bottle before tipping it into her mouth.

"Alright, stupid idea," Tessa said, water dripping down her chin. "What if we burned the vines away?"

"Wow, when you say stupid idea, you really mean it."

"I'm being serious!"

"So am I! If we set this place on fire, I can only pull you out once the flames have eaten away at the vines. By then, you'll already be significantly burnt, if not dead!" Amara stood up, pacing back and forth, her tail flicking in frustration. "I can't believe you! Telling Vee I'm a demon is too far, but sure, let's set you on fire and see what happens!"

"Can you just shut up for a second? I didn't say set them on fire, I said 'burn them away'." Tessa's tattoos flared, and she made Amara look at her. "Look at these vines: they're vibrant and healthy. If they weren't, they wouldn't be this strong. Even if we introduce fire, they're going to resist it, which means controlling the flames will be easy. How much control do you have over your fire, anyway?"

"I'm honestly not sure. I can move it around easily enough, but I don't know what happens when it spreads. I might have control over all fire, or just mine, but right now I don't know."

"How about we test it out? You got any paper on you?"

Amara opened her backpack, ripping a page out of a notebook before sitting next to Tessa. "Alright, what are we doing?"

"It's easy: Just light a corner on fire, let it spread, then see if you can stop it."

Amara nodded and took a deep breath. She summoned a small flame, which took more effort than expected, and lit the paper on fire. The flames caught quickly, latching onto the sheet before it started to spread. After a few seconds, once the fire was approaching the middle of the page, she reached out and tried to pull it back.

She immediately noticed a few differences, the most obvious of which was the color. The fire she summoned had a slight purple tint, whereas the fire that spread afterward looked much more natural. Although it was difficult for her to judge temperature on feeling alone, she could also tell that the natural fire was less intense.

Connecting with the new fire was tough. She could sense its presence, but it took a few tries to extend her own control over it. Once she'd established the connection, the fire took on a purple hue, and she was able to extinguish it just before losing the paper entirely.

"It worked!" Amara brandished the paper, unsure where Tessa's line of sight ended. She also found herself yawning, which was surprising given the time of day.

"See? The vines are gonna be even easier—they won't catch the same way the paper does." Tessa was clearly excited, but Amara could tell she was also feeling a little smug.

"Okay, fine, you were right. I'm sorry I snapped at you; I just can't stop thinking about Vee, about Derek." Amara felt something squeeze her arms, then looked up to see Tessa's tattoos glowing.

"Hey, I told you: We'll figure something out." Tessa paused. "What if we just—"

"We're not killing him, Tessa," Amara said quickly, cutting off her friend.

"Ugh, fine, just stomp all over my dreams."

Chuckling, Amara moved closer to Tessa and looked for a good place to start. She found a slightly smaller vine curled around her friend's chest and wrapped a hand around it. Carefully lighting her palm on fire, she squeezed the vine as she tried to burn it apart. It took a few moments, but soon she was able to close her fist entirely, the vine having been severed.

"Okay, one down. How did that feel? Not too hot?" Amara asked.

"Pretty warm, but nothing I can't handle. Now get me out of here already!"

Moving to the next vine, Amara prepared to repeat herself. When she tried to pull more fire into her palm, however, she couldn't find any.

"Shit."

"C'mon, what is it now?"

"I, uh...I'm tapped out."

"You're out of fire? Now?"

"I just figured this out today! I have no idea what my limits are!"

"So, what now? Do you need a nap? A protein bar?"

"I don't think that would work; my powers come from...you know..." Amara watched as Tessa slowly figured out what she meant.

Tessa tried to speak a few times, the words needing more time to catch up. "By yourself?" she finally asked.

Amara shook her head. "Doesn't work; I have to feed on someone else's arousal." She coughed awkwardly, unsure how to proceed. "I could try to get Nick down here? I'd have to leave to get a signal, though."

The thought clearly made Tessa uncomfortable. "Look, can we stop beating around the bush? There's an obvious solution here."

The two locked eyes, and Tessa's growing aura made her insinuation more than obvious. Amara moved closer, the smell of arousal already filling her senses. "Is that so? What do you mean?" She leaned in, trying to hold back a smirk.

"I-I mean, we're alone down here and—" Tessa paused, finally piecing together the look on Amara's face. "Wait, are you fucking with me?"

"Me? I would never! I'm just waiting for you to finish." She paused, her words dripping with sarcasm.

"You're gonna make me say it, aren't you?"

Amara nodded. She watched as the helpless witch briefly struggled against the vines and noticed another pulse in her aura.

She's talked a few times about loving to be submissive. This might literally be a wet dream for her. Well, when in Rome...

"Look, it was only a matter of time, alright? I've always thought you were hot, but sex didn't seem like something you wanted, so I thought maybe you were ace or something. I tried not to push it, but then you turned into a demon and now, when we hang out—"

Amara pushed a finger against Tessa's mouth, stopping her nervous rambling. "I think what you're failing to say is that my being a demon turns you on, and every time you see my real body, you get flustered? And it's been getting worse recently?"

"How did—" Amara's eyes flared briefly, and Tessa sighed. "Right, the aura reading. So, when I tried to steal looks..."

"I noticed every time," Amara laughed, then moved her tail closer, letting it caress the side of Tessa's face. "Whatever should we do with you? The would-be demon fucker that's all tied up?" She wanted to straddle Tessa, but remembered that her hips were still pinned down by vines. It was time to get creative.

"I've half a mind to punish you, to show you how bad I can be." Her tail moved to her friend's neck, slowly wrapping around it. Leaning in, she felt Tessa's hot breath tickle her own lips, and held her back as she tried to steal a kiss. "You don't deserve that yet. Now tell me, what's your safeword?"

"F-fuck, I...red. It's red. Stoplight system. Or snapping."

Amara's words, and more likely her tail, were already having a significant effect. She needed to keep pushing, to arouse Tessa even more so she had something to feed on. Leaning back, she pulled her shirt off, revealing a black sports bra that showed off her cleavage surprisingly well. With her shoulders now exposed, she manifested her wings with a shower of embers.

Whew, that took more effort than usual. I'm really running on fumes here.

Amara's tail, still curled around Tessa's neck, repositioned so that its tip lay near her mouth. "Since you're so eager to taste me, open wide."

She pushed her tail into her friend's mouth, grinning as she elicited a soft moan. She'd never acted so dominant before, and she knew she would have to do this again.

She flexed her tail, taunting Tessa with how much control she had over her. Her tail began slowly thrusting in and out, exploring the strange feeling of being in someone else's mouth.

"Do you like being a demon's little plaything?" she asked, pulling out.

Tessa gasped, spit already running down her chin. "Fuck, I like this side of you."

"I thought you liked me more before I turned? Something about being too 'confident and assertive' now? Maybe I should stop..."

"No! I'm sorry, I didn't mean it!" Tessa stammered.

She's practically melting in my hands already, and I've barely touched her. I could get used to this.

Amara grabbed Tessa's face in her hand. "Ask nicely, and I'll keep going."

"Please Amara, I'm so fucking horny, don't stop!" Another strong pulse in Tessa's aura, her smell filling the air.

Unable to hold back any further, Amara leaned forward and kissed the desperate witch. Her lips were soft, almost delicate, and Tessa sighed with relief as she eagerly kissed back. There was a surprising grace to her passion, an elegance that seemed at odds with her typically brash demeanor.

Amara's tail loosened its grip, then left Tessa's neck. Traveling down, it soon found the distracted witch's thigh, wrapping around it slowly. It pushed higher, underneath the blanket of vines, drawing closer to Tessa's covered sex.

She was wearing tight black jeans, and Amara knew she wouldn't be able to get inside them with only her tail. Content to tease the outside of her crotch, she found that her friend's aura was now potent enough to feed on. She connected with it, pulling its energy into herself as she felt her strength return.

Amara shifted closer, kissing her friend harder. She playfully licked Tessa's lip ring, pulling it into her own mouth before biting the lip it belonged to. A loud moan encouraged her to keep going, and she pushed Tessa's head to the side. She drank in the witch's scent, her arousal intoxicating, as she peppered her neck with soft kisses. Her tail continued its teasing, and she allowed herself the guilty pleasure of biting heavily into Tessa's neck.

"UuunghFUCK!"

"Hope you don't mind a few marks!" Amara said, giggling.

"If that's the price for living out this tentacle fucking fantasy, I'll happily pay it back tenfold."

"I take it you're ready for more?" Amara pulled back, sitting up as she cracked her knuckles. Reaching down, she grabbed one of the many vines holding Tessa, then lit her palm on fire once more. After another few severed connections, she had given herself access to Tessa's writhing hips.

Their lips met again, the excitement growing. Amara repositioned slightly to give her tail a better angle, while her hands unbuttoned Tessa's pants. Vines still pinned down her legs, but there was enough room to pull her pants down to her thighs.

Amara broke the kiss, shifting down to appreciate the view she'd just uncovered. Her friend was wearing surprisingly elegant black lace panties, with intricate designs tickling the inside of her thighs. As Amara explored Tessa's exposed skin, sliding behind to massage her ass, she confirmed it was a thong.

"Are these your 'fuck me' panties? That you only wear to parties?"

"I-I wear them outside of parties!"

Amara smirked, knowing that Tessa only wore these when she was hoping to get laid. "You didn't plan all this, did you?"

"Absolutely not! I mean, not the accidental bondage. I...might have been trying to work up the courage to make a move for the last week or two."

"Since when were you the bashful type? You've propositioned me dozens of times since we met!"

"As a joke! It was funny making you blush and squirm! Now you're a literal sex demon, and that's really fucking intimidating."

"Well, as flattering as that is," Amara started, her tail moving higher, "I think you've earned a bit of punishment for your deception." With a quick thrust, she pushed her tail back into Tessa's mouth.

As her tail thrust, she leaned in to explore Tessa's hips. She kissed her exposed thighs, biting them softly to test how sensitive they were. With each bite, her friend twitched slightly, her gasps muffled by the tail filling her mouth.

The smell of arousal finally proved too much, and Amara pulled her friend's panties down as much as the bondage allowed. Tessa's sex was glistening, eager for attention after the last few minutes of teasing. Amara continued kissing closer, and soon her lips found Tessa's clit, sucking it lightly before running her tongue over it. A loud moan filled her ears, and the sexual aura surrounding her grew significantly more potent.

She noticed immediately that Tessa had a very different taste than Nick. She was sweeter, and it was easier to enjoy the taste when it wasn't being pushed deep into her throat. That same taste was reflected in her aura, which Amara eagerly tapped into.

She faintly heard Tessa snap her fingers and pulled her tail out of Tessa's mouth. "Everything okay?" Amara asked.

"Everything's...fuck...it's great, but my mouth is getting tired. That flared end is really something else."

After drying off her tail on her pants, Amara lightly stroked Tessa's cheek again as they talked. "Thanks for telling me! Now, where was I..." She pulled her friend's clit back into her mouth, her tongue massaging the entrance below it.

Tessa moaned again, her voice no longer muffled by Amara's tail. Her legs continued twitching, doing their best to buck against the vines still pinning her down.

The witch's arousal flooded Amara's senses, her strength growing steadily as she pleasured Tessa. Still, the biggest payoff always came from orgasms, and Amara was very aware that Tessa had far more experience than her. "So, I've never done this before. With another woman, I mean. What do you like?"

"Fuck, that's right. I keep forgetting you were a virgin until like, last month."

As the girls talked, Amara slowly pushed a finger into her friend.

"I-I tend to like penetration the most, though everything feels good. Once I'm warmed up I can be a real size queen too. Fuck, keep going..."

Amara continued pushing into Tessa, her finger slick from her friend's warm sex. She was watching carefully, trying to see how her friend's body responded to everything she was doing.

Hearing that Tessa liked penetration, Amara decided to push a second finger into her. The witch groaned even louder, and she felt Tessa's warm embrace squeeze her tight as she pushed deep.

"So, are you just a size queen, or do you also like those toys with all the weird shapes and sizes?"

"Anything and everything! I've got a knotted dildo, one that's supposed to look like a dragon's dick, but I've always wanted to expand my collection." Tessa spoke with an unnatural cadence, her words periodically stopping and starting as Amara continued fucking her. "Nothing like your tail, though. Closest I could probably get is some kind of tentacle toy, but those don't normally flare at the tip."

After pushing a third finger into Tessa, Amara moved higher to steal another kiss. She flourished her tail, letting it tease Tessa's neck again as she spoke. "Well, what I'm hearing is...we have something we need to try?"

Tessa's aura pulsed again, betraying her excitement at the idea. "Unless that's weird! I don't want to make you uncomfortable!"

Amara leaned in for another kiss, cutting Tessa off while she pulled her fingers from her friend's pussy. "Tessa, just shut up and let me fuck you silly, okay?" She licked Tessa's juices off her fingers, the delightful taste pairing with another jolt of strength. She lit her fingers on fire to clean them off, then quickly burned away a few more vines holding down her friend's chest.

Finally able to straddle Tessa, Amara took her place while her tail moved down between her friend's legs. Her tail circled Tessa's entrance, teasing her for a moment before slowly pushing inside. "How's it feel?"

"It's...I can't even describe it. It's just as warm as the rest of you, and the flared tip is like nothing I've—Fffuck! Do that again!"

Amara twitched the end of her tail one more time. She loved watching Tessa try to talk while they fucked, and it was amusing that she could stop her train of thought completely. She slowly thrust her tail in and out, and found she was getting used to the feeling of her tail being inside someone else. It wasn't directly pleasurable, but it was still exciting to know that Tessa had been so heavily fantasizing about her demonic attributes.

Tessa's moans grew louder, and Amara stopped trying to ask her questions. She knew her friend was close, and it was time to figure out what made her cum. She continued fucking her, slowly introducing new tricks and watching how Tessa's aura responded to them.

She continued flicking the end of her tail, exploring the inside of Tessa's pussy to see where her buttons were. Eventually, she started twisting, letting the ridges of her flared tip turn as she pushed in and out.

While this happened, she leaned in and continued to kiss Tessa. Her screams of pleasure were like music, and they only grew louder when Amara began biting her neck again. "I want you to fucking cum for me, Tessa. Cum like the horny little slut you are, cum on my tail!"

She continued to whisper into the witch's ear, demanding her orgasm, and soon the combined pleasure proved to be too much. A final, deafening scream echoed throughout the empty room as Tessa's orgasm started.

Amara kept fucking her, keeping the pace consistent to extend the orgasm as long as she could. A waterfall of sexual energy poured into her, practically overwhelming her senses as her own arousal grew in response. She reached for more vines, the ones holding Tessa's arms, and burned them away. While still nervous about the fire, she found that her control had increased exponentially now that she was properly fed.

Tessa kept cumming, her orgasm lasting longer than Amara had ever seen before. For the first time, she had to try and cut herself off from her friend's aura, as she was worried about taking in too much. She could feel her strength, her inner fire, eager for an outlet as it roared inside of her. It was unwieldy, and Amara knew just what she needed to try and tame it.

Amara slid off Tessa, desperately pulling off her own pants. She watched as her friend's orgasm started to fade, and moved in to straddle her face. "Time to return the favor!"

Tessa's arms, now free, moved to Amara's ass and pulled her close. Her tongue reached for Amara's clit, playing with it softly as she finally got a chance to explore Amara's body. Tessa's hands moved across her ass, her thighs, finally moving up to push her sports bra off. Her hands cupped her tits as they fell free, pinching her nipples eagerly.

It was Amara's turn to gasp and groan, and she reached down to run her fingers through her friend's hair. It was immediately apparent that all of Tessa's practice had paid off; she seemed to know exactly how to get Amara off, despite this being their first time together.

Tessa reached underneath Amara, her fingers pushing inside her pussy as her tongue continued teasing her clit. Amara had grabbed Tessa's hair, and was thrusting her hips in time with the fingers eagerly fucking her. It barely took a minute before Amara was screaming out in pleasure, her body shaking from the orgasm her friend was giving her.

She felt fire shoot from her horns, filling the room with demonic light as her moans echoed off the many steel structures. Her tail wrapped around one of Tessa's legs, squeezing tight as her entire body tensed and released.

It took several minutes for her body to stop twitching, and her own orgasm to finally fade. Once it did, she shifted back slightly so she could look down at Tessa.

"I, uh...wow," Amara said, panting heavily.

"How's that for your first lesbian experience?"

"I think it's unfair of you to set the bar that high, honestly. What about you?"

"Let's just say my curiosity is thoroughly sated." Tessa smirked, licking her lips as her hands moved to pull her pants back up. "Can this not be a one-time thing? Is that greedy to ask?"

Amara shifted once more, leaning to the side until she was no longer straddling Tessa's neck. "Not at all! I'm just glad I didn't embarrass myself."

As she spoke, she quickly burned away the last few vines holding her friend down. She did one last check for any accidental burns, and was thrilled that she couldn't find any.

"Small tangent, but are you okay? Your horns, like, exploded when you came."

"I'm fine! My powers always do weird things when I cum. Like they're recalibrating or something."

"Hey, as long as the fire stays away from me. Speaking of your horns, can I touch them?"

Amara nodded as she finished getting dressed. She leaned her head forward, and felt Tessa's hands run through her hair before finding her horns. She grabbed them tight, giving them a quick tug.

"Hey!" Amara said.

Tessa laughed before returning her hands to herself. "Sorry, just testing a theory. I know what I want to try next time!"

"So, we're back to openly perving on me again?"

"Old habits die hard, I guess." Tessa grabbed the rest of her things, pulling them free of some vines with Amara's help, before the two headed for the exit.

10

SNARES & SULFUR

"The blue or the red?"

"Are you serious? The blue!"

"You sure? I kinda like the pattern on the red."

"You have green eyes, Nick. When she's staring longingly into them, do you want her thinking of Christmas?"

"Alright, fair point. Blue it is."

Nick hung the red shirt back up, then pulled the door closed. He dressed himself in the mirror hanging on the back of his closet, making sure every detail was perfect. The dark blue button-down shirt went over a thin white tee, and he spent several minutes rolling up the sleeves just the way he liked.

"So, when do I get the full story about you and Tessa?" Nick asked.

"What, like a play by play of how we hooked up? Pervert." Amara laughed, sliding to the edge of Nick's bed. She was laying on her stomach, flipping through social media feeds as she helped Nick get ready.

"Please, I could get that from her if I wanted. Do you know how she told me that you two hooked up? She sent me a picture of the bite mark you left on her neck, saying 'Guess who I just did!' I want to know how you feel about it. This is the first time you've slept with someone other than me."

"I dunno; maybe it's my succubus blood, but it all feels kinda normal. I needed to get her out, we're into each other, it just made sense."

"What about your abilities? Do they feel any different?"

"Will you stop fussing about me? I'm a grown woman, and I can take care of myself. Maybe you should focus on, I don't know, your date with one of the hottest girls on campus?"

"Hey, I can be nervous about two things at once!" Nick protested.

"Look, I get it. This last month has been a lot, but I'm not the only person in your life. Today is about you, not me."

Nick sighed. "I know, I know. It's just...it's weird, right? How mundane this all feels? Like demon puberty is just a thing people do, no biggie."

"You want to complain that stuff isn't weirder? Are you trying to tempt fate?"

"I'm just nervous that we're missing something. Something waiting to bite us when our backs are turned."

Amara stood up, moving to Nick and hugging him tight. "Nick, I know you like being prepared, but that can't stop us from living our lives."

A moment passed, the two leaning on each other as Amara's words hung in the air. Nick paused, letting his thoughts wander as his friend tried to calm him down. It struck him that their dynamic had returned to normal—or at least close enough to what had been normal previously. With Amara more in control of her abilities, much of the initial confusion and terror had passed.

"I won't lie, it'll be nice to do something normal for a change," Nick said.

"Something? Or someone?" Amara said, smirking as she jumped back on his bed.

"That's not what I mean!"

"Uh huh, suuure. You think she's secretly a total animal in bed? Maybe she's got, like, a huge pain kink."

"Amara, I'm being serious. I don't want to sleep with her today."

"Well, does your libido know that?" Her eyes flared with recognition. "Your aura doth protest, m'lord."

"Hey, I'm used to sidestepping my body's craven desires. Before you turned all demonic, I was actually in a bit of a dry spell."

"It won't be distracting? Wondering what her body feels like? Picturing her hot breath tickling your neck as she inches further and further down?"

Nick couldn't help but notice that, halfway through speaking, Amara's voice had pitched up. When he turned back to the bed, Vee was staring back at him, a devilish smirk on her face.

"You're not helping, Amara. Quite the opposite, in fact."

"Oh, c'mon, can you honestly say you're not curious?" Amara rolled onto her back, kicking her legs playfully in the air as she traced Vee's curves with her hands. "That you don't want to know what this body feels like?"

Nick swallowed nervously. He was telling the truth about his plans, but Amara's relentless teasing wasn't making that decision easy. He continued watching, aware that this wasn't Vee, but unable to look away from her objectively enticing body. "That's not what I'm saying. What is the goal here? To make this date even more stressful for me?"

"Absolutely not! In fact, I know just the thing to get you ready."

Amara slipped off the bed, onto the floor, and slowly crawled over to Nick. "Let me take the edge off. Your libido will be happy, letting you focus on the date. Plus, it'll get you to stop worrying about me and Tessa."

"An ulterior motive? How devilish of you!" Nick watched his friend move closer, licking her lips in anticipation. "Alright, fine, if you insist. On two conditions."

Amara sat up, now directly in front of Nick, her eyes reluctantly moving away from his bulging pants. "A foolish play, to bargain with a demon such as I! But fine, name your price, and perhaps I will take mercy!" Her hands traced up his legs, grabbing his thighs as her eyes flared with excitement.

"I already showered, and I don't have time for another, so only oral. I'm not going on this date reeking of sex." He paused, waiting for Amara to nod before continuing. "Secondly, you turn back. I'm not doing anything while you look like her."

Without a second thought, Amara shifted back into herself. "Ha! You fell into my trap! That's exactly what I wanted you to say!"

Nick watched as the demon reached for his pants, unbuttoning them quickly before pulling them to the floor. He had already been struggling to keep his libido in check, and her teasing had pushed him over the edge. By the time his cock had been freed, it was already quite hard, and he couldn't help but moan when her eager hands wrapped around it.

Amara leaned in, her eyes bright, and kissed the tip of his cock, slowly teasing it with her tongue as she continued stroking him. She appeared to be taking her time, mimicking what he'd done their last time together.

"Fuck, that feels good..." Nick muttered. His hips were already moving along with her hands, subtly asking for more as she teased him.

After another kiss, Amara pushed forward, her tight lips pulling his cock inside her mouth. She moaned loudly, letting the vibration tickle his shaft as her tongue reached for more. After a deep breath, she began moving back and forth, sucking him off in earnest as his breath quickened.

A burst of embers suddenly appeared, and Nick watched as Amara's horns manifested again. He flinched in surprise, still not used to the fires of her transformation, but quickly saw that he was unharmed.

"Those for me, or for you? Nick asked quietly.

Amara pulled off his cock, stroking him as they talked. "Well, a little of both, but mostly for you." With another kiss, she wrapped her tongue around his shaft and sucked him back into her mouth. As she did, she reached for his hands and moved them to her head, wrapping them around her horns.

"Someone's feeling feisty today. You sure about this?"

A soft pop filled the air as Amara pulled off his cock again. "Oh, I'm positive. Don't you want to take out some aggression? Get back at me for my relentless teasing?"

Nick tested his grip on her horns, and found they were much more comfortable to hold now that they were longer. "The thought might have crossed my mind. You sure you can handle it?"

Without saying anything, Amara dug her nails into Nick's hips. Her intent was obvious; she was trying to push him, and wanted him to stop asking questions. She did this frequently; it was her way of bullying him to be more decisive, though it had never been this sexually charged in the past. Knowing it was foolish to try and argue now, he figured he might as well enjoy one of his favorite fantasies.

Gripping tight, he pulled Amara back so just the tip of his cock rested on her lips. After a moment, he pushed her down, testing to see where her limits were. She gagged softly, and the sound fueled Nick's aggression.

He continued like this for another minute, slowly moving her up and down his shaft, pushing a little bit deeper every time. He let himself move faster, trusting that Amara would speak up if she were uncomfortable, and soon he had successfully lodged his entire cock in her throat. Her eyes were flaring with pride as he held her down, and he took care not to keep her there for long.

"Fuck!" she gasped, spit dripping down her chin, "That's more like it! Put this little demon in her place!"

Responding with only a smirk, he pulled her down again. Her throat opened easier now, and he decided to test how rough he could get. Redoubling his hold on her horns, he began fucking her face in earnest, watching as his entire shaft slid in and out of her mouth.

Nick's breathing grew more erratic as he started losing control, his orgasm only seconds away now. With a final thrust, Amara's head firmly planted against his crotch, he grunted loudly and started cumming.

His cock twitched as it emptied itself, the demon's throat massaging it eagerly. He felt her swallowing every load of cum, the sensation unlike anything he had felt before. Another burst of flame filled the room, and soon her tail was wrapping around his leg, refusing to let him go. He knew from experience she was feeding on him in more ways than one, and was happy to let her decide when she had gotten her fill.

After barely a minute, Amara's tail relaxed. She had stopped swallowing, and Nick had long ago stopped cumming. She pulled back, happily wiping the spit off her chin.

"Mmm, fuck! I didn't know you could get so aggressive!"

"Are you okay? I thought that's what you wanted and I—"

"Oh, shut up and enjoy the afterglow. This might be the last time you get to pound my throat like that!" Amara smirked as she stood up, running to the bathroom.

When she returned, she had a small washcloth. It was already damp with warm water, and she kneeled one last time to clean up Nick's dripping cock. He paused, taken aback at his friend's attentiveness. "Amara, I can clean up after myself; you really don't need to do this."

"I want to! Besides, like you said, you don't want your first date to reek of sex." Amara stood up, happily kissing Nick on the cheek as she finished. She paused briefly, her face betraying a hint of vulnerability. "Look, everything about this is weird, I get it, but I can take care of myself. I just want you to be happy. You and Vee will be really cute together."

"And...you'll be alright if we stop all this?" Nick gestured to his pants as he finished buttoning them.

"I'm in control of my shapeshifting now, remember? I don't have to worry about outing myself when I hook up with someone! Plus, Tessa's a total monster fucker and she'll happily keep me fed. It's time for this little demon to spread her wings."

Once Nick had cleaned himself up again, he checked his phone. After a few quick texts, he pocketed it and took a deep breath. "Well, that was Vee. Looks like it's time to head out!" He opened his arms, silently asking Amara for a hug, and she eagerly jumped in to accept.

"Also, you'd better appreciate how lucky you are. Vee is an absolute sweetheart, and if you hurt her, I'll never let you live it down!"

The two friends laughed as they locked up Nick's apartment. After making plans for lunch the following day, with Amara eager to wait as little as possible for news about the date, they went their separate ways.

By the time Nick caught up with Vee, she was leaning against a brick wall near the entrance to the restaurant. A thickly knit sweater hugged her body, fending off the impending chill of autumn, and a simple pair of jeans framed her legs flatteringly. Her eyes lit up when she saw him, and he swore her smile alone made his heart skip a beat.

"So, this is the place?" Nick asked.

"Yup! I've never been here myself, but I've always wanted to, and I'd say this is a pretty good excuse."

"As long as that's not the only reason I'm here, I'm more than happy to be a guinea pig with you!" Nick laughed as he let Vee lead the way. She held open the door for him, and soon enough they were sitting at their table.

The restaurant was nothing unique, essentially just a bar and grill serving the usual American fare. They placed their order quickly before catching up with each other as they talked about classes. Nick felt it was strange, being on a first date with someone he'd already known for a while, and he wondered if Vee had the same butterflies in her stomach.

"So, full disclosure, but I'm a little nervous about today. I feel like we've been casual friends for a while now, and I'm not entirely sure how to switch over to dating," Nick said.

"I'm glad it's not just me!" Vee relaxed slightly, as if some invisible burden had just been lifted. "Like, obviously I want things to change so we're not just friends anymore, but also I don't want them to change too much, so where's the line?" She took another drink, then sighed. "Honestly, I'm just happy we agreed to take this slow. I don't need more unpredictability in my life right now."

"How are things with you-know-who?" Nick asked, reaching across the table to take Vee's hand.

"They're not good. I'm not going to jail, and he's not pursuing formal charges, likely because he has no proof, but he's still telling everyone that I'm at fault. I'm just trying to keep my head low, and avoid busy spots on campus when I can."

Vee had picked this restaurant partially because it was off campus, and partially because it was a little pricier than other places nearby. Hopefully, the broke college masses would avoid this place in favor of something cheap and close.

Vee turned her arm, lacing her fingers between Nick's as she smiled at him. "But I'm not here to talk about that bullshit. How are you? Amara still dealing with...what was it, family stuff?"

Nick smirked. He'd mentioned a few times that he was helping Amara through some vague problem, and he'd avoided saying anything other than nondescript family drama. "I think she's finally moved past the bulk of it. We had a few weeks of doing nothing but dealing with that, figuring things out, but recently things have mostly gone back to normal."

Well, as normal as they can be when your best friend is a succubus.

"That's good! I'm really happy she's moving past it. It might not be the same, but I understand the stress a family can bring."

"Oh? I don't think you've ever talked much about your family."

"I try to keep quiet about it when I can," Vee mumbled.

"We can talk about something else, if you like. I don't mean to pry."

"No, I want to. Plus, if we're gonna be dating, we should learn to lean on each other, right?"

Nick caught himself blushing, giddy they were actually committing to starting something. "I'm all ears."

"My family is...well, it's complicated. This may sound a little silly, but because of who my parents are, there's a lot of pressure on me to live up to certain expectations. I try my best to stay on top of everything, but it can be exhausting at times."

"I don't think that's silly. Tons of people have parents trying to push things on them. Are they, like, public figures of some kind?"

"I guess you could say that. I'm also not entirely their kid, which can be a bit odd at times."

"You mean you're adopted? Or they used a donor?"

"Something like that. Let's just say I have a pretty confusing family tree."

Nick noticed that they seemed to be veering into uncomfortable territory, as Vee had pulled away from him. "We can leave it there, if you like. Just know that, whatever you're feeling, it's valid."

"Thanks, Nick, I really appreciate it." Vee paused, her nose twitching as she looked around the restaurant. "Do you smell anything weird? Like, kinda foul?"

Nick paused, focusing on the smells around him. "I don't think so? Though, my sense of smell has never been the best."

"It's probably nothing. Forget about it." Vee repositioned in her seat. "I'm glad Amara is doing better. What'd you guys end up doing?"

"Well, it was just a lot of very sudden changes all at once, and eventually she got used to the new normal. It's funny, at times she almost seems like a completely different person now."

"I'm sure being sick in the middle of that wasn't helpful."

"Sick?" Nick paused, briefly forgetting that they'd told everyone she was sick when her wings first appeared. "Right, the week off. Yeah, that wasn't ideal. Still, it gave us more time together, right?"

Vee smiled, pushing some loose hair behind her ear. "That was definitely an upside, though it's a shame she had to lock herself away for a week for you to finally ask me out. I'll be sure to thank her the next time we hang out!"

"I think she'd appreciate that. It's weird how excited she is for us to get together."

"She's really something, isn't she? Sometimes I see you two and wish I had a friend like that—someone who knows absolutely everything, and sticks around anyways."

With a questioning look, Nick tried to figure out if she was joking or not. Within moments, Vee's face broke into a smile, and his laughter joined hers. They quickly pushed away from each other as the food arrived, and the conversation veered into other topics.

They talked about classes, complaining about teachers and unfair deadlines. They talked about what might happen after college, what they hoped to do once they had their degrees and were out in the world. Nick found himself going on small tangents about his love of architecture, sharing his thoughts on various structures around campus.

Vee seemed quite interested in hearing him talk, though he couldn't help but grow self-conscious about taking up too much of the conversation. He periodically tried to ask her similar questions, about what she saw for her future, hoping to learn more about her.

The first time he tried, she only mumbled something vaguely about 'the family business'. Each time after that, she would happily share a quick thought or two, but always redirected the conversation back to him. Once he noticed this happening, he did his best to ask questions that she seemed more interested in answering.

He also noticed that, every few minutes, her nose would twitch and she would quickly look around the restaurant again. Though she never mentioned the smell again, it's obvious it was on her mind.

They had just about finished their meal when a small group of students approached the table. The one in front, a shorter girl with medium-length brown hair, spoke up first.

"Wow, Vee, it's so crazy running into you here!"

"Yeah, Tania, what are the odds?" Vee shifted uncomfortably as she spoke, her voice quiet.

"So, this place serves arsonists now? I don't know if I feel safe eating here anymore."

The group of students around her snickered.

Nick pushed his chair back, standing to face the group. "Hey, how about you leave us alone? It's hardly our fault Derek got drunk and decided to play with matches."

"Oh, we were just leaving. C'mon, girls, let's eat somewhere a little safer tonight!"

Nick stood tall, watching Tania and her friends leave. Once they were out the door, he sighed heavily, then turned back to Vee. She was in the middle of standing up, her purse already hanging across her body.

"Vee, wait, they're not gonna bother us anymore."

"No, I knew this was a mistake." Her voice was shaking, a precarious mixture of rage and despair.

"You don't mean me, do you?" Nick asked quietly.

"No, not that." Vee took a deep breath, seemingly pulling her nerves together. "Never you. I just meant...all this. Trying to have a normal life, thinking I could avoid...it's nothing. I'm getting out of here. Do yourself a favor: You'll have an easier time if we don't do this."

Vee pushed past him, her strength catching him off guard. He chased after her, tossing a credit card at a waiter, and caught up about half a block away.

"Vee, wait!" he said.

She paused, still facing forward.

"I'm not here because it's easy, or convenient, or anything like that. I'm here because I like you, I want to be a part of your life. Everyone has baggage. That's why we lean on each other, right?"

Vee turned quickly, burying her head in Nick's shoulder. She was almost as tall as him, though her defeated posture made it easy to wrap his arms around her. He felt her shoulders twitch, her body fighting to hold back tears.

"There's so much I want to tell everyone, to tell *you*. Things are just so complicated, and I feel so alone."

Nick paused, trying to find the right words. "Look, I get not wanting to share everything. Believe me, I've seen some crazy shit this year, but I can still be a part of your life. I can make this easier for you."

Vee shifted, turning to look at Nick. They locked eyes, their faces now unexpectedly close, and she pushed forward.

When their lips met, a thousand thoughts raced through Nick's head. The intimacy was beautiful, it was everything he'd imagined, but he could feel the weight she carried. Her sweater was soft, easy to hold tight, to pull her in as they kissed. Her perfume washed over him, filling his senses briefly before she pulled back.

Her nose twitched.

She froze, her eyes wide with shock as she stared at Nick. "No..."

"What's wrong?" Nick asked, trying to hold Vee tight.

She pushed harder, brushing his arms off as she stumbled backward. A tear finally fell. "You...you too?"

"Vee, what do you—"

"Stay away! Leave me alone!" Vee turned again, breaking out into a sprint.

For a split second, Nick thought about following, but he knew it wouldn't do any good.

After parting ways with Nick, Amara had met up with Chloé and Tessa for dinner. The girls idly gossiped about the date, wondering what their friends might be up to, and eventually switched to more mundane topics. Chloé took up most of the conversation, eagerly sharing updates on her school project, and Amara was happy that she could contribute simply by listening.

Her thoughts lingered on Nick, on his date with Vee. She honestly hoped it was going well, but knew that things could easily change moving forward. Without Nick, she'd need to find new ways to keep her demonic needs sated.

After her week without sex, when Nick had been visiting family, she'd been paying close attention to her libido. In hindsight, the discovery that sex was a literal need wasn't all that surprising, but at the time it had caught her off guard. On several occasions, she'd experimented with avoiding sex to test how it affected her, and had learned several important things. Depending on how much she fed, she was able to go about two days without sex before the side effects kicked in. The most obvious effect was, unsurprisingly, being incredibly horny, but it was hardly the most annoying.

Without sex, her body started shutting down. Food gradually lost its flavor and wasn't as filling, while sleep quickly lost its restorative effects, if she could even manage to fall asleep. Her ability to read sexual auras intensified, becoming something that she couldn't turn off, and she found it increasingly difficult to ignore the urge to feed.

She never went long enough to test the more severe effects, but worried that her self-control might vanish if her needs went unattended for too long.

I don't think I can rely entirely on Tessa, she's got other partners. I've never bothered looking for other people to hook up with, since I would have to explain my tail, but now I've got my shapeshifting under control! I suppose I could start—

"—isn't that right, Amara?"

Amara shook back to her senses, looking around to see Chloé and Tessa staring at her. "Sorry, what was that last bit? I spaced for a second."

"I was telling Chloé that you and I were heading to the library after this, right?" Tessa said, obviously hinting at the correct answer.

"Oh, y-yeah," Amara mumbled, trying to pull herself together. "I've got some class stuff I need to catch up on, and after my week off, I'm trying to avoid staying home."

"Well, you two have fun with that! I've got plans, unfortunately, otherwise I'd love to join you." Chloé smiled, grabbing her stuff and getting ready to leave. "Tessa at the library, who would've thought..."

Amara stifled a laugh as Tessa glared at her, joining Chloé in picking up their things. After a few minutes, the girls said their goodbyes and parted ways.

"So, the library? When did this happen?" Amara asked.

"Well, for one, there might be a circle there. But even if there isn't, I want to see if I can find the schematics for some of the original buildings."

"Dang, that's a good idea. Looking for the hidden rooms?"

"That's the plan, but honestly I doubt I'll find anything. This feels like something they wouldn't want records of."

"Who do we think 'they' are? The creators of the circles?"

"Eh, not sure I care. I want to know why they exist, not who made them."

By the time the girls made it to the library, the crowds had thinned out slightly. Most students preferred spending time there between classes, and Tessa had hoped that they might have the basement archives to themselves now that it was later in the evening.

They slowly walked through the library, doing their best to stay inconspicuous, when Amara noticed a group of three guys at a table in the corner of the main floor. Through their auras, she could tell they were all mildly sexually frustrated, but that wasn't her main concern. One of them, the one with short, brown, lightly tousled hair, was looking straight at her with wide eyes.

It's that Brandon idiot from before! Fucker!

Amara snarled at him, flaring her eyes for a moment, and he nervously buried himself back in whatever book he was reading. Amara hated the thought that such a creep was still roaming around campus, but as long as he was too scared to approach her, she figured it wasn't a big deal.

As they walked down the main stairs to the basement, Amara noticed that her friend seemed nervous, and was looking behind them every few seconds.

"Hey, Tess, you alright? You're acting like we're being followed."

"I mean, I hope we aren't, but I'm worried. We just found proof that people are fucking with the circles, and in case you forgot, we made a bit of a mess under the cafeteria. Whoever these people are, they might know we're onto them."

"That's why you've got me, right?" Amara flashed a cocky grin, manifesting her tail as she tried to strike an intimidating pose. "Your own personal demon bodyguard!"

Tessa couldn't stop herself from laughing. "True, I feel a lot better with you here. Though, no offense, but have you ever actually been in a fight?"

"Well, no, but I did a bunch of sparring practice with Nick. I'm also hoping that, between my fire and my appearance, I can just scare people away before anything actually starts."

They made sure that the archives were empty before entering, Amara eager to keep her horns and tail out. The two of them decided to start on opposite sides of the room then work toward each other, and had no illusions that this was going to be a fun experience.

The archives weren't the most organized area in the library, and often served as a place to put materials that the staff couldn't find space for. For every well-labeled filing cabinet filled with helpful information, there were at least two boxes stuffed with random paperwork. Some were filled with receipts, some with old promotional materials, and everything seemed to be at least a few dozen years old.

Amara was almost impressed at how old everything smelled as she searched. She found a few drawers of old newspapers, several collections of out-of-date textbooks, even a few geological surveys. That last item seemed promising, given everything Tessa had told her about magical leylines, and she made a mental note to try to look through them some time.

"I think I've got something!" Tessa called out.

Amara, eager for something to break the monotony, rushed over to her friend, who was moving stacks of paper out of the drawer.

"It looks like this whole drawer is old schematics, but I'm not sure how they're organized. How about you take the back half, I'll take the front, and we'll start by looking for buildings where we've already confirmed there are circles."

"Can do, boss!" Amara was thrilled to have the scope of their work narrowed, and quickly got to work.

This collection ended up being exactly what they were looking for. The drawer wasn't well organized, which was expected, but it seemed to contain a very thorough history of various building schematics for their campus. Frustratingly, the files seemed to have been organized differently at different times in the library's history: Some files contained all schematics from a certain year, while others contained all the schematics for one specific building.

As they pored over all the yellowed papers, they soon came to one concerning conclusion: None of the files had the original schematics. They had found renovations, newer buildings, additions, but never the original plans for the original campus.

"Ugh, this has to be intentional, right?" Tessa groaned, tossing her head back.

"But intentional on whose part? The founders of the university? Or the people who are fucking with the circles?" Amara wondered.

"There's no way to know." The witch groaned, throwing some papers to the ground in defeat. "We're back to square one. This is bullshit!"

"Hey, we're way past square one. We've already found multiple circles, you're learning how they work, and we've confirmed that someone is trying to weaken them. You did that almost entirely on your own!" Amara moved closer, wrapping her tail around Tessa and pulling her in for a hug.

"Y'know, it's hard to throw a pity party when you're being this compassionate and optimistic." Tessa leaned into Amara's shoulder, sighing heavily. "But yeah, I guess you're right..."

"Look, we've already been here for a while. How about we call it a night?"

"What about the circle? We haven't even tried looking yet."

"If there's one down here, it's not going anywhere. You've pulled too many all-nighters looking for them, and you need to get some sleep. C'mon, up!"

Amara started putting all the papers back, and Tessa reluctantly joined in. They finished relatively quickly, and it only took a few more minutes to clean up the other messes they'd made in searching the archives. The witch was still worried about being followed, and she was adamant they leave as little evidence as they could.

Amara hid her tail and horns before leaving the archives, then paused as they entered the hallway. "Hey, let's use the back staircase. If there's actually someone following us, it'll be less obvious if we leave that way."

"There's another staircase down here?" Tessa asked.

"Yup! Originally it was the only one, but the renovation added the bigger staircase by the front entrance. I have a friend who used to work here; she said the back stairs are mostly just for troublemakers now." Amara couldn't help smirking as she spoke, remembering the last time she'd shown this to someone.

"Are you hiding something from me? Are you a troublemaker?" Tessa nudged her ribs, eager for gossip.

"I...may have brought Nick here once."

"Amara! You're such a slut!"

The girls laughed as they pushed into the old, decrepit staircase. Amara summoned a ball of flame so they could see, and they started climbing. "It was just the one time, right after we decided I was likely a succubus. I pulled him back here and—"

The instant Amara stepped onto the middle landing, a burst of light exploded from the ground. It was impossibly bright, blinding her even when she closed her eyes. The light lingered, bending in on itself before latching onto Amara. She screamed, falling to the floor as pain shocked her body, her limbs seizing uncontrollably. She felt Tessa's hands grab her, preventing her from falling down the stairs, but they did nothing to stop the pain.

The light vanished quickly, leaving Amara writhing in darkness while Tessa scrambled to get her phone out.

"Amara! Say something!" the witch cried.

Amara couldn't form words, as her body was too preoccupied with its efforts to keep breathing. Every few seconds her muscles twitched of their own accord, the strange energy running circuits through her body.

"Fuckfuckfuck this is bad, this is really bad!" Tessa cried.

"What happened?" Amara whispered, managing to sit up slightly as the seizing stopped.

"Things just got a whole lot worse. I'm so sorry, we need to—"

"Cut the bullshit and fucking tell me!" Amara hissed. Another spasm hit, and she grabbed at Tessa to steady herself. Her fingers tensed, digging into her friend's leg as the magic attacked her. After another few seconds, the effects calmed down enough for Amara to come back to her senses.

She realized that Tessa was grabbing her wrist, trying and failing to pull it away. She was also staring at Amara, eyes wide with a mixture of shock and fear. "Fuck, Amara, let go!"

"I-I...the magic, it—" She couldn't finish her sentence. When she pulled her hand off Tessa's pants, she saw traces of blood on her nails. There were several small gouges in her friend's pants, exactly where her fingers had been. "Tessa! I'm so sorry, I don't know what came over me!"

Tessa slid away from Amara, wincing in pain as she raised her leg to inspect it. Amara caught another glimpse of the injury, and saw just how deep her nails had punctured. Blood pooled on Tessa's leg, soaking into her jeans, and Amara tried to reach up to help. Tessa, however, twitched with fear as Amara moved closer.

"Amara, what was that?!" Tessa asked nervously.

Seeing her fear, Amara moved to the other side of the landing. "I'm sorry, I'm sorry!" Amara repeated.

A minute passed in silence while Amara watched Tessa tend to her injury. Eventually, the witch sighed and looked up at Amara. "It's okay, Amara. I don't think this is anything serious, you just... you scared me, is all. Are you still you?"

They locked eyes, Amara fighting the urge to reach for Tessa for comfort. "Still me. Promise."

The witch sighed heavily, tension leaving her body. "It might not be your fault. This trap, I'm pretty sure it was Enochian. It's the language of the angels."

"Seriously? Please tell me that doesn't mean what I think it means."

"It might not. I honestly don't even know if angels roam the earth anymore. Most mortals can't read, yet alone understand Enochian, but it's not unheard of. Every once in a while, supposedly, someone has enough holy juice in them to be able to speak it."

"So, what did it do to me? I didn't mean to hurt you, I swear. I don't even know what happened!"

"It was dark, so I couldn't see exactly, but it felt like your nails grew? Just for a second, long enough to puncture my jeans. You also, like, growled at me. It's hard to describe."

Another shock, smaller this time, jolted Amara. "But you're...fuck...you're okay?"

"I'll be alright. Promise. I'll bet this is just the holy magic fucking with your body."

Amara crawled to a corner, leaning against a wall. She gestured to the landing around her before speaking again. "What do you think this was? They trying to kill me?"

"I wish I could say, but Enochian is a huge mystery." Tessa moved closer, pulling Amara into a hug before touching their foreheads together. They rested like that for a few minutes, Amara's breathing slowly returning to normal. "You're alive, though, so we avoided the worst."

Amara pulled out her phone, texting Nick an update while assuring him that she was safe. Cautiously leaning forward, she tried moving her body around to see if anything was still hurting.

"How's everything feeling?" Tessa asked.

"Surprisingly okay, which is a little concerning." As she tested various muscles, she remembered that she was still hiding her demonic aspects. "I'm gonna pull out my demon bits—back up a little?"

The witch nodded, then moved to sit higher on the stairs. Amara moved further away from the wall, pulling her shirt off to prevent her wings from destroying it. After a deep, nervous breath, she tried to manifest her true form.

She immediately cried out in pain as another shock surged through her. Bolts of white energy flashed across her body, her muscles seizing once more as she doubled over from the shock. "Fucking...wow, that hurts."

Tessa was immediately beside her, grabbing her shoulders to steady her. "I hate to say it, but I think I know what's happening here."

Still breathing heavily, Amara met her friend's gaze and nodded in agreement. She made sure to keep her hands to herself. "Are you thinking that all my demonic traits are being blocked? Cuz that's what it feels like."

The witch nodded, her face full of concern. "I wouldn't be surprised if the trap had a couple different effects. Obviously there's the magic blocking your demonic nature, but that initial blast of light seemed pretty intense. I wonder if it would have been able to banish a lesser demon altogether."

"I'm sorry, did you say *banish*?"

"Like, back to Hell. That's normally what these religious fuckers want. Best-case scenario, whoever's on campus isn't strong enough to do that. I'll bet you're magnitudes more powerful than, like, a random imp or whatever."

Amara winced, another trace of holy energy sparking off her body. "That's a terrifying thought."

"Can you stand? We need to get you home."

Tessa pulled Amara up to her knees, then helped put her shirt back on. Although she was still fairly weak, walking felt comfortable, as long as she was leaning on Tessa.

Every few minutes, another jolt of pain shot through her. Tessa confirmed that, if someone were looking closely, they would definitely be able to see the strange flickers of light when it happened.

The walk home felt impossibly long, Amara's paranoia reminding her of when her tail first appeared. She was scared of everyone they passed, nervous they might see the magic sparking, unsure who might be hunting her.

Her thoughts drifted back to the last time she'd left the library with Nick.

"I keep worrying about other students finding out, but maybe we should be worried about bigger things?"

Sometimes she hated being right.

II
EXPOSED

Amara stumbled through her front door, her body weak from the trek home. Even with Tessa helping her walk, she could feel the lingering radiant energy sapping her strength. Its sting came in waves, and a particularly nasty shock ran through her system just as she collapsed on the couch. She gestured to her front door, silently asking Tessa to close it.

"Another one?" the witch asked.

Amara nodded silently, clutching her sides as she waited for this spasm to fade. She briefly lost track of time, and when the episode passed, Tessa was sitting next to her on the couch. She happily reached for the glass of water that had appeared nearby.

"Don't suppose you know how long this'll last?" she asked, already knowing the answer.

"Not even a little. I know more about nuclear physics than I do about Enochian. Plus, y'know, never met a demon before."

Amara sighed. "Yeah, yeah, I know: stupid angel bullshit. What have I even done? Defend myself against Derek? What gives them the right to hunt me down like some kind of animal?"

"Look, I hate to say this, but that's probably all you are to them."

Another few seconds passed as Amara shifted on the couch, sitting up completely. "I still don't know how they found me. Have they been after me my whole life? Or just since I started turning?"

Tessa turned to face her, taking her hands and pulling her close. "I know this is frustrating, but there's no way to know. What if we focus on something else?

Maybe we can try to find a way to fight whatever's going on right now? For all we know, it might not go away unless we do something.

"I'm open to ideas," Amara grumbled. "This sucks."

"Well, fighting back is normally easier if you're stronger, right? Do you think you can still...feed?" Tessa's voice grew quiet, almost as if she were embarrassed to ask.

"Is that a serious question? Or is someone feeling a little frisky?" Amara teased.

"I mean it! You get stronger by fucking—it's not a weird question!"

Amara laughed, still surprised at how flustered Tessa could get about sex when she wasn't the one in control. "No, it's a good question, and a good idea. Presumably, whoever's hunting me isn't going to stop, so I should learn how to recover from this."

Tessa blushed. "So, how should we—"

Without waiting for Tessa to finish, Amara leaned in and kissed her friend. They stayed like that for a moment, enjoying the intimacy, before she pulled back and began speaking again. "My room?"

The witch nodded eagerly.

Amara had butterflies in her stomach as she walked Tessa back to her room. She had no idea why she was nervous, as they'd already fucked before, but something about this felt delightfully mundane. There were no magic circles, no vines, and she didn't even have her demon bits. It would just be two girls, alone in a bedroom, having a good time.

"So, my feeding: I'm drawing from your arousal, not mine, which means the more turned on you are, the better. The more open you are about what you like, and what you want, the easier this will be. I know you really like my demon bits, but sadly those are out of the picture."

"Amara," Tessa started, "the horns, the tail—they're not the only reason I'm into you. Like I said last time, I thought you were crazy hot even before you turned."

Amara found herself blushing. "Well, all I'm saying is, what do you want to do?"

"I think...last time I got a lot of attention. I want to explore you and see what makes you tick. Have you got any toys?"

Amara nodded, reaching under her bed for her toy box. As she opened it, showing everything to Tessa, she reminisced about how different her sex life used to be. For years, her body had known nothing but the touch of these toys, and now they were practically useless in the face of her demonic libido. It also occurred to her that she'd stopped watching porn. She had all these memories of her solo sex life, yet they seemed so foreign now, as if they belonged to someone else.

"Oooh, you've got plugs? I didn't know you were into butt stuff!"

"I never used those, actually. Bought them on a whim, but trying them on my own felt...I dunno, not worth it?"

"Want to give it a shot?"

Amara could see the excitement in Tessa's eyes, but also noticed the vibrant aura growing around her. "Let's do it! I can see your aura, so let's hope that's a good sign."

With the logistics out of the way, Tessa eagerly took the lead this time. She leaned in, kissing Amara slowly before pushing her onto her back. The witch straddled her, moaning softly as their bodies pushed against each other. Their lips met eagerly, over and over, while their hands explored each other's bodies.

Tessa brushed a hand against Amara's cheek, softly holding her before turning her head to the side. She leaned in, kissing her neck, biting the sensitive skin. Amara gasped, quietly moaning in pleasure as she felt Tessa smirking in satisfaction.

"Can you feed yet? Just a tiny bit; maybe that won't trip the magic."

"I-I can try. You saying you're sufficiently horny?" Amara teased. She moved her hands to her own legs, worried about what happened back in the staircase, and cautiously reached for the witch's aura. Tessa seemed to be right; by playing it safe, the holy magic left her alone. She could still sense its presence, and felt like she was navigating around an electric fence, but she was able to form a connection.

The aura, and its energy, tasted delicious, but it came slowly. "Mmmm, that seems to be working," Amara said. "You can't feel anything, can you?"

Tessa shook her head. "Nothing. For all I know, you could be making it up to get laid." She pushed her hands under Amara's shirt, grabbing her waist and pulling her close as they repositioned their legs.

"Oh, woe is me! I'm afflicted with a terrible weakness! If only I had a hot young nurse to tend to my every need!"

"That how you want to play this?" Tessa asked, smirking. She moved down, peppering Amara's neck with kisses before pulling her shirt off entirely. "I'm afraid I left my nurse costume at home; got any other fantasies?"

"Wait, do you actually have—Fuck!" Amara couldn't finish her question as Tessa's teeth had found her midriff. She bit hard, just underneath her bra, making the demon shriek in surprise. After the initial shock, Tessa lightened up, teasing and kissing her friend's stomach before reaching up to undo her bra.

Amara continued feeding, and while the process was frustratingly slow, she appreciated the extra energy. She noticed that the magic shocks had stopped, and hoped that their plan was working.

Tessa's mouth moved further down, her lips teasing Amara's stomach, then her hips. She would still bite, occasionally, but she always kept it tame. Amara loved the attention, the teasing, and had to fight to keep her feeding under control. Tessa began undoing her pants, and soon after Amara saw the familiar glow of the witch's tattoos. She felt another pull, and smirked as her jeans slowly pulled themselves off her body.

"That's a neat trick; I'll bet your partners love that," Amara purred.

"They, uh, don't know I'm a witch."

"What! No way!"

"No one does, Amara. Well, no one used to. You and Nick were the first."

With Amara's pants now on the floor, Tessa began tracing the inside of her legs.

"Well, either way, I'm glad you told me."

"It's nice to be open about it. More than I would have guessed." Tessa bit the inside of Amara's exposed thigh, causing her to jump in surprise.

"Be careful, I'm really sensitive there!" Amara yelped, her legs twitching as the witch continued biting her. She squirmed, giggling as Tessa held her down, unable to deny that the torture felt good.

Eventually, Tessa took mercy on Amara and stopped her assault. She hooked her fingers into Amara's panties, pulling them down before tossing them aside.

Now fully on display, Amara reached down to play with Tessa's hair, then pulled her closer so they could kiss again.

Their legs intertwined, both girls slowly grinding against each other as they kissed. Amara's hands explored her friend's body, eagerly pulling off her shirt, then her bra, so they wouldn't have anything between them. Finally, with Tessa topless, she leaned in to kiss her breasts, biting her nipples to return the earlier teasing. The witch moaned, her body twitching, her hands grabbing Amara's hair to keep her from pulling away.

After a minute, Tessa released her hold, pushing Amara back to the bed. "Alright, I'm done waiting, I want to fuck you!" She grabbed for the box of toys, pulling out two in particular, along with some lube. The first was a small bullet vibrator, the second was the smallest plug of the set.

"What do I need to know?" Amara asked, readjusting the pillow under her head.

"Just keep breathing and relax." Tessa squeezed some lube onto the small plug, then moved it into position.

"Oh! That's cold!"

Tessa laughed. "Lube tends to do that. Here, use this vibrator; it'll make it easier to adjust to having something in your ass for the first time."

Amara nodded, taking the bullet and turning it on. She held it against her clit, letting out a moan as the vibrations began working their magic. As she settled in, she felt Tessa pushing the toy, its slender tip working into her ass. The smooth plastic felt odd, but not entirely unwelcome, and Amara did her best to keep breathing.

"How's it feel?" Tessa asked, slowly pushing the small tip in and out.

"It's odd. Not really pleasurable, but I don't dislike it. You were right about the vibe; much more enjoyable this way."

Tessa moved a hand toward Amara's chest, massaging her breasts and pinching her nipples as she pushed the toy further in. Amara gasped, still adjusting to something being in her ass. The extra attention, from the vibe, from the pinching, did wonders. Were the only stimulation the anal play, she doubted she would be won over by it.

As the toy pushed in, bit by bit, Amara found herself growing used to the strange sensation. It still wasn't directly pleasurable, but the stretching made a fascinating addition to the vibes coursing through her clit. Once enough of the toy was inside, Tessa began properly fucking her with it, moving it back and forth slowly. The conical shape meant that each thrust pushed her ass open a little further. She wondered what anal would feel like with a real cock, knowing that most weren't shaped like cones, and decided it would be a very different experience.

"The toy is almost all the way in. How are you feeling?" Tessa asked.

"I think the stretching is actually kinda nice. I have a bigger one, right? That's the same shape?"

"You do! Want to step it up?"

Amara nodded, and while her eyes were still closed, focused on the vibrations and the toy, she could sense another pulse in her friend's aura. "I swear you're enjoying this as much as I am."

"I'm fucking a smoking hot chick in the ass. This is a dream come true!" Tessa pulled the first toy out, set it on the nearby towel, and grabbed the bigger one. Soon it was covered in lube, and taking its place at Amara's tight entrance. "Aura reading still kinda freaks me out, though."

"Oh, yeah? Why's—oh fuck, that's interesting." Amara's thoughts were cut off by the bigger toy pushing into her. Even with Tessa taking it slow, the stretching was much more intense.

"Still comfy?"

"Yeah, it's just...new. Still getting used to it."

"I'll just tease you with the tip for a bit, let you get used to it. You tell me when you want more."

Amara nodded, repositioning the bullet vibe slightly. "So, aura reading is freaky? Why's that?"

"It's like you're reading my mind. You're seeing parts of me that no one has ever seen before. I know it's strictly a sexual thing, but it's still odd being so...visible."

Amara reached for Tessa, gently holding the side of her face. "Want me to talk about it less? I'd hate to make you uncomfortable."

Tessa laughed. "No, you're fine. Just getting used to my bestie being a sex demon, as you do. Ready for more?"

"Give it to me!"

The witch pushed deeper, the plug stretching Amara open as she gasped.

"Ohhh, fuck, that's big. Keep it there for a sec," Amara whispered.

She felt Tessa hold the plug at its current depth, slightly rocking it back and forth to help her adjust. Amara turned up the intensity on the bullet, moaning loudly, her hips rocking with Tessa's movements. The plug still felt odd, but she was starting to see why people liked anal play. The stretching, the fullness, paired amazingly well with the bullet, and she could feel hints of an orgasm approaching.

"Someone's enjoying herself," Tessa smirked. "Have we got an aspiring little anal slut here?"

"Didn't...fuck...take you for a dirty talker, Tess," Amara groaned, her body twitching. The vibrations were coursing through her body, desperately reaching for an orgasm, and she was eager to surrender it. Tessa's hand returned to her breasts, pinching her nipples hard before moving further down. The witch grabbed her waist, holding her tight before starting to properly fuck her with the toy.

Amara gasped louder, feeling the toy work in and out of her tight asshole. She thrust harder, bucking her hips to try to take more of the plug into her ass. She maxed out the intensity of the bullet vibe, eager for her first anal orgasm. Tessa's nails dug in, and Amara finally lost control.

She screamed out, body convulsing with pleasure. Her legs grabbed Tessa, pulling her close as wave after wave of orgasmic bliss cascaded through her. She felt the witch's hands grab her waist tight before the feeling of teeth on her nipples returned.

Amara grabbed Tessa's hair, holding her down as she continued biting. The added sensation was incredible, pushing her orgasm to new heights as it lasted long past anything she'd ever felt before. She held tight, Tessa's hands moving to her breasts and squeezing them while her tongue explored her nipples.

They stayed locked in that position for minutes, Amara squirming and moaning, before her orgasm finally faded, her body completely spent from the process.

"Fucking...wow...Tessa, that was incredible!" she whispered between labored breaths.

The witch looked up at her, releasing her grip on Amara's waist. "Oh, you're definitely an anal slut now."

"If that's what an anal orgasm feels like, then you're absolutely right." Amara pushed herself up on her elbows, running her hands through Tessa's hair. "Wait, how are you holding me? Wasn't one hand holding the toy?"

"Oh, you bottomed out a while ago. You were fucking back so eagerly that it slipped in."

Surprised, Amara moved her hand between her legs. Sure enough, the butt plug was completely inside of her. "That's crazy! No wonder I came so hard."

Tessa crawled closer, eagerly kissing her again. Lying down on Amara's chest, the witch wrapped her hands around her torso and began relaxing. Their breathing slowed, eventually synching as they reveled in a post-orgasmic stupor.

"Wait!" Amara said, "You didn't cum yet!"

"Oh, believe me, I've had more than enough fun." Tessa reached up, playing with Amara's hair while they talked. "Plus, I don't want to risk you feeding too much and triggering more holy magic spasms. How's that feeling, by the way?"

"I mean, I didn't have any attacks while we were fucking, but otherwise it's hard to say." She sighed, matching Tessa's gaze. "I should probably check, but that requires leaving bed."

"Just get it over with! I'm not going anywhere." Tessa pulled back, and Amara was now free to sit up. Before sliding off the bed, she cautiously pulled the butt plug out, working it slowly to avoid any painful surprises. When it finally popped out, she tossed it on a nearby towel, and moved to the middle of the room.

Standing tall, she stretched her arms above her head, her back cracking as she did. Closing her eyes, Amara connected with her inner fire, which was much stronger after her recent feeding. She tried to pull it forward, ever so slightly, trying to manifest a tiny flame in her palm.

The holy magic fought back, restraining her magic and zapping her for her efforts. This time, however, the shock felt manageable, perhaps even surmountable. She could feel her own fire straining against the Enochian magic, eager to break free, and she felt confident enough to try. With a deep breath, she pulled more fire out, igniting her hands further. The shocks continued, and she winced, but knew she could keep pushing.

"Tessa, back up," Amara said, her body tense. After making sure her friend had moved away, she summoned all her energy and tried to manifest her demonic aspects. The magic fought back, its vicious sting desperate to punish her, but she knew she could beat it.

Her body warmed rapidly. While she couldn't feel the heat directly, her awareness of her abilities told her that heat was pouring out of her body. Her fire grew, eager to break free, and she directed it to her wings, her horns, her tail. Holy magic attacked her, running circuits through her body as it fought her. Finally, when her flames were at their hottest, she found the breaking point of the Enochian restraints.

With one final push, she felt her true form return, her entire body cloaked in flames. Her eyes shot open, watching as the blinding light of the holy magic left her body, fading into nothing while she stood triumphant in its wake.

"Ha! I'm back!" Amara yelled. She flexed her tail, pulling it close to examine it, before doing the same with her wings. Nothing seemed out of place, and she did one final spin before turning to face Tessa again. "How do I look?" she asked, seductively stepping closer to her friend.

"Fuck, Amara, that was...really fucking hot. In every sense." Tessa's naked body was glistening, drenched with sweat that definitely hadn't come from the fucking.

"Shit, are you okay? I may have lost track of how much heat I was pumping out."

"I'm fine! Just a little surprised, I guess. It was practically a sauna for a minute. I'm glad nothing caught on fire. Although..." Tessa crawled to the edge of the bed, "it looks like the carpet and the ceiling got a little singed."

Amara groaned as she saw what Tessa meant. A vague circle of discoloration was burned into the carpet, and the paint on the ceiling seemed to have warped slightly. When she moved, she also saw two distinct shapes where her feet had been during the transformation. "Ugh, this poor landlord." She paused briefly. "Think insurance will cover this as an Act of God?"

It was Tessa's turn to groan as she fell back on the bed. "Amara, that was terrible. You're above that."

"I'm a demon! I'm above nothing!" She wrapped her tail around Tessa's ankle, pulling her close before jumping on the bed with her.

"No! Let me go, foul beast!" Tessa screamed. The girls wrestled for a moment before their laughter overtook them. When Amara finally collapsed next to her friend, their lips met once more before Tessa spoke again. "So, at the risk of killing the mood, I desperately need a shower."

"You should definitely do that before I do. I'm pretty sure I drain the entire building's hot water supply every time I shower." Amara finally sat up, grabbing a spare towel for Tessa.

"It's a shame you can't just, like, heat your own water," Tessa said.

"Right? Like, I love that I can summon fire but damn, I wish it were more useful."

As Tessa showered, Amara happily played with her tail as she examined her body in her full-length mirror. At first she was looking for any possible damage, but soon her gaze turned from one of caution to admiration. She was happy to have her body back, to an extent that surprised her. She eagerly traced her eyes over her tail, her horns, and her wings, even though she couldn't fully extend them. A sense of pride overtook her, and she even made a few poses in the mirror before laying back down.

When Tessa finally left the shower, she found Amara lying down, lazily drawing shapes in the air with her flames. They switched places, and soon Amara was back to cursing her building's water heater.

Vee quickly tapped the door with her knuckles, then went back to nervously fiddling with the straps on her backpack. She looked up and down the hall, scared she might find someone watching her, and cursed herself under her breath. She had thought about placing tracking runes around the dorms, but in the excitement for her date, she hadn't gotten around to it yet.

Maybe I deserve this. I let my focus slip, I tried to give myself a sliver of a normal life, and now Nick is wrapped up in all this.

When Amara finally opened the door, Vee jumped forward, wrapping her arms tight around her friend. "I didn't know where else to go," she mumbled into her friend's shirt.

Amara wrapped an arm around Vee, closing the door quickly. "Hey, is everything alright? I heard the date was...not the best time."

What do I say? Do I tell her about Nick, that he might be lost?

No.

I need to stay focused; I can't allow myself to get distracted. There's so much more at stake than one person.

Vee took a deep breath, then pulled away from the hug. "It wasn't that bad, I just...I had to leave."

Amara took her hands, holding them tight as she walked them both to the couch. Vee noticed how warm Amara was, how nice it felt.

"I know about the assholes at dinner, but is there something else? Something other than this mess with Derek?"

Vee set her backpack down, then joined Amara on the couch. "I guess you could say that. I've got a lot going on right now—more than you know."

"Well, I'm not going anywhere. Talk to me, Vee."

"I wish I could, Amara. I really do, but I can't. Things are just so complicated, and I'm being pulled in so many different directions. When I was out with Nick, something clicked and...and I realized I can't do this right now."

Without saying anything, Amara pulled Vee in for another hug. She was so warm, so relaxing, Vee had to fight the temptation to fall asleep in her arms, to try to escape her life. Unfortunately, she knew that her problems followed her into her dreams, and there was only one way out of this prison.

"This may sound a little random, but has Nick been seeing anyone recently?" Vee asked.

"Like, dating? No, just you. It's all he can talk about."

"He hasn't hooked up with anyone at a party recently? Maybe within the last month or so?"

Amara paused, shifting uncomfortably in her seat before speaking. "N-nothing like that. He actually told me he's been in a bit of a dry spell recently. Vee, what's really going on here?"

I wish I could tell you, Amara. You're such a great friend, I can see how worried you are, but there's nothing you can do to help me. If you haven't noticed anything different about Nick, then the succubus must be doing something else. Maybe she's in his dreams?

Vee sighed, giving up her train of thought. She leaned against Amara, her friend's warmth washing over her. "It might be nothing, I don't know. I feel like I'm falling apart, Amara." Vee's body twitched slightly, tears threatening to form.

"Hey, it's gonna be okay. I'm sorry things didn't work out with Nick, but that doesn't mean you have to give up. We've still got each other, right?"

The girls stayed quiet for a few minutes, holding each other. Despite her best efforts, Vee felt tears falling down her cheeks, and eventually she pulled back to avoid rubbing her tear-stained face on her friend.

"Do you still keep tissues in your bag?" Amara asked, holding Vee's face and brushing a tear away.

Vee nodded, sniffling as she curled into herself.

Amara zipped open her bag, reaching in to dig around. Before she could get started, however, Vee heard a small shock, and watched as Amara flinched, pulling her hand back quickly. "Shit!"

"What's wrong?"

"Just a little shock! It's been pretty dry recently, I should actually get some lotion real quick." Amara jumped up, hurriedly walking to the bathroom. As she got up, her phone fell from her pocket.

That was odd. Why was she in such a rush?

Shrugging, Vee pulled her bag closer to look for the tissues herself. When she looked inside, however, she froze.

No.

She'd forgotten to take out her Enochian Texts.

No no no no.

The holy book was glowing, its magic recently activated.

That's not...that doesn't make any sense, how would she—

Her breathing quickened, her pulse racing as she quickly scanned the apartment.

She saw Amara's phone, its case blackened and warped. In the corner of the kitchen sat a fire extinguisher, clearly recently used. The walls were covered in scratches, and several portraits lay broken on the floor.

My nightmares started the night of the party. The party that Amara left early. With Nick.

Vee heard the water in the bathroom running; she likely didn't have much more time alone. She zipped up her bag, her panicked thoughts racing, and prayed she was wrong. As she tried to calm her breathing, she realized that her senses were no longer enhanced. In fact, this was the first time she'd been to Amara's since she'd started enhancing her senses.

She swallowed nervously, starting the prayer to enhance them once again.

Please be wrong, please be wrong, please be wrong...

Divine energy flowed into her body, amplifying her senses, and Vee was immediately overwhelmed.

Amara's apartment reeked of sulfur.

She broke the spell, unable to withstand the overwhelming stench. The door to the bathroom opened, and Vee watched Amara walk back to the couch.

I can't let her know. I have to get out.

"Ah, much better." Amara paused, studying her face. "You alright? You look like you've seen a ghost."

"I have to go." Vee stood, her body tense as she grabbed her backpack. She moved quickly to the door, fighting every urge to sprint from the building.

"Wait, what? Please, just talk to me!" Amara tried to catch up but paused in the doorway.

Vee was halfway down the hall when she stopped. The sun was already setting, its absence covering the halls in shadows. When she turned back to look at Amara, she saw only a darkened silhouette, a vague suggestion of a person. Their eyes met, but Vee no longer saw the comforting gaze of a friend.

She only saw the glowing, amber eyes of a demon.

12
MASKS

"—and then she just said 'I have to go' and ran off!"

"That's almost exactly what happened on our date. She didn't say anything else?"

"Nothing!" Amara collapsed onto her couch, her tail grabbing the water bottle from the floor. "I've been texting her, and I asked Tessa and Chloé to do the same, but no one has heard anything. I'm really worried, Nick."

Nick sighed. "I am too. I just don't know what else we can do. If she's not willing to let us help, what are our options?"

"Can't we just...I dunno, get everyone to corner her?"

"An intervention? That's certainly dramatic." Nick paused, likely considering the logistics. "Maybe it's worth thinking about. If everyone is at the party tomorrow, we can ask what they think?"

"The party's tomorrow?! Shut up!"

"Shockingly, yes, the Halloween party is on Halloween."

"I still don't have a costume!" Amara groaned, grabbing a pillow and pulling it close. "And how am I supposed to focus on partying when I'm so worried about Vee?" She smashed the pillow against her face, letting out a scream of frustration.

After a few moments, Nick spoke up again. "Y'know, someone told me once that I can't let my worries stop me from living my life."

"Yeah? Well, whoever that person is, I bet she hates having her words turned against her. Hypothetically. But also, she sounds super fucking hot."

"Eh, maybe like a seven. Seven and a half if you're into brunettes."

Amara grabbed the pillow with her tail and chucked it at Nick. "Oh, shut up! I'm at least an eight, and you know it!"

Nick caught the pillow easily, tossing it back on the couch before sitting next to her. "Look, I'm not gonna keep quoting you, but you made a lot of good points before my date. Life keeps going, whether you want it to or not." He paused, placing a hand on Amara's tail. She looked over at him, the facade of indignancy breaking as their eyes met. "We'll check with Chloé and Tessa tomorrow, see if they're on board, and then try to talk with Vee next week."

"No, you're right, that sounds like a good plan." Amara finally sat up, her tail curling around Nick's waist as they talked. "I still feel bad I haven't tried to fix things with Derek yet. I promised her I would, and I thought I might be able to use my powers to do something, but I've been so busy with Tessa and...ugh."

They leaned against each other briefly, letting the silence hang in the air, before Nick spoke up again.

"You know what might cheer you up? I had a feeling you'd forget about your costume, so I threw something together for you."

"Seriously? This isn't just, like, a weird fetish thing, is it?"

"I would never!"

Nick stood up and moved to the kitchen, grabbing his backpack off a chair. As he opened it, he continued speaking, his voice slightly quieter. "I was just thinking back to when this all started. When you first got your tail, your horns, and you were so nervous about staying hidden. What if, to celebrate this new you, you just went as yourself? No more hiding?"

"Nick, I say this with nothing but respect for you, but that sounds like a terrible idea."

"Just hear me out!" Nick cleared a space on the counter. "It's Halloween, so everyone is already primed to assume that everything is a costume. All we have to do is give them enough reasons to believe you're wearing one!"

"I'm still skeptical, but alright. Keep talking."

After dumping out his backpack on the counter, Nick walked through his plan. He had craft glue for her horns, to make them look fake, and contacts that she could pretend were glowing instead of her eyes.

He also had a large black belt, lined with thick pockets. The pockets were filled with random pieces of circuitry and wiring, and a large hole had been cut out of the back for her tail. Ideally, he explained, it would look like she'd simply bought a really fancy tech tail from a costume company.

The last item was legitimately a cheap costume piece; a pair of plastic succubus wings, probably from the pop-up Halloween store down the street.

"Is this where the money ran out?" Amara said, smirking.

"No, this is the most important piece! If the wings are this cheap, it'll make everything else look fake too. Plus, let's face it, your wings are way too big to have out at the party."

"They are pretty fucking massive," Amara mumbled, looking over the disparate costume pieces. "You really think this will work?"

Nick moved closer, pulling her in for a hug before speaking. "I think you deserve a night to be proud of who you are. If that's not tomorrow at the party, then when is it?"

Amara buried her face in Nick's chest, mulling over what he'd said. She thought about the last month, realizing that his words rang true; she'd been incredibly nervous every single day, worried someone might find out. The constant cramps from tucking her tail in her sweaters, the frustration of locking herself away for a week when her wings appeared, and never being able to take her beanies off. A lot of that stress had faded once she figured out shapeshifting, but after falling in love with her demonic aspects, it got frustrating hiding them away constantly.

Am I proud of being a demon? Do I want to brag about it to the whole school?

The instant she asked the question, the answer was obvious. The thought of everyone seeing her real form, fawning over her horns and her tail, sounded amazing. Whatever being a demon meant, if it meant anything, she didn't care. For now, she was proud of who she was. Nick was absolutely right: Why should she deny herself this chance?

"Alright. Let's do it!"

"Great! Want to try some of it on? Get ready for tomorrow?"

"Actually, I think I have a better idea." Amara smirked, her tail snaking around Nick's torso again, pulling him close. Their lips met as she ran her fingers through his hair, savoring the intimacy as she felt his aura stir. "I don't know if we'll have time to fuck before the party tomorrow, so I need as much energy as I can get before then!"

Nick responded by running his hands down her back, grabbing her ass and pulling her close before leaning in to kiss her neck. "One of these days I'll get used to you saying that."

"Aww, is it still weird that you're fucking your best friend?" Amara teased, turning around. She pulled him with her as she moved to the couch, then pushed him down.

"Hey, I'm not complaining, it's just...I never thought this would be us."

"Nick, if you don't stop talking, I'm calling Tessa over here to fuck my ass again and making you watch." Amara started undressing, tossing her clothes aside. "Unless you're into that, in which case I'll make you sit outside."

"Tessa did what? I didn't know you were into that!"

"Don't get your hopes up, buster—it's still new, so you're not getting that today. Now what did I say about talking?"

Nodding, Nick closed his mouth and started pulling his own clothes off. He'd only managed to remove his shirt before Amara climbed on his lap and pinned him to the couch. Their lips met again, their kissing more intense as their excitement grew. Amara had noticed an instant surge in Nick's aura at the mention of anal, and she knew she would need to get more practice in so she could try it with him soon.

He reached behind her, undoing her bra and freeing her breasts. Once out, she sat up straighter, encouraging him to lean in and taste them. His hands ran up her waist, grabbing her tits before kissing them, his tongue running over her nipples. Her fingers continued playing with his hair, holding him down as he started biting.

"Fuuuck, just like that, you know what I like," she whispered, eager for more.

He sucked on her nipples, switching between them before pulling them into his mouth and biting them again, harder. She could tell he was growing bolder; he had never bitten her like this before.

She squeezed hard with her thighs, grinding against him as she felt the bulge in his pants grow. His breathing quickened, matching hers as they pleasured themselves against each other. Their lips met again, then their tongues, as Amara ran her hands down Nick's stomach, eagerly reaching for his pants. She undid them slowly, then hooked her tail in his waistband and pulled them off.

With Nick now almost naked, she reached into his boxers and readjusted his cock, angling it up so they could keep grinding against each other. She moved closer, pushing their bodies together, eager to feel as much of him against her as she could. She could feel her pussy soaking through her panties as she pushed against Nick's cock. He was incredibly hard, clearly ready for more, but she knew from experience that she'd be able to feed more if she prolonged the experience.

His hands, which had been massaging her ass, began traveling up her back. He dug his nails in, scratching deep from her shoulders to her waist, causing another loud moan to fill the apartment. After another pass, he reached higher and grabbed her hair, pulling at it to expose her neck.

He'd only managed a few teasing bites when he finally spoke up. "I want more, Amara."

She giggled, leaning in and whispering into his ear. "Thought you'd never ask!" She quickly repositioned enough to pull her panties off, helping Nick to shed his last article as well. When she climbed back on top of him, there was nothing between them.

His hands tried to move to her waist, but she met them with her own and pinned his arms over his head. "I'm in charge today, mister," she whispered.

Her tail holding his cock in position, she teased the tip with the folds of her pussy, moving as slowly as she could. His hips bucked, trying to push inside, but she managed to stay one step ahead of him. As his desperation grew, so too did his aura, and she finally reached out to start feeding on him.

Now that they were connected, she sank down, his cock disappearing inside her. Their faces were still next to each other, and his moans were like music to her ears. He tried again to move his hands, putting in more effort this time, and Amara found she was still able to overpower him. She held him still, taking the chance to lean in and bite his neck in retribution. As she did, her tail moved higher, curling around his arms to help hold him in place.

"Do you like the struggle?" she asked, slowly riding Nick. His cock pushed deep into her, scratching that most persistent itch. "I hope you're not holding back just for my amusement!"

Their eyes met, Nick eager to call her bluff, and she felt his arms strain. His muscular physique tensed, pushing hard to try to break free of her hold, but he couldn't move his hands away from where she was pinning them.

"That's...surprisingly hot, Amara. I think you're finally stronger than me," he whispered, his hips still matching her movements.

"Oooh, that's an exciting thought," Amara said, picking up the pace.

Her hips bounced higher, almost pulling away entirely before sinking down again. The control felt amazing. It was practically addictive, and she wanted more. She manifested her wings, a shower of embers washing over her as they appeared.

She hooked her feet under Nick's legs, adjusting her tail so it was wrapped around his torso rather than his arms. With a powerful thrust of her wings, she briefly lifted both of them up, her pussy pushing hard against Nick as they fell back to the couch. A wicked smile crossed her face, and she locked eyes with Nick to make sure he was still enjoying himself. His look, and his aura, clearly indicated he was having the time of his life, so she tried again.

Another heavy push, and the two of them were thrown off the couch again. She knew she couldn't attempt to fly inside, but the added thrust made the sex so much more enjoyable. She was reveling in her control, fascinated by her own strength as she fucked Nick faster. Her wings matched the pace of their frenzied fuck as they drew inevitably closer to their climaxes, both moaning louder with each thrust.

"Fuck...cum for me, Nick, give me what I want!" she moaned, her body twitching as she rode him.

"Amara, I—" Nick was unable to finish his thought, his words cut off by the sudden overwhelming pleasure coursing through his body. His orgasm overtook him, his hips bucking into Amara as he came hard.

Amara, still connected to his aura, felt all his pleasure pour into her, empowering her, expanding her awareness again. Its intoxicating scent filled her senses, and she began cumming as well, her pussy eagerly gripping Nick's cock. The two stayed like this, twitching and moaning against each other, as Amara continued pulling energy from Nick's orgasm.

Her wings, no longer pulling them up off the couch, tensed along with the rest of her. They arched high, extending to their full length as an unexpected surge of energy caused them to ignite. She moved her tail away from Nick, worried it might do the same, but the flames seemed content to stick to her wings this time.

Eventually, their orgasms passed, and the two friends caught their breath. Amara pulled back the fire from her wings, extinguishing them quickly. Once finished, she leaned in and kissed Nick again, her smile frozen on her face.

"Fuck, that was absolutely delicious!" she whispered.

Nick was unable to respond, his chest still heaving as he leaned his head back on the couch. He stayed there for another few moments before mustering the strength to speak. "That was...fuck, Amara. I've had plenty of sex, but it's really something else with you. Are you okay? Is the apartment okay? That was a hell of a lot of fire."

She took another look around. Other than some minor discoloration, everything seemed to be in order. "I think we're all good! Plus, even if something catches, I practiced putting out fire when I freed Tessa from those vines." She let herself collapse on Nick, closing her eyes as she listened to him breathe. They stayed like that for another few minutes, both slowly relaxing as they recovered from their fuck.

It was Nick who pointed out how sweaty they both were; Amara from the fucking, and Nick from the inferno that had erupted from her. Eventually, they had to get off each other. The only question left was who got to shower first.

The roof of Amara's apartment complex was flat, covered in gravel, with its only notable features being a couple of air conditioning units and the door to the stairwell. One corner of the roof extended higher than the rest, solely to house the entrance, and it was on top of that highest point that Amara now sat, closer to the center of the roof than the actual edge.

One leg dangled off the edge, the other rested atop it. She leaned against her raised knee, burying her chin in the crook of her arm. She felt a heavy breeze dance across the roof, ruffling her hair and passing over her horns. She sensed the air pressure, felt it change, and understood its temperature just as intimately as she did her own body's. She unzipped her hoodie, let it slide down until it was resting on her waist and her elbows, and manifested her wings. Angling them toward the wind, she closed her eyes, and imagined she was flying.

The sun had set hours ago. Nick had originally been over for dinner, but they'd spent quite a bit of time catching up, among other things.

Quiet footsteps echoed from the staircase, and the door pushed open.

"Amara? Where are you? I got your text," Nick said, looking around.

"Up here," Amara replied. She didn't know if Nick had a way up, and she moved her tail closer, gesturing for him to grab it.

"You really should have put those away; what if I'd been someone else?" he said, grabbing her tail. She wrapped it tight around his wrist and pulled him up to join her.

"I could smell you."

"Ah. I always forget you can do that."

"Mmhm."

Nick settled in, his legs hanging over the door, and he took a deep breath. "It's nice up here."

"I've been coming here a lot lately. It's pretty high, and it's the only place I can feel the wind on my wings." Amara sighed. "I like watching the clouds. I think about flying up to them, then I wonder how high I'd need to climb before nobody could see me anymore. High enough where I could just...be. Just riding the wind, not a care in the world."

"You're awfully contemplative tonight. What's on your mind?"

She didn't respond. Her eyes were fixed on the sky, tracing shapes in the clouds.

They both sat there for a while, the minutes passing in silence as her wings shifted with the wind.

Her tail curled around her raised knee, and she squeezed herself tight. Another deep breath, another sigh.

"Am I different?" Amara finally asked, eyes still locked on the sky.

Nick looked at her, his eyes moving from her tail, to her horns, to her wings. "Is that a trick question?"

"I'm not talking about all this," she said, gesturing to her various demonic limbs. "I mean...*me*. As a person."

Another breeze passed across the roof, the rustling of nearby leaves filling the silence while Nick thought about his answer. "You seem brighter. Like there's more of you than there used to be, if that makes sense."

"Honestly, it kind of does." She paused before speaking again. Her words came slowly, carefully, as if she were scared of saying the wrong thing. "Recently, I've been thinking a lot about...before all of this. Back when I thought I was just a regular college student, with nothing to worry about other than homework, or losing my virginity."

Amara smiled, wiping her nose on her sleeve before continuing. "If you'd asked me then if I was happy, I would have said yes. Without hesitation. But when I think back, when I put myself in those shoes again, I feel like I knew something was off."

"Off?"

"Just different, somehow. It's hard to explain."

"Give it a shot. I'm not going anywhere."

"It's...ugh, I'm terrible at this. Like, pretend everyone is a puzzle. You spend your life trying to put together the pieces, to figure out who you are, and eventually you see the picture. Everyone else? They've finished their puzzle, but not me. They clearly know who they are, so am I doing something wrong? Maybe I just haven't figured out where all the pieces go yet. Maybe they're all faking it, and everyone feels the same way I do."

The wind died down slightly, and Amara tucked her wings behind her again.

"Then suddenly, WHAM. It turns out there's a missing piece—it's been in the box the whole time. I had no idea it was there; it didn't make sense to look when everyone else had all their pieces from the beginning, but suddenly everything makes sense. The piece clicks into place, and I see...myself."

"But that's a good thing, right? You're happier now?"

"Well, like you said, it's as if there's more of me. I feel more connected with myself than I've ever felt before. When this whole demon puberty thing started, I sometimes worried that I might lose myself, turn into something I didn't recognize. But recently, I've been worrying about the opposite; that I'll be myself the whole time, but blind to how much I'm actually changing because it feels so natural."

"What changed?"

"I've been getting angry recently. I've snapped at people more in this last month than I have my whole life. And then, after I stepped into that weird angel trap, I...I hurt Tessa."

"What did you say?"

"Well, I yelled at her, but that's not what I meant. I actually hurt her: My fingers became, like, claws, and I drew blood. I didn't even know they could do that!"

"But it was an accident, right? I'm sure she understands, and believe me, I would know if she were angry with you."

Amara sighed in frustration, falling back on the rooftop behind her and splaying out her wings. "Ugh, I know, it's just...my mind has been all over the place recently. And now I've got this great costume that you threw together, and you're telling me to be proud of what I am, which made me wonder if I even *should* be proud of all this and—"

Nick interrupted her, placing a hand on her leg. "Hey, I've said this before, but you're a good person. If you really were changing into something else, something evil, we wouldn't be having this conversation. You wouldn't be thinking twice about accidentally hurting someone. That's more than enough proof for me."

She leaned forward, her wings propping her up, before looking at Nick. "Have I thanked you yet? For everything?"

"Hey, that's what friends are for."

"No, I'm being serious. Your best friend turns into a demon, and you barely even flinch. You've been here every step of the way, every weird change, helping me make sense of it all. I might never have figured out I was a succubus, or realized that my tail can be helpful, and now it's like my favorite thing about me. You had a thousand chances to bail, and you didn't. So, y'know, thanks. I really appreciate it."

Amara finally sat up all the way, moving next to Nick and wrapping a wing around him. They leaned against each other, looking out over the campus, quiet apart from the occasional car horn or train whistle.

"You want to hear something funny?" Amara asked.

Nick looked at her, waiting for her to speak.

"So, I mentioned that my anger's been a little unpredictable recently, but honestly, all my emotions have been like that, to a lesser degree. A few weeks back I was at Tessa's for movie night, and they put on something called Homeward Bound. It was a cute animal movie about pets trying to survive a wilderness journey to get home, and in the end they all tearfully reunite with their owners. Anyways, for some reason, watching this movie *devastated* me. I bawled my eyes out for, like, ten minutes."

"Because all the pets made it home safe?"

"It's ridiculous! I felt so silly afterward, but in the moment, it was just so overwhelming!"

After a moment of stunned silence, Nick's composure finally broke. He started laughing, harder and harder, until tears ran down his face. His arms clutched his ribs, and Amara wrapped her tail around his shoulders just to make sure he didn't fall. Eventually, his laughter infected her, and they both fell backward on the roof while they waited for the fit to end.

It was several minutes before Nick finally managed to speak again. "Wow, I needed that. I'll be sure to warn you if that Sarah McLachlan commercial ever starts playing."

"Ha, ha, very funny, Nicholas," Amara said dryly. "By the way, what's your costume for tomorrow?"

"I've got an old Beetlejuice suit that still fits; probably just going to do that. I didn't have the money for anything new after I threw that belt together for you."

"I knew it! You did run out of money!" Amara said, jokingly punching Nick's arm.

"I don't really care, to be honest; Halloween is just another party to me. I mean, don't get me wrong, I love seeing everyone get creative with their costumes, but I guess it's just not that big a deal to me."

"You mean you love seeing how slutty all the girls dress?"

"Your words, not mine." Nick paused for a moment. "Speaking of slutty, what are you wearing tomorrow? I hope it's more than just that belt and a smile."

"Psh, you wish. I've got a few bodysuits that might be cute, and a whole bunch of tights and shoes to sort through. I was thinking of pulling those out tomorrow, unless you want to watch me try them on now?" She winked at Nick, always happy to fluster him.

"I haven't got any plans, so sure!" Nick planted his hands on the ledge and pushed forward, effortlessly catching himself as he turned back to Amara. "Want any help down?"

Rolling her eyes, Amara stood up and jumped. Her wings caught the air, and she landed on the other side of the roof, dozens of feet past where Nick had landed. She took her time walking back to him, de-manifesting her wings before opening the door with her tail.

"Showoff."

"Nerd."

13
HALLOWEEN

Amara pulled on her second boot, the top of it resting just beneath her knee, and zipped it closed. This pair was one of her favorites; all black, slightly ruffled, with a thicker heel that was quite comfortable to walk in. Standing up, she looked at herself in the mirror, letting her eyes take in the final outfit.

Black fishnet leggings emerged from her boots, showing off her shapely legs. They soon vanished into her bodysuit, a single piece of faux leather that sat high on her hips. Her cleavage was on full display underneath the lacing on the front, which was pulled tight so as to not come undone at the party. Two small straps traveled from the top of the bodysuit to her neck, where they met a simple black collar.

The back of the outfit was practically non-existent. Quite a bit of her ass was visible, and she felt like she was wearing an exceptionally revealing swimsuit. Her entire back was exposed, save for a single strap that held everything together.

The belt had been fitted over the bodysuit, and she was happy that it didn't seem to chafe her tail. The fake succubus wings were strapped to her shoulders, the contacts were comfortable, and they'd successfully drizzled fancy glue around the base of her horns. As skeptical as she'd been, she could no longer deny that Nick had put together something ingenious.

As she stared in the mirror, appreciating how good she looked, she couldn't help but think about the last time she'd dressed up for a party. Almost a full month ago, her friends had dragged her to the Jade Palace's homecoming bash, and she'd been nothing more than a nervous virgin worried about letting loose.

Her friends had helped her with makeup, offered outfit suggestions, even given her advice on who the hot singles were. Amara had, for the most part, gone along with everything as an excuse to do something new and exciting with her friends.

Now, although she was proud of the person she'd become, it was hard to ignore the emptiness of the room around her. Vee was still ignoring everyone, and Chloé couldn't see her getting ready without learning the true secret of her costume. Was this the start of everyone drifting apart from each other? She wanted desperately to embrace her true nature while also keeping the same friends she'd grown to love over the last year, and she hoped such an outcome was still possible.

She turned to Nick, her tail twitching with excitement. "Maybe I should drape my tail over my arm? Then I don't have to worry about people stepping on it."

"I could see that working. I was thinking either that or wrap it around a leg."

"I think I'll just hold it, that feels easier." Amara moved her tail to the crook of her arm, draping it like a fancy scarf before letting it fall limp. "Still wish I could have my wings out, but that would be such a bad idea."

"I know it's not ideal, but you still look fantastic without them." Nick jumped off the bed, standing briefly in front of the mirror to adjust his black and white striped suit. "How about me? Looking good?"

"You look great! I still think you should have let me do some face paint."

"Eh, I just really don't want stuff on my face. I've got the green wig, though. Isn't that good enough?"

"Hey, if you're fine settling for good enough, that's on you." Amara turned back to the mirror, smiling as she admired herself. "I could never, and thankfully I don't have to. I look fucking amazing!" She checked her phone, noticed she had just gotten a text, and got the rest of her things together. "Alright, time to head out! Tessa and Chloé are here!"

They left the apartment, Amara taking a moment to lock up, then headed for the entrance. She paused at the front door to the building, looking at her friends outside.

Chloé's never seen me like this before, but if anyone were to notice, it would be her, right? She's always drawing; I've seen her sketch me before. What if she sees right through the costume? Can I tell her? No, idiot—Tessa warned you about that.

Just go outside, be confident, sell the outfit. Remember, tonight you're not Amara the Human, you're Amara the Succubus. Not that there's any difference, but they don't know that.

She felt Nick grab her shoulder, giving her a knowing look. "Hey, you ready? It's not too late to turn back."

"No. I want this. I'm...I'm ready." She moved her tail to her arm, let it go limp, and left the building.

Walking down the sidewalk, Amara took a moment to admire her friends' costumes. Chloé was wearing a simple long white dress that ended around her shins, showing off her comfortable brown boots. A short-sleeved red leather jacket covered most of her upper body, though it hung open to reveal the dress underneath. Her hair had been braided, and a bright pink ribbon had been clipped to the base of the braid.

Tessa's outfit was much less elegant, and Amara was hesitant to even call it a proper costume. She wore her usual black combat boots, with intricate stockings covering her legs. An incredibly short skirt left little to the imagination, and a frilly black bra was doing its best to put her cleavage front and center. She'd done nothing with her hair, save for a black hairband that held a tiny, off-center witch's hat.

The two girls seemed to be bickering about their outfits as Amara moved closer.

"Look, all I'm saying is that guys want to see skin, but you're covering most of it!"

"Tessa, not all of us are here to get laid. Maybe I just want an excuse to go out in a fun costume!" Chloé protested.

"Yeah, Tessa, there's more to life than sex," Amara said mockingly.

Tessa turned to face her. "Oh, that's rich coming from yo—holy shit, Amara, you really went all out, didn't you?" As she talked, Tessa nervously looked at their other friend.

Chloé's eyes were wide, darting between all the pieces of Amara's so-called costume. After a few seconds, she finally spoke up. "Wow! Amara, you look incredible! Are you a tiefling?"

"What? No, I'm a succubus. What's a tiefling?"

"Ohh, that makes sense. I'm used to succubi having thinner tails, but this one looks so real! Where did you get it?"

Amara looked at Nick nervously. "I, uh, Nick actually took care of that."

"Gotcha. I'll bug you for the link later, okay?" Chloé said to Nick. She immediately jumped into a lengthy monologue about what tieflings were, with Amara vaguely remembering that she'd heard this explanation before.

They took off for the party, which required them to walk across most of the campus. Chloé's explanation about tieflings soon gave way to general gossip, with Tessa still trying to push her into showing off more skin. Amara, on the other hand, had little to say. She kept glancing around, curious if other people were looking at her. Whenever she did catch someone staring, she realized that most people were much more eager to see the revealing outfit than her tail.

After passing the first few groups, Amara's nervous energy vanished. She began walking with more purpose, thrilled that she could just be herself tonight. She looked up at the sky again, remembering last night's talk with Nick.

He was absolutely right. I should be proud of myself.

To name a building The Jade Palace is a bold choice. Such a dignified name might instill visions of grandeur; perhaps a maze of lordly halls decorated with emerald tapestries, or a series of regal chambers designed to host exalted dignitaries. To the students of Aurelius University, such a description couldn't be farther from the truth.

The building in question was, in reality, a run-down manor that had long ago been converted into a frat house. The more prestigious fraternities had buildings on campus, which came with additional pressure to keep a clean, wholesome appearance. This meant that, while parties were sometimes hosted at such residences, they could never be as raucous as most students would prefer.

In contrast, The Jade Palace was off campus, and belonged to a less notable fraternity. The entire building had been retrofitted to serve as the perfect party house. The main floor had several rooms dedicated to hosting, providing space for everyone to mingle, along with a pool table that frequently hosted drinking games. A large breakfast bar had been added to the kitchen, though breakfast would be the strangest thing to order there. A nearby tip jar ensured that the Palace always had a well-stocked liquor cabinet, and students were eager to contribute.

The centerpiece of the house was originally a large living room, with a vaulted ceiling and visible second-story loft. The towering walls of this room had been painted bright green, and had been the inspiration for the name of the University's most notorious party house.

For students eager to let loose, the massive basement had been equipped with an impressive sound system, along with a series of lights that could be changed to fit the mood, or even synched with the music. A second bar in the back corner made sure the crowds stayed tipsy, and it wasn't uncommon for other substances to be readily available as well.

The second story of the Palace held four bedrooms, along with the loft. Very few members of the fraternity actually lived here, and the rooms contained incredibly few personal effects, as everyone understood what they were meant for. It had been in one of those very rooms that Amara had lost her virginity to Nick. As she walked to the Palace, she briefly lost herself in memories of the first party. With the benefit of hindsight, it was obvious that the party, and being surrounded by so many horny college students, would have caused her dormant succubus heritage to stir. Now that she was a full-fledged succubus, she was determined to take proper command of this party and show off her new self.

By the time Amara and her friends arrived, the party was already in full swing. Before they even reached the main entrance, she already had dozens of people complimenting her outfit, stunned at how realistic everything looked. While it was obvious that most of them, mainly the men, were more interested in how revealing her clothes were, it was clear that her "costume" was drawing a lot of attention.

Amara had never felt more alive. While her first party had been a little awkward, and mostly spent with her friends, tonight she found herself invigorated by how many new people she was meeting. The attention was intoxicating, and she got used to answering all the questions people had about her various accessories.

Initially, she'd been nervous to let people feel them, but as the night went on, she carefully let more people touch her horns, hold her tail, all of them marveling at how lifelike they were. On several occasions, the crowds cleared a space so she could let her tail down and walk, showing off how "ingenious" and "reactive" the technology in the tail was. She stressed that she'd spent good money on it, but always refused to say where.

She noticed a few strange things after the first couple of hours. Firstly, she noticed just how powerful her new demonic senses had become. Over the last few weeks, in her attempts to stay inconspicuous, she'd tried her best to keep her eyes from glowing. Even then, she had still gotten quite skilled at reading people's auras. Now, as she needed to sell the illusion that she was wearing glowing contacts, she kept her eyes fully engaged, and found that her senses had expanded far beyond what she'd previously known.

In addition to her usual talents, she had increased insight as to where people were directing their attention. Previously, auras only seemed to mix once people had fucked, but now she saw infinitely more subtleties. Two people might lock eyes across the room, and their auras would slightly shift to similar tones. She even began to see what she assumed were shades of her own aura, solely due to these strange reflections.

Secondly, no matter how much she drank, she never felt drunk. She was no stranger to alcohol, but due to the chaos of her transformation, she simply hadn't gotten around to it recently.

That feeling of material intoxication, while she did miss it, had been replaced with something far more delicious. The auras of everyone around her were so strong that she was actually able to feed in small quantities. Every person she playfully kissed, every eager partner that she danced with, and dozens of random other students that she simply walked past, every one of them fed her appetite.

She was in the middle of dancing with a particularly attractive red-haired cheerleader when something caught her eye. Above her, looking down from the loft, was a beautiful woman with curly, medium-length blonde hair. A short, pure white skirt accentuated her gorgeous legs, and matched the elegant white wrap that hung just off her shoulders. Her torso was covered in some kind of leather armor, and a gold circlet rested atop her head, its filigreed leaves interwoven with her hair.

Vee!

Quickly excusing herself from her conversation, she ran up the stairs as quickly as the crowds would allow. Within minutes, she'd found Vee, who was now leaning against the back corner of the loft.

"Vee, I didn't know you were coming tonight!"

"I guess we're all full of surprises, aren't we?" she said softly.

Amara was unsure what to say after their last conversation, stammering slightly before managing to speak. "You, um, look amazing. Are you, like, a Valkyrie?"

Vee walked past her, toward a nearby bedroom. "Something like that, yeah."

Opening the door, Amara looked inside and saw the room was empty, save for the bed in the back corner. Vee gestured for her to go inside, and she eagerly accepted.

"Well, I'm a succubus!" Amara said, showing off her tail as she walked into the bedroom.

"Oh, I know," Vee said, her voice unusually monotone. She closed the door behind them, the noise of the party muffled by the barrier. As Amara turned to face her, eager to ask if things were better, she instead watched as Vee planted her hands on her shoulders and shoved hard.

Stumbling backward, a flash of light filled her vision, and she collided with the wall behind her. At least, she thought it was a wall, but it felt softer than it should have. When she opened her eyes, she saw she was standing near the edge of a bright, glowing circle, and ethereal walls looped around her, trapping her inside. She watched as Vee locked the door, then circled Amara, keeping a healthy distance between them.

"Vee, what is...are you a witch too?" Amara asked.

"You can drop the act, Hellspawn. We're alone."

"Vee, I don't know what—" Amara took a step forward, reaching out for Vee, but before she could take another, her friend snapped her fingers. A terrible blinding light erupted from the circle, and a painful shock ran through Amara's body, one that was all too familiar. She fell to her knees, now in the middle of the room, clutching her ribs in pain.

"Do you think I'm stupid? That I'll just keep falling for your lies?" Vee hissed.

Another shock coursed through Amara's body, followed by a horrid realization. "This magic...the Enochian, that was you?"

"Stop fucking lying to me!" Vee screamed. She stepped closer, striking Amara across the face. Amara gasped, shocked at how angry Vee was. Their eyes met briefly, but Amara was forced to close hers when another burst of light appeared. She braced for a shock, but none came. Instead she saw that a glimmering sword had appeared in Vee's hand.

Before she had time to react, Vee drove the tip of the sword into her hip. Amara screamed as Vee quickly slashed upward, slicing through her belt. It fell to the ground, her tail now completely exposed, and soon Vee did the same with her fake wings. The energy from the sword was almost unbearable, its burn noticeable even when it wasn't touching her.

Amara fell to her hands and knees, gasping as she tried to recover from the stinging cuts. "Vee, please, why are you doing this?"

"You want to keep pretending? Fine, I'll humor you."

Amara felt the radiant sting of Vee's sword under her chin, raising her face until the two girls locked eyes.

"I'm a fucking angel. But you've known that for a while, haven't you, Hellspawn?"

Vee's eyes were filled with unbridled rage, on a scale Amara had never seen before.

She keeps calling me Hellspawn. Maybe she's just like Brandon! He thought I was a demon pretending to be someone I wasn't!

"This isn't what it looks like, Vee. Put the sword down, let me explain."

"So you can fill my head with more lies? Tch." Vee turned away, the sword leaving Amara's neck. Kneeling on the floor, she pulled a massive book out from under the bed, one that thrummed with the same radiant energy as the sword.

I just have to convince her I'm still me.

"Okay, yes, I'm a demon. I know how that sounds. But I'm still Amara! Other than a couple of new limbs, I'm still me!"

Vee pivoted quickly, glaring at Amara. "Is that supposed to make me feel better?! I know you are! This would be so much easier if you'd been replaced, or possessed, but no matter how I look at this, I can tell it's you!"

"Then why are you doing this? We're friends!"

"Do friends impersonate each other? Frame each other for assault? I came to you, scared and confused, cried on your shoulder, and you lied to my face!"

"I-I didn't know what—"

"After my date, I ask you about Nick, and more lies! How long has he been your thrall? Since the party?"

"He's not a thrall! I don't even know what that is!"

Vee paused, her intense glare unyielding. "Even now, with everything out in the open, you don't even respect me enough to speak the truth." Her voice was shaking, and Amara swore she saw her eyes water. "I'm done with your lies. I'm finishing this."

Opening the book in front of her, Vee turned to a specific page and started speaking. The words that came from her mouth were objectively beautiful—it almost sounded as though she were singing—but to Amara they were accompanied by a piercing shrill inside her head.

"Vee, w-what are you doing?" Amara asked, voice shaking with fear, hands trying to block out the noise.

"You're a demon. Demons belong in Hell."

Banishment.

After everything she'd learned about herself, after all the effort she'd put into controlling her abilities, Amara was once again trapped in a circle, opposite someone who didn't see her as human. Nothing she said mattered, and her friend was trying to cast her into Hell.

Why does this keep happening?

The Enochian grew louder, and Amara saw sigils light up around the circle. She had no idea how much time she had left, and she knew nothing about how to stop this.

I can't go to Hell. There has to be something I can do!

Amara clenched her teeth, focusing on the radiant energy binding her to the circle. The magic continued to assault her, attempting to hold her down, but she reached deep and tried to connect with her inner fire. As she grabbed hold, its heat spreading through her, she felt something else, something primal. A deep-seated anger began to spread, more intense than anything she'd ever felt before, and her instincts told her it was time to fight back.

I broke through this magic before. I can do it again.

She held her hands out in front of her, willing the flames to manifest. The Enochian magic continued to attack her, but the more she pushed, the closer she got to finding its limits. Her hands ignited, the purple flames casting an ominous glow on her face. She looked at Vee, and could tell she was already starting to sweat.

More.

She needed her true form, wanted it desperately. Her wings were still locked away, and she reached for them. Another series of shocks, another piercing sound as Vee continued chanting, but Amara pushed through it. She pooled all her strength together, everything she'd siphoned from the party guests, and bucked against the holy restraints. With one final scream, she shattered the magic of the Enochian circle, feeling her wings appear once more.

Vee watched as the demon held out its hands, trying to focus its energy. She had no idea how strong it had become, and she hadn't gleaned any helpful information from their conversation. She hoped her circle would buy her enough time to finish the banishment spell.

In only a matter of seconds, she felt the heat in the room grow exponentially, and then the demon's hands caught fire. The flames were extraordinarily hot, and had an unnatural purple tinge.

How is it breaking through the Enochian? It shouldn't be that strong!

Vee spoke louder, willing the magic of the book to hold the demon down as long as possible, but she could sense it was only a matter of time before it broke free. She was only seconds away from finishing the ritual when the entire circle shattered, the demon's wings appearing in a burst of flame.

The magic shock that emanated from the broken circle threw Vee backward, colliding with the far wall of the bedroom. Her book fell from her hands, but she managed to keep hold of her sword.

The demon looked at her, its features twisting in the light of its unholy hellfire. Its horns seemed even longer now, the whites of its eyes had turned completely black, and its fingers had elongated into incredibly sharp claws. Its wings were gigantic, far bigger than Vee had expected, and they cut off her path to the bedroom door. Most dangerous of all was the hellfire; it enveloped the demon's horns, poured from its eyes, and embers periodically traveled down its wings and tail.

Change of plans: Kill the demon if possible, escape if not.

Thankfully, Vee had come prepared for a fight, even if she'd done everything in her power to avoid it. Bright lights started flashing, the fire alarm having been triggered by the intense heat, and within seconds water was pouring from the sprinkler system.

The demon screamed, its unholy voice stinging Vee's ears as she took the opportunity to attack. She had the advantage of surprise; it was clear the demon hadn't expected the sprinklers to be loaded with holy water, and its flames were already weaker in its presence.

Vee aimed her sword at the demon's chest, hoping to end this quickly, but its speed caught her off guard. The sword missed its mark, piercing the demon's shoulder as the radiant energy started hissing. In combination with the holy water, she could tell the demon was in rough shape, but she knew she didn't have much time before the holy water ran out.

Pulling the sword free, Vee tried to focus on weakening the demon as much as possible. She had the clear advantage: The demon was moving much slower than she was, and she threw everything she had at it.

Moving quickly, her sword sang through the air as she landed strike after strike. She did her best to push the demon into a corner, but it continually managed to sidestep her as it parried her blows. The demon clearly had no fighting experience, and was using its arms to block her sword when dodging was impossible. After a series of successful cuts, however, Vee noticed the demon start to change.

Its claws and the back of its wrists began to calcify, growing a black, bony material that matched its horns. With this new change, the demon was able to meet her sword strikes with its fists, deflecting her attacks.

While the hellfire was still held at bay by the holy water, the two now seemed to be on somewhat even footing. They danced around each other, trading hits as each tried to gain the advantage. Vee was unquestionably the superior fighter, but she had no practice fighting against a demon like this. Every time she thought she'd gained the upper hand, the demon's tail or wings would knock her off balance. She had no idea what to do against an opponent that had three extra limbs to fight with.

After a brutal couple minutes of fighting, Vee could sense that the holy water had just expired. With the tide of the fight about to change dramatically, she managed to push the demon away, and tried to run for the door.

With surprising speed, the demon lunged forward, tackling her from behind, sending them both crashing through the door and into the second-story hallway. After they both staggered to their feet, it let out a roar, another burst of flames erupting from its body, and then realized that its hellfire was no longer being stunted. Its hands ignited once more, and it leaped forward.

Vee just managed to dodge the attack, jumping toward the loft. She pulled out a bottle of holy water, sliced the top off, and threw it at the demon to try and disorient it. The water hit its mark, and bought her enough time to move closer and grab the demon's face, letting loose a powerful blast of light.

The demon screamed in pain, and Vee took a moment to look around. The building had been evacuated, thankfully, but it was catching fire. Without a reserve of holy water, the sprinklers simply couldn't handle the overwhelming heat of the demon's infernal flames. As much as she wanted to help, she knew this might be her last chance to escape.

Running for the edge of the loft, Vee jumped over the railing, landing softly on the first floor below. She stumbled, briefly, and registered she was likely more hurt than she realized, but she was thankful the demon hadn't gotten any truly devastating hits in.

She ran for the back entrance, and was only a few steps away when it erupted in hellfire. Looking behind her, Vee saw the demon standing on the loft, having just kicked the railing to the floor. Soon the other entrance caught fire as well, and Vee realized she was trapped.

The demon jumped from the loft, landing in front of Vee as the two stared at each other. They were both panting, covered in sweat, and while the demon had sustained more injuries, Vee could tell its wounds were already mending.

For several moments, neither spoke as they slowly circled around the room. Vee was hesitant to make the first move, already scared at how much she'd underestimated the demon, but she knew time was not on her side now that the house was burning down. She reached into her belt, pulling out a small bag, and the demon finally lunged at her.

Vee jumped out of the way, spilling the contents of the bag on the floor as she did. A heavy line of salt followed her, and she extended it as long as she could before turning to face the demon, who had just charged again.

When it crossed the line of salt, Vee saw it flinch with pain and took her chance to attack. Brandishing her sword, she managed to catch the demon's waist, her sword hissing as the holy energy worked its magic. She'd been so focused on her successful strike, however, that she failed to see the demon's tail lash out. It grabbed her ankle, knocking her off balance before throwing her against a nearby wall.

Vee screamed out as she collided with the wall, her vision briefly blurring as she fell to the ground. Thankfully, due to the line of salt it had just crossed, the demon was too disoriented to capitalize on her moment of weakness.

Her supplies dwindling, Vee grabbed her last item from her belt, a small rosary, and wrapped it around her offhand. She rose to her feet, moving close to the line of salt, hoping it would continue to act as a deterrent to a direct attack. She whispered another prayer, empowering the rosary, and prepared to continue. The heat was getting to her, and her stamina was fading fast.

The demon lunged again, apparently deciding it was fine suffering the effects of the salt line. Its speed, unfortunately, had not dwindled since the fighting began, and it managed to catch Vee off guard.

Vee fell backwards, the demon on top of her, as she landed a punch on its jaw. The magic on the rosary detonated, its holy light stinging the demon, but it wasn't enough. She tried to follow it up with another strike from her sword, but the demon grabbed the blade, stopping it dead. With a flick of its wrist, it threw the sword across the room.

The demon's tail snaked around her offhand, and her other hand was soon pinned as well. The demon clenched its free hand, its bone-covered knuckles striking Vee's brow with a sickening crack. Her head hit the ground, disoriented, as another strike met her chin, cutting into her lip.

She looked up at the demon, barely able to see as her damaged eye started to swell. She was trapped, pinned beneath the demon's body, and she had no more energy left to keep fighting.

This is it? This is how I die?

The demon grinned, its black horns wreathed in hellfire. She felt its terrible hands close around her neck, its claws pushing deeper into her. With one last smirk, the demon's eyes flared, her bright amber irises glowing.

"Amara, please..." Vee whispered, barely able to speak as Amara's hands threatened to finish her off.

Her blood raced, fire coursing through her veins. There was freedom in her movements, true freedom that came only from complete abandonment of pretense, and her thoughts were fixated on stopping Vee.

I can't go to Hell. I don't belong there! I won't let her!

She barely registered what was happening, as her instincts had long ago taken control. She hardly even felt the dozens of scratches that covered her body.

Pain.

The heat felt incredible, and she'd never felt so at home.

Fire.

Something wet covered her fists.

Blood, fresh.

Her vision was blurred, not from injury or holy magic, but from overwhelming rage. Everything was red, and she could feel her hatred reflected in the flames that consumed the building around her.

"Amara, please..."

Her heart skipped a beat.

No. Something's not right.

Amara shook her head, doing everything in her power to stop, to pull herself back to her senses. When she finally looked down, she saw a horrible scene.

She was sitting on top of Vee, pinning her down. Her hands had warped into a twisted parody of themselves, blackened bone claws pushing into Vee's neck, drawing blood. Vee stared up at her, tears running down her face, mixing with the blood that poured from a deep cut on her brow.

Her face was full of terror, overwhelming despair, and worst of all, resignation.

Amara let go, watching as Vee gasped for air. Horrified, Amara stood up, stumbling backward as she looked around at the house, now engulfed in flames.

Amara panicked, unsure what she should do, before reaching out and trying to connect with the roaring inferno. She saw the color change, and she was able to extinguish a small patch of fire near the front exit, but the door caught again in mere moments.

"It's too much! I-I can't...I can't stop it!" Amara cried, her voice shaking with fear. She looked over to Vee, still lying on the ground, and realized that the loft above her was buckling from the fire. She heard a loud crack and watched as the structure started falling to the floor.

"No!" Amara screamed. She jumped forward, moving much faster than she thought possible, and grabbed Vee off the floor. She curled her wings around her, hugging her close to her chest, and ran for the back entrance.

She crashed through the door, rolling across the back lawn a few times before finally stopping. She laid Vee on the ground, watching as she slowly opened her eyes.

"Why?" Vee asked, her throat clearly damaged from the smoke.

Amara fell backward, scrambling to her feet as tears attempted to form, but were quickly burned away by the flames around her eyes.

Sirens sounded in the distance, quickly moving closer as the flames from The Jade Palace climbed higher in the sky. Amara locked eyes with Vee, then turned away. She broke out into a sprint, wings ready, and leapt into the air.

Her wings carried her higher and higher, the smoke hopefully hiding her escape as she kept ascending. The hot air from the fire pushed her skyward, and the wind filled her wings as she fled, the open sky welcoming her for the very first time. The sirens of the emergency vehicles seemed to follow her, drowning out her thoughts as she desperately tried to flee.

She was having trouble thinking straight, her mind replaying past conversations and thoughts.

"You don't understand, Nick. I was itching for an excuse to hurt him."

"Demons are fucking terrifying. Every instinct in my body is telling me to run, that I shouldn't have freed you."

Without realizing it, Amara found herself descending onto the roof of her apartment complex. She crashed shoulder first into the gravel, skidding to a halt as her tears finally appeared. They ran down her face, cutting through the soot as she screamed up into the sky. She curled into herself, grabbing her knees as her tail wrapped around them, and she wept.

What am I becoming?

AMARA'S STORY WILL CONTINUE IN:

CIRCLES
OF CHAOS

THE AURELIUS ARCHIVES: BOOK TWO

ACKNOWLEDGEMENTS

I never thought I'd be a writer. I mean, isn't writing done by serious people with literature degrees? Who are actually well-read? While I think, on some level, writing and storytelling always appealed to me, it was hard to picture myself behind the wheel. I came close once or twice, I think I've got the rough outline of a YA story buried in a notebook somewhere, but it just never happened.

Then, in late 2023, I found a story prompt about a young woman discovering she was a succubus. I started writing it partially as a joke, assuming that "I wrote smut once" would simply be another funny anecdote to bring out at parties. I nervously posted it online for other people to read, and a funny thing happened.

People really liked it.

And it inspired me to write another chapter. I outlined the entire first book, then the second, and it became clear that this was a story with serious staying power. I realized that I could fill these pages with everything I've always wanted to see in stories, things that typically get cut from shows and movies. I want to see polycules, trans characters, queer people in happy relationships, and sex that puts an emphasis on communicating with your partner.

I hope from the bottom of my heart that you've enjoyed this first part of Amara's story. If I've got you hooked, and you're looking for more, I would be remiss not to mention my Patreon! There you can find first drafts of future books, behind the scenes thoughts on each and every chapter, and even possibilities to join in the creative process. I also have a Discord for everyone that enjoys my work, not only my Patrons, and we're always happy to welcome more enthusiastic readers to the community.

To join in the fun, visit NyxNyghtingale.com. Hope to see you soon!

In addition to my wonderful Patrons, I want to thank each and every person who's ever taken the time to read my work. I'm thrilled to have reached so many people, and there simply aren't enough words in the English language to express my gratitude to everyone that has enjoyed my stories.

Another huge shout out to Linda Bulickova | Noeran who designed the cover art for this book. She's a phenomenal artist that worked tirelessly to bring Amara to life, and I couldn't be happier with the results. There's no stronger incentive to publish more books than the chance to work with such a gifted individual.

To all my friends, colleagues, acquaintances, and anyone I've ever trapped in a conversation about my writing, thank you so much for putting up with me. I'm sure many of you feigned interest to keep me around, and I appreciate your sacrifice.

To all my commenters, beta readers, and fellow writers, your feedback has and will always be invaluable. There's nothing quite as special as celebrating the art of storytelling with other people just as passionate as I am.

Most importantly of all, I could never have found this opportunity without the support of my loving wife. She puts up with so much, and this book simply would not exist without her. I hope to one day adequately express the depths of my affection for her, but for now, I'll have to settle for a quick acknowledgement in a smut book.

Until next time! Nyx <3

ABOUT THE AUTHOR

Nyx Nyghtingale is an Urban Fantasy writer who focuses on romance, passion, and self-discovery. After getting her start through online fiction sites, she's very excited to have added self publishing to her list of accomplishments. When not writing, Nyx can be found lurking the aisles of bookstores in pursuit of every sapphic Cozy Fantasy book in existence.